Death of the Elver Man

Death of the Elver Man

Jennie Finch

IMPRESS
BOOKS

First Published 2011
by Impress Books Ltd

Innovation Centre, Rennes Drive, University of Exeter Campus,
Exeter EX4 4RN

© Jennie Finch 2011

Typeset in Sabon by Swales & Willis Ltd, Exeter, Devon

Printed and bound in England by imprintdigital.net

British Library Cataloguing in Publication Data
A catalogue record for this book is available from the British Library

ISBN 13: 978-1-907-605-07-9 (paperback)
ISBN 13: 978-1-907-605-11-6 (ebook)

Acknowledgements

I would like to thank all the people who have taken the time to answer my stupid and seemingly endless questions whilst writing this book. In particular my thanks go to Dai Pearson for his knowledge of pike, Paul Humble for the Normark knife and ex-PC Stuart Smith for his knowledge of poaching laws. Thanks to everyone at Keiths Sports for your patience and good humour especially Jonathon Bonas and James Freeman for help with guns and fishing – your knowledge is tremendous!

Thank you to Carol Clewlow for the amazing 'Detective Fiction' module at Teesside University. I would never have managed without all your help and support.

I owe a great debt to the Lit Award Ruhr – without the award I would have struggled to complete this book and many thanks to Drina Paulovic for her support and help at the London Book Fair.

Special thanks go to Lynn McCormick, my avid reader, for your enthusiasm and encouragement.

Finally I would like to dedicate this book to Jackie. Her knowledge of the Criminal Justice system in general and the Probation Service in particular has been priceless. Thank you – this really would never have happened without you.

This is a work of fiction and I have occasionally taken perfectly good information and altered it to fit the story. Any errors or omissions in the book are mine.

Chapter One

The Somerset Levels are strangely flat. Once located below sea level, they emerge crouching but defiant due only to the graces of the great drainage ditches that cut through the area. Below the Zoy, an island hummock of land, the canal stretched into the distance, its water grey and thick with curdled mud. At one end was a sluice gate, over six feet tall and dulled by exposure to the harsh elements of this stolen land. The water flowed almost silently; the only sounds birds and occasional small animals burrowing into the surrounding reeds. A soft wind set the witheys and willows swaying, a constant background for eyes and ears. Above her the sky stretched away into the distance, but somehow the land did not, sight brought up short without an horizon as if at the edge of the world. It was a timeless landscape, untouched by modern life, carrying its human residents like ticks on its back.

The gear stick was fighting back again as Alex struggled to change down. She braked, stamped on the clutch and just slowed sufficiently to take the bend on the wrong side of the road.

'Stupid piece-of-shit car,' she muttered, as the aging suspension wallowed on the curve and one wheel dipped into a pothole. There was a clanking noise as she pulled away along the straight, a warning from the loose exhaust. Peering into the emptiness, she crossed her fingers in futile superstition against breaking down so far from anywhere. She slowed the car, wrestling with the gears again as she searched for the turning. Off to her right was a gap in the verge and a gravelled road ran away into the distance. There was no signpost and she hesitated before plunging off, leaving the main road's minimal sense of civilization behind.

The cottage seemed to emerge from the land itself. Set in a hollow off to the left it huddled as if hiding from prying eyes. She stopped the car and got out into the chill November wind. The silence was shocking after the rattling and grinding of her aging Citroën, which was emitting soft ticking sounds as the engine cooled. She wondered whether she should pull off the road, but the ditch ran hard up against it on the right and the yard and drive of the cottage she had come to visit were piled high with the rusting remains of other vehicles. She'd seen no-one for several miles, so she decided it was probably safer to leave the car where it was.

The smell she had noticed when she opened the car door, the smell she had attributed to the drainage ditches, became noticeably stronger as she picked her way towards the front door. Keeping a wary eye out for dogs, she reached the front step and pressed the doorbell. Her finger stuck to the greasy surface as she pulled it away. There was silence from inside the house. She glanced at her watch, relieved to see she was on time despite the journey. Deciding the doorbell probably didn't work anyway, she tried knocking on the door, politely at first and then with increasing force. Just as she decided to abandon all dignity and shout through the letterbox an upstairs window flew open.

'What's you wanting then?' demanded a female voice. A middle-aged woman glared down at her, her ample figure quivering inside a lime-green housecoat.

'Good afternoon,' called Alex, trying to inject some friendliness into her tone. 'I've come to see Kevin.'

The woman stared at her and shook her head. 'Kev's not here. Not today.'

She began to close the window and Alex said, 'But he's expecting me! I wrote last week and made an appointment. I'm his new probation officer.' The woman gave her a look of condescending pity. 'Wouldn't make no matter – Kev can't read. Anyway, 'tis Carnival.'

She tugged at the window as Alex called up, 'What do you mean, Carnival? He's supposed to meet me every week. I'm going to have to take him back to court if he misses again.'

The woman laughed, a wide-mouthed cackle that revealed several brown teeth and a wasteland of gum.

'You'm not from round here are you? Ain't no judge'll send anyone down for going to Carnival. Come back next week maybe. I'll tell him to be here.'

The window slammed shut leaving Alex alone and shivering in the icy wind. She had expected the West Country to be warmer than London but November in Somerset could be bleak, very bleak, and cold.

It was just gone four when she got back to the office after a long, long drive across the Levels, for there was nowhere on the track wide enough to turn round and she had been forced to wrestle the car along a surface more suited to horses and carts than motor vehicles from the 1970s. She was in a vile mood as she pulled into the almost empty car park. The desk was deserted apart from Lauren, her diminuitive and indispensable assistant.

'Where the bloody hell is everyone?' Alex demanded.

Lauren looked up from her specially designed desk and shook her head. 'Why are you back here? It's Carnival tonight.'

'Don't you start,' said Alex. 'I've already had this conversation with Kevin Mallory's mother. The little bastard was out – again.'

3

Lauren slid off her chair and crossed to the counter, climbing on to a stepped stool to reach the safety latch and buzz Alex in.

'You should try to go now,' she said. 'It's impossible to get out of town after about 4.30. They'll close the roads and you'll be stuck here until after the squibbing.'

Alex closed the door behind her and blinked. She was getting a headache and her eyes were itching horribly.

'Is there another language I don't know about being used around here?' she asked. 'Everyone keeps saying "Carnival" like it means something special. And what the hell is *squibbing*?'

'Believe me, you don't want to know,' came a voice from the main room. She turned to see Jonny, Lauren's elder brother, leaning on the counter. Tall, dark and with Lauren's soft brown eyes, he was popular with the younger girls in the office and even managed to get a smile from Pauline, the formidable senior administrator.

'After the parade they all gather in the High Street,' he said. 'Then they all light squibs – like roman candles on poles but much bigger. About a hundred they have, all going off at once with an explosive maroon in the base. Someone gets burnt nearly every year but it's a real sight to see. Ready Sis? Come on, let's get out of here. I've got the car outside.'

Lauren clambered down the steps, grabbed her bag and trotted out under Alex's arm, which was stretched out to hold the door open for her.

'See you,' said Jonny. 'You really should get off now. It's . . .'

'Carnival. Yes, I know.' Alex gathered her files and headed for her office on the top floor of the building. At least she'd be able to get some work done this evening, free from the constant phone calls and flow of inarticulate and stubborn youths that comprised most of her case-load.

At half past six she dropped the last forms into her basket and locked her filing cabinet. She considered going to look at the

Carnival but the lure of her own space, a glass of wine and a good book in front of the fire was stronger than the amateurish antics of a bunch of small-town exhibitionists. She was turning off the lights and locking up the top corridor when Bert, the evening janitor, appeared at the top of the stairs.

'Evening Bert, I'm just off. I think everyone's gone early this evening,' she said cheerily. Bert looked at her. 'What're you doing here then? Didn't no-one tell you – 'tis Carnival. You'm not going nowhere now 'til after midnight.'

How much disruption could a small town procession cause, she thought with rising irritation. She was crossing the car park, fumbling for her keys, when a blast of music, bone-jarringly loud, caused her to swing round towards the gates. The sky lit up with coloured lights and there was a roaring of applause and laughter. She peered around the gateposts and felt her mouth drop open in astonishment. The High Street was packed with onlookers, a solid mass of bodies jammed six or seven deep on each side of the road. Gliding slowly down the centre was the largest, brightest and noisiest float she had ever seen. Forty feet long, fifteen feet high and lit by hundreds of light bulbs, it was pulled by a tractor. A cast of thirty men in immaculate costumes danced and sang along to 'I'm a Yankee-Doodle Dandy', whilst a diesel generator crawled behind providing the power needed to run this monstrosity. Behind it came another, then another, all with different themes and conflicting songs. The resulting cacophony rose from the long line of floats that stretched as far as she could see, down the quayside and off out of town. Bert materialized at her shoulder.

'Told yer,' he yelled above the din. ''Tis Carnival night.'

A young man stood, deep in the crowd. He was thin and ragged with spiky, home-cut hair and dirty hands, a scarecrow of a lad who watched with his mouth open as the floats glided past.

'What you think then?' he shouted to his mate next to him. His companion shrugged his shoulders and yelled back.

'Dunno. Maybe if you could raise the subs or had something special to offer. They's all right picky mind and hard to impress.'

A man appeared behind the boys and laid a hand on each shoulder. 'Now lads, how's it looking then?'

He was a big man, heavy set with red, meaty arms and wrists. His hair was jet black and his eyes, a startling shade of blue, were hard and calculating.

'Looks fine, Dad,' said the second boy, a lean young man with russet hair and a disarming grin. When he started school several older, bigger boys had dubbed him 'Carrots' a name that stuck for less than a week. Even at the age of six Billy was fearless and although he rarely started a fight he never failed to finish one. 'Kev was just wondering about joining a gang, maybe Watermen. What you think?'

Kevin looked at the man hopefully.

'I could raise the subs, Mr Johns. I've plans for that, in the spring. I just need someone to speak up for me with the gang men.'

Derek Johns looked at the scruffy waif in front of him and felt nothing but contempt for this sorry specimen. Kevin looked younger than his age, still too young to drink, and seemed small and insignificant next to his friend. Why his son chose to hang around with the Mallory boy was beyond him, but then Billy had always had a soft streak in him. He tugged at the boys' shoulders and steered them out of the crowd.

'Come with me. We'll find a quiet spot in the Judge Jefferies . . . get a pint in while the rest of the world freezes out here. See what we can work out, eh?'

In the relative calm of the pub, Kevin sipped his half of cider and waited to see if Derek Johns was going to help him. If he was honest with himself he was scared of Billy's dad, deep down cold afraid. He'd grown up with Billy and his younger brother, known locally as Biff on account of his short temper and readiness to apply force to any obstacle. Billy was a different character entirely, a more thoughtful boy who resembled his mother, unlike Biff who was a miniature version of his dark, menacing father. Despite their physical differences they were both prone to occasional fits of wild humour and lived their lives with a reckless disregard for authority. Billy was nicknamed 'Newt' by his friends, a title earned by his ability to shin up the sheerest of walls, his hands and feet sticking to any surface. It was rumoured he could shed body parts and re-grow them overnight, so easily did he slip through the hands of the law. Newt, at just twenty-one, was already the finest cat burglar in the county and he always had plenty of money in his pocket. His father's connections helped smooth the way for his various enterprises and somehow Newt had never been fingered successfully by the police. Kevin's dad had vanished when he was six, unmourned by his long-suffering and over-protective mother. He envied the Johns brothers their support network but was privately relieved he did not have to live with a father like theirs.

'So,' said Derek, taking a deep pull from his pint and wiping the foam from his upper lip, 'you fancy joining a Carnival gang eh?'

Kevin nodded his head, as outside the noise of the crowd swelled to greet the town favourites, makers of the largest and most elaborate floats. Derek watched the boy's face, his mind flicking over the possibilities. The lad was no use to him, he decided. No point in wasting any more time with him. Next to him, Newt nudged Kevin very gently in the ribs. Derek turned his cold gaze to his son, who looked at him quizzically.

'Well now, seems you need to raise your money first,' he said. 'How much you got?'

'About thirty quid,' said Kevin proudly. Derek gave a cruel smile.

'You'll need more than that lad. About ten times as much at least.'

To his surprise Kevin didn't seem crushed by this impossible amount.

'I'm going to get it in the spring,' he said, trying to whisper above the growing din. 'Goin' elvering. Got a nice little pitch sorted and my cousin, he knows the Elver Man so I can sell on without no problems.' This was more initiative than Derek had expected and he cast a second look over the boy. His father had been a dismal failure – still was actually – a petty thief who didn't know when to keep his mouth shut. Derek and his friends kept well clear of the Mallorys and their associates. They couldn't be trusted. He shook his head, dismissing Kevin from his plans.

'Well, you let Billy here know when you've got your money and we'll see,' he said, getting up. He drained his glass and turned to the door. 'Come on Billy-boy. They're about ready for the squibbing.'

Billy rose to follow his father, nodding to Kevin as he trailed obediently in the big man's wake.

Outside, the shouting became a chant as the fireworks were lit and the sky filled with a hundred explosions. Kevin sat at the table in the empty pub hugging his glass and dreaming of the day he would march into the square, squib-pole slung over his shoulder.

Alex approached Monday afternoons with dread. Garry, the senior probation officer, held his weekly meeting and it was always *his* meeting rather than a forum for the team. Here he doled out instructions, new policies from the ever-increasing bureaucracy and shared out new clients and assignments. She sat in the staff room waiting for his arrival and considering her colleagues. There were four other officers, two short following recent resignations and transfers. She was the only first-year officer and was still on a light case-load as she felt her way around the system. The others were all handling extra clients and she wondered how they managed the sheer volume of work. Paul Malcolm dealt with the youngest offenders, lads who were the bane of Social Services. Thin, rangy and always slightly untidy, he wore an air of perpetual hope. Paul Malcolm believed in his work with a missionary zeal that carried him through setbacks, disappointments and the constant battles he fought against the lures of cider, glue and, increasingly, petrol sniffing.

Eddie handled category 'B' offenders, the bread and butter of probation work. Most of his case-load was repeat offenders on licence or those on their last chance before imprisonment. He was short, rotund and padded around the office looking rather like an amiable teddy bear, but his wrath was fearsome and most of his clients treated him with respect. Despite his girth, Eddie had a fondness for walking, hiking and camping, and frequently hauled small groups of wayward youths off into the wild for some character-building outdoor living. Alex was using every trick she could think of to avoid being dragged along on these expeditions. She rarely agreed with her clients but she was also of the opinion this sort of activity came under the 'cruel and unusual punishment' heading.

The only other woman on the team was Margaret, and Alex looked at her as she sat upright and self-contained in the corner and wondered what on earth had brought her into this line of work. Margaret specialized in serious offenders – violent or sexual offenders, often with multiple convictions. She dealt with their mental states, kept them to their licence conditions, breached them with cool efficiency when necessary and still had time to lecture part-time at several regional universities. In her neat suit, court shoes and perfect make-up, she was the complete opposite of Alex, a fact they both acknowledged by a polite nodding of heads in greeting each morning.

Alex was slightly in awe of the final member of the team, a long-serving and supremely capable man named James by his parents but known generally around town as 'Gordon' Bennett. Dressed in a tweed jacket with leather patches, a hand-knitted waistcoat and sporting a neat beard, Gordon looked more like a visiting academic than a probation officer. He was unfailingly polite to everyone he encountered, lived his life by his own strict moral standards and was generous with his support. On several occasions he had taken Alex to one side and offered the benefit of his experience and she had never regretted taking his advice. Gordon was the core of the team, the man they all relied on, but he was by no means a push-over as many clients (and occasionally officers) had found to their cost. Gordon was living proof that it is a stupid person who mistakes gentleness for weakness.

It was Gordon who leaned over and said to Alex, 'Have you got your SNOP with you?'

Alex looked at him, startled. 'My what?'

Gordon grinned, transforming into a mischievous faun for a moment. 'The Statement of National Objectives and Priorities. That tedious government summary they sent round last week.' He reached into his briefcase and withdrew a battered looking document. Alex rose from her chair hoping to dash to her office and locate her copy before the meeting began, but the door opened and Garry entered, followed by Pauline, the senior administrator who was carrying a full copy-box. Eddie sprang to his feet and took the box, huffing in surprise at its weight, and Alex sank back down hoping Garry wouldn't notice her empty hands.

'Here,' whispered Gordon, and thrust a sheaf of papers at her. 'I always keep a spare copy in case Garry wants to borrow one of mine. I wouldn't want him reading some of the comments in the margins.'

Garry looked around and nodded approvingly as the team settled into their chairs.

'Thank you Pauline,' he said, without looking at her. 'Perhaps you could arrange some coffee?'

Pauline looked around the room, her face devoid of expression as the officers glanced at her and then back to the SNOP papers. Only Alex met her eyes as she tried to convey sympathy for Garry's boorish attitude. Pauline was a vital part of the office, hugely experienced and highly skilled. Treating her like an inexperienced trainee was, in Alex's mind, not acceptable. Garry waited until the door closed behind Pauline before beginning.

'I trust you have all read and considered the new Statement of National Objectives and Priorities,' he said. 'As you probably know, this is an exciting new approach to our work and will allow a more unified and cohesive strategy to underpin the changes taking place in the criminal justice system.'

Alex wanted to close her eyes and drift away. Garry was one of the most tedious speakers she had ever encountered. The man could sound pompous reading out a menu.

'We have been working to develop a local initiative that, whilst keeping to the ideals of the national strategy, is appropriate to our need here in Somerset,' Garry continued. He reached into the copy-box and drew out a number of identical buff folders, passing them round to the team. 'This is the result, the Statement of Local Objectives and Priorities.' He sat back looking very pleased with himself as the officers flipped through the document in a desultory manner.

'This is purely a local scheme?' Margaret asked, in an attempt to appear enthusiastic. Garry nodded as Eddie said cheerfully, 'So this would be SLOP then?' Garry's smile vanished as a fit of sniggering broke out around the room. Ignoring his Senior's expression, Eddie grinned and said, 'Maybe we should do a special version for our team. We could call it the Statement of Team Objectives and Priorities. That would make it . . .'

'Stop that!' snapped Garry. 'That's quite enough acronyms, thank you.' Eddie nodded, 'exactly. SNOP, SLOP and STOP. It's got quite a nice ring to it don't you think? After all, this is the pointy end of probation work and the buck stops here.'

It was unfortunate that Pauline and Lauren chose that exact moment to deliver the coffee.

Alex had not wanted to go back home for Christmas. She knew her parents had been expecting her but the thought of the long journey to London and then the battle around the North Circular road to get out into Essex was depressing beyond measure. Her brother was there, her perfect brother with his perfect wife and their two perfect children. Brother was something successful 'in the City' and brought home an obscene income. He had recently adopted the grey suit and red braces look of the new generation of money men and

Alex loathed everything he stood for. Predictably he poured scorn on the idea of rehabilitation of offenders, thought the courts were too lenient and was in favour of capital punishment. It had been a miserable few days and she was glad to be back in Somerset, her main emotion being relief as she turned into the lane and bumped her way up the track to her rented home. She loved her parents very much, but they had so little in common now that she found the hours dragged by, each a lost opportunity as much as a wasted holiday. She would have stayed in Somerset for Christmas but was rather chastened to realize how few people she could honestly consider friends. She'd never been wildly sociable she realized, as she poured a glass of guilt-free wine and settled in front of her log fire, but at least she always had people around her at college. It was a few days shy of the New Year and she was sitting in silence, drinking alone. Her mind wandered back to the last New Year with its long, warm night of revelry holding so much promise. Broken promises, she thought bitterly as she dragged her thoughts away from that horribly painful memory. There were worse things than being alone she decided.

She recounted this to Lauren over coffee and mince-pies the next morning, brooding on her parents' lack of understanding for her career choice and her lack of any real alternative to the trip back for the festive season.

'I don't know, is it me perhaps?' she asked.

Lauren was brutal in her honesty.

'Thoroughly tiresome, that is, and fully deserves the wrong answer. You don't exactly get out much and the only people you meet here are either staff or criminals. And between you and me, I think you'd have more fun with the criminals. Do you want that last mince pie?'

Alex hesitated, a fatal error, and Lauren continued as she munched away.

'Why are you living way out in the sticks anyway? You should look for some place a bit closer so you can go out, have a drink sometime. Buses is rubbish round here you know and there's no taxi driver going all that way late at night so you pretty well stuck.'

Alex was doubtful. 'I don't know, it's not a good idea living on your patch. We were always advised against it at college.'

Lauren waved a scornful hand. 'College,' she scoffed. 'What do they know. Is not like some big city here. Why, is scarcely any trouble for those in town. Let's face it, most times they're too pissed to find their way home never mind track down their probation officer.'

Alex sat in her office, picking away at the small mound of paperwork on her desk. On her arrival she had taken a short-term lease on a converted forge out in the countryside. It had been a beautiful and tranquil retreat during her first stressful weeks at work. Set at the foot of the Quantock Hills, it was the complete opposite of the endless flat of the Levels. An Essex girl born and bred, Alex still found hills rather a novelty. She loved their solid presence at the back of her home, the way the trees rose in layers as they sought the sunlight. She had watched the evening sun cast cloudy shadows across the broad sweeps of heather and bracken and marvelled at the way the day cast the face of the hills into ever-changing patterns, an infinite swirl of colours.

But as winter closed in she began to regret her choice. The forge was cool in summer but bitterly cold in winter and she had been cruelly misled over the supposed mildness of the West Country climate. By the beginning of December she was giving serious consideration to dragging her bedding into the front room to sleep in front of the wood-burning stove, the forge's sole source of heat. Whatever the drawbacks in visiting her parents, at least they had central heating and they even ran it occasionally. The next morning, when she woke to find ice inside the bedroom window, she spent her lunchtime visiting the few estate agents open over the long Christmas break. The market was slow, interest rates were higher than most people could countenance and she was able to grab a bargain, a small terraced house on the banks of the River

Parrett, five minutes walk from her office. It was a funny, crooked little house with a tiny back garden, no parking and a loft conversion with windows that threatened to slip into the street if opened. She loved it, and in February, helped by Gordon and his family, Lauren and her brother Jonny, she bid the forge farewell and moved into the heart of town.

The next day, tired and aching, she sat in at the afternoon meeting trying to nod intelligently when she really wanted to put her head down and doze off. She was imagining her new front room, freshly painted with a wooden dining set and matching dishes when she realized Garry was talking to her.

'Right,' she said and flashed him a bright smile.

'So you'll liase with Eddie and Paul on this?' Garry asked suspiciously, 'This is potentially a serious matter and I need to be sure you can handle it.'

'Of course,' she said, wondering what she'd agreed to take on.

'We can have a quick meeting in my office,' said Eddie nodding in her direction. 'Make sure everyone's informed of events and histories.'

'Especially histories,' muttered Paul into his notepad.

The team meeting was blessedly short and Alex hurried after Eddie and Paul to the relative safety of the Eddie's office. It was very masculine she decided looking at the leather chair by the desk and the series of photographs from long, hard walks. Tousled and grubby faces grinned down at her in triumph as they stood on a succession of bare and windswept peaks. In the centre of each group stood Eddie, clad in a cagoule. Orange, she thought privately, was really not his colour.

'Right,' said Paul seating himself next to the desk. 'This needs careful handling. How much do you know about the Johns family?'

Alex hesitated, blinking in confusion. 'Well, not much. Actually nothing. Sorry.'

Eddie snorted and reached into his filing cabinet. 'Lucky

you,' he said as he dropped a thick, battered file onto his desk. 'There you go. Bedtime reading.'

Alex reached out and pulled the folder across the desk, opening it gingerly.

'That's just the stuff we can prove of course,' said Paul. 'There are a lot of false alarms with the Johns family. This is mainly about Derek, their father. A nasty piece of work by all accounts and he has been inside several times. We've nothing on the boys except the stuff from Social Services. You know, family with absent father, school avoidance; young Biff was always a bit too handy with his fists on occasions.'

Eddie leaned over and turned to one page near the middle, 'This is all we've got on the elder boy, Billy. He was caught shoplifting once, let off with a caution. Nothing at all since then but he's known as Newt around town. Bit of a legend in his own way.'

'Newt?' asked Alex.

Eddie nodded, 'Yep. Like the pond lizard? Word is he can climb a sheer wall as if his hands and feet stick to the surface. He's smart, quick and charming and so far he's run rings round the entire county police force. Derek Johns got pulled for a bit of dodgy lead theft but he's due out again any day and this is going to hit him very hard. He adores his boys despite being such a nasty piece of work so be careful and play it absolutely by the book. For some reason, Newt is pleading guilty and you've got him so you get to do the report. Lucky girl.'

Alex opened her mouth to protest the 'girl' when Paul interrupted.

'I'd go as soon as possible,' he said, his face serious. 'They've let Newt out on bail to be with his mother so you have to visit the Johns' home and that's better done without Derek there. He's a bit – volatile, especially where the boys are concerned. And there are whispers about this whole business. It seems the police were waiting for them. Someone's "bubbled". Wouldn't like to be them when Derek gets out.'

He took the file and flipped through it. 'No, I've got most

of this already,' he said to Eddie. 'I'll go and see Iris Johns, offer our support if she needs it. I had a bit of contact with Biff last time he was excluded from school. He was placed in the special unit for a while and we got on quite well the times I was visiting. Poor lad.' He shook his head. 'There'll be hell on about this. Someone didn't do their job properly at the station.'

Eddie nodded as Paul got up to leave.

'Hang on,' said Alex. 'I'm sorry, I've missed something here. What's going on with this family?'

Eddie looked at her with sad eyes. 'They were caught coming out of a post office down the other end of the county,' he said. 'No way were they going to walk from that regardless of their father's "connections". The boys were separated at the station and Biff was locked up alone. Someone decided to let him stew, so they just left him. They found him in the morning, dead. He'd hanged himself with his blanket.'

Mindful of Paul's advice, Alex arranged to see Billy 'Newt' Johns the next afternoon and spent an unsettling evening skimming through the file for his father, Derek Johns. It made uncomfortable reading. Derek began as a snatcher – grabbing bags and purses and running away – whilst still at school. He'd been excluded permanently for assault when he was thirteen, after beating another boy unconscious and then punching a teacher in the face when she tried to intervene. The next few years were filled with shoplifting, petty theft and drunk and disorderly charges until he was sent to borstal for burglary aged fifteen. On his release he surrounded himself with like-minded people, loud, arrogant men who took what they wanted and did what they liked. He'd spent over half his adult life behind bars and his two sons ran wild, skipping school to shoplift, stealing fruit and eggs from local farms and drinking home-made cider, known as 'natch', to the locals.

Natch, Alex knew, was a problem particular to this part of the country. Brewed by many farms and small-holdings, it was sold in gallon containers to anyone with the few pounds it cost. Over half of her younger caseload had committed their offences under the influence of Natch. She's never tried it herself and had no intention of indulging. Some 'natural ciders' reportedly had eight units of alcohol in a pint. By her reckoning this made a gallon container as potent as a bottle of whisky – and it was consumed with relish by children as young as ten.

Neither Biff nor Newt had any criminal record apart from Newt's collar for shoplifting a handful of sweets then he was eleven. Cryptic notes from Social Services suggested this was mainly because they had never been caught, or by the time anything came before the magistrates the witnesses forgot vital and incriminating details. Maybe that was why Biff hung himself, she thought. No chance of escaping this time and no father to protect him, he was heading for some kind of secure unit or Young Offenders provision. Newt was about four years older – he'd be off to 'proper' jail somewhere and Biff would have to fend for himself. He must have been terrified if killing himself was the better alternative. She turned out the light and tried to settle into sleep, but the unfamiliar sounds of the river outside her window kept her awake and she lay on her back, eyes open as she tried to get the thought of young Biff Johns out of her head.

'Phone call, Alex,' called Lauren, as she pushed through the front door the day after the Easter break. She waved a hand in acknowledgement and pointed upwards to indicate she's take it in her room. She hauled her overloaded briefcase across the reception area as Lauren said, 'Just transferring you now', into the telephone. In her room she dropped the case onto the desk and groaned as the contents spilled out over it and onto the floor. Snatching up the receiver she tried to sound calm and professional.

'Hello? Alex Baker here.'

''Morning,' came an unfamiliar male voice. 'You are the probation officer for William Johns I understand?'

Alex had to think for a moment – William . . . of course, Newt.

'Yes that's right. I'm due to visit him later this week. Sorry, you are . . .?'

'Chaplain McCausland, Dartmoor prison. I'm calling to let you know you'll have to reschedule. I know sometimes the authorities forget to inform people with appointments so I thought I'd make sure you knew.'

Alex felt her heart race, memories of Biff flooding through her head.

'Knew what please?' she said, trying to keep her voice steady.

'Why, about the escape. Young William's in solitary for two weeks but you should be able to see him after that. Though he'll be on special measures for a bit, silly boy.'

Newt had been dismayed at his sentence. He'd hoped that by pleading guilty he'd be treated more leniently, especially in light of what his brief referred to as 'this poor young man's tragic family circumstances'. Unfortunately the judge was not swayed by this, remained unconvinced of his well-acted penitence and actually hinted he was fortunate not to receive a longer term. The only concession made was the speed with which his case had been handled. Pleading guilty helped to move things along but the prosecutor had pushed for a quick trial and sentence. Derek Johns was due for release in the next few weeks, he told the judge behind closed doors. The family had a history of witnesses developing total amnesia or conveniently vanishing just before they came to give evidence. Much better get it all sorted out before Johns could organize his supporters and colleagues. Everyone except Newt agreed this was for the best.

Two years was bad enough but two years in Dartmoor was a real blow. Newt had hoped for Pucklechurch though he was just over the age limit for a Young Offenders Institution. Even Bristol or Exeter would have been okay – not too far for his mother to visit. But the prisons were filling up, space was at a premium and the only berth available on the day of his sentence was the grim Victorian mausoleum that was Dartmoor.

'Don't worry Mum,' he'd said at their last meeting, 'I'll be alright. Just you hang on until Dad gets out.' He watched her walk out of the visiting room, her face streaked with tears, and realized she looked old. Like a little old woman struggling to face the world alone. Anger burned in his heart and he vowed to find out who had set them up. Someone had – the police were there almost before the alarm was triggered. And that someone was responsible for his little brother's death. Newt seemed much calmer, more easy-going than the rest of his family but when he did finally become angry he could be just as dangerous and now he was very, very angry.

Dartmoor was a shock, especially as his experience of prison was limited to a few hours in a police cell and his time on remand awaiting sentence. It was cold, it was grey and it smelt. There was no privacy, little to do and precious little dignity to his life for the first few days and he was relieved and grateful for the protection offered by one of his father's colleagues. Big Bill Boyd was a stalwart of Derek Johns' 'organization' and he took Newt under his wing, explaining the system and introducing him to the people he needed to know in the prisoners' hierarchy. Big Bill had access to his own sophisticated channels of communication and one morning as Newt queued for his breakfast the man next to him passed him a tiny slip of paper. Newt carried it in his pocket until he could read it late that night by the sliver of light that shone through his window. It was a message from his father telling him to keep his ears open for any information regarding the disastrous post office job. There was a rumour going around the Levels that a tip-off had come from a warder at Dartmoor and Derek Johns wanted to know if it was true. Newt read the note twice before spitting on it, chewing it up into tiny shreds and swallowing the pieces.

The next morning he began a concerted charm campaign on the warders, the teachers and the Chaplain, with the sole aim of worming his way on to the outdoor details. It took him a few weeks but as the cold weather continued to bite, several men dropped out of the garden projects on the prison farm and Newt stepped forward, an eager volunteer. It was a job for a 'trusty' and by rights Newt shouldn't have been eligible, but he'd been well behaved, hard working and in every way a model prisoner. He got the placement.

For three weeks Newt shivered in the biting wind as he dug, hoed and weeded around the vegetable gardens. The garden workers were issued with overalls and donkey jackets but the wind cut through the layers of clothing and by the end of each day Newt's hands were blue and stiff with cold. He was seriously considering chucking it for something indoors – even sign painting would be preferable – when he got his first piece of luck. He was leaning on his hoe out of sight of the warders, who were huddling in the relative warmth of the greenhouse door. As he glanced around he spotted a familiar figure. Newt turned his head slowly, looking around casually whilst allowing his eyes to run over the man being escorted to an unmarked van, through the fences and across the road. The man was older than he recalled, thin and unhealthy looking and he'd lost most of his hair, but Newt was sure. He watched as Kevin's dad, Frank Mallory, was helped into the van, his bag placed in the boot before being driven off towards the town.

'Bastard,' came a mutter next to him. Newt glanced to his left at the prisoner who had materialized next to him. The man nodded and then spat into the line of cabbages Newt was supposed to be hoeing.

'Fucking grass,' the man added. Before he could say any more there was a call from the warders, who emerged from the greenhouse warmed and eager to spur their charges on to greater efforts.

Newt spent his social time drifting around the open landings, exchanging a few words, offering his cigarettes around and fishing for tiny snippets of information. By the end of the week he had enough to piece together a reasonable story. Frank Mallory had washed up in Dartmoor several months ago. A petty thief of weak character and few connections, he was the butt of numerous practical 'jokes'. After several weeks he was transferred to the Infirmary and thence on to the VP wing. Although it was supposed to be a secure and safe environment, news and gossip about the Vulnerable Prisoner block still leaked out into the main population and Frank's transfer had raised a few eyebrows – he wasn't a sex offender, drug dealer or a disgraced copper so why was he there, people were asking. Frank, a nonentity most of his life, was the subject of intense speculation. It was obvious to all that he was ill, very ill and he was desperate to secure a release on compassionate grounds, but his history worked against him. Every time he was released he re-offended, mainly dumb, petty crimes involving little or no skill, imagination or even profit. He was separated from his wife, never saw his family and had nowhere to go. It was doubtful he would survive long on the outside, so limited was his experience of independent living. Better he stay in prison where he was warm, fed and looked after was the general consensus, but Frank had one great burning desire. He wanted to spend next Christmas, his last Christmas, as a free man. He wanted to see Kevin once more and give him a present, some small token to balance against the years of abandonment and neglect. He was a driven man and was willing to do anything to make his dream come true.

In his first few weeks, Frank picked up snippets of talk from the general population. Most were of no use to him but he started out on the same landing as Big Bill and he heard him boasting of Newt's exploits. Three post offices turned over, all at night with the culprits getting away clean – the coppers were desperate for a break in the case. Frank was careful. He knew the Johns gang could reach him even in Dartmoor, and they were noted for their imaginative brutality, but the information was a gift he could not ignore. He took his chances with a soft word to the prison doctor and eight weeks later he was in the back of a plain blue van, a new identity in his pocket and a place on a secure protection scheme awaiting him. He glanced back at the prison as he drove away. He knew he'd never go back inside. He might just make it to Christmas if he was lucky. He didn't see Newt's eyes following him down the road, he didn't know Biff was dead and he had no idea Derek Johns was out of prison and looking for the man responsible.

In one of those sudden climatic shifts, Dartmoor was flooded in sunshine for most of February. Warm breezes blew in from the Gulf Stream and walkers and climbers were often sighted following the trails across the moor and through the village. Newt, on his outside work party at the prison farm, bided his time, lurking by the pig-pens until a fight broke out on the other side of the gardens. As the warders hurried over to separate the culprits he stripped off his jacket and overalls, shivering in the breeze. Dressed in white prison vest and navy boxer shorts he looked at first glance like one of the occasional joggers, lean and hardy runners who used the footpaths and trails for long-distance training. Slipping under the fence and crouching until he was clear of the garden area, Newt set off at a steady pace for the village a mile down the road.

The phone box was at the other end of the short row of houses, most of them homes for prison warders and other staff. Newt felt his heart race as he jogged as casually as he could past the closed doors. It would take just one glance from a window and he would be caught, but luck was with him. He reached the box, stepped in and dialled for a reverse-charge call. When the call was accepted he delivered his message as swiftly as possible, replaced the receiver and stepped out into the winter sunshine. He waited, leaning against the glass of the phone box until the warders picked him up a few minutes later. Ushered him into an isolation cell they shook their heads at his folly.

'What did you do that for you daft lad?' one asked.

Newt shrugged. 'Just fancied stretching my legs a bit. You was quick though, spottin' I'd gone.'

The warder stared at him and burst out laughing. 'You looked the part, until you got out on the road. Then you was easy to see. Not many joggers around here in wellies.'

Newt smiled to himself as they closed the door and went off to tell their fellow guards about the Somerset lad's 'great escape'. He'd done what was needed. It was up to his father now.

Chapter Two

Kevin shivered in his thin jacket as the March night turned cold and squinted at the nets in the muddy river. This was the delicate bit. Pull them in too soon and you only got half a catch, leave them too long and the homemade frame might give way and that was a night's work swimming away downstream for someone else to harvest. The moonlight faded as dark clouds rolled in from the west and he decided he'd had enough. Hauling at the square net he tipped the contents into several plastic boxes stamped 'Property of Highpoint Fish Quay'. He hefted the boxes into an old pram careful to keep the baby eels upright as they squirmed and rolled in their hundreds. Not bad, he though as he packed up his gear, stowed his nets in the reeds and began to push the pram and its precious cargo along the towpath. Nearly three boxes – might be over thirty quid. It was nearly a mile to the underpass where the Elver Man waited each night and he put his head down and plodded steadily along in the dark, watching for any signs of the river wardens as he went.

The Elver Man's van was parked in the shadow of the motorway bridge, lights off to avoid attracting unwanted attention. Kevin pulled his pram up to the back and rapped on the door. When there was no answer he went round to the driver's window and peered in. The seat was empty but he spotted the keys in the ignition. It began to rain and the wind was getting up, blowing the water sideways under the bridge. Kevin hesitated for a moment but as the rain increased he opened the door and slid inside. He'll be back soon, Kevin reasoned. The keys were there so he'd not be far. He glanced in the wing-mirror to make sure his precious elvers were safe and felt in his pocket, pulling out a fistful of money. Over two hundred quid now he gloated, running his thumb over the edges so the notes rustled. Another fifty or so and he'd have his dues. He would be a fully paid up member of the Watermen, the best and finest Carnival gang in town. He shoved the money back into his pocket and settled back in the worn seat. It had been a long night and the interior of the van was warm. In the dark, with the rain pouring down he didn't notice the blood as it dripped from the back doors to gather in a sticky pool around the van. He didn't realize his shoes were splashed with it where he'd circled the vehicle. After a few minutes he drifted off to sleep.

Alex gazed from her office window at the grass along the banks of the River Parratt. Bright daffodils, blocks of vibrant gold and cream, had sprung up seemingly overnight and there was real warmth in the pale spring sunlight. Her phone rang and she turned back to her desk as she saw the clock. Kevin, she thought. Bloody Kevin's late again.

'Message from Kevin,' said Lauren's voice. 'He's got himself arrested and won't be in.'

'I'm coming down. Don't let his mother leave,' Alex said, and dived for the stairs. The main room was empty by the time she got there and Lauren was leaning on the counter looking anxious.

'You let her go!'

Lauren shook her head and beckoned her over.

'Never mind that, she's gone off to find a solicitor.'

Alex stopped and asked, 'What's wrong with old Smythe? He's been Kevin's solicitor since – well, for ever.'

'I think Kevin's going to need someone a bit better than Smythe,' said Lauren. 'He's on his way to Bristol as we speak. Word is, he's murdered the Elver Man.'

Alex took a deep breath, confounded by yet another unknown in this strange world but was distracted by the main door flying open. Three young men sporting Mohican haircuts and leather jackets swaggered in and flung themselves onto chairs in the waiting area. They were full of themselves, laughing about the 'Lorry Boy' they'd left standing outside, too scared to come in. The leader, a tall rangy boy with broken front teeth, shouted across to the office window.

'Mornin' Bridget. Tell him I'm here, right?'

Lauren glanced in his direction and waved vaguely before turning back to Alex.

'Hang on – Bridget? Why Bridget?' Alex asked. The whole office fell quiet and suddenly everyone was busy, their attention fixed on papers and typewriters.

'Lauren! Why did he call you Bridget?' Alex insisted. Lauren looked up at her defiantly.

'Like the song. You know – "Bridget the Midget", okay? It's a joke.'

Alex was scarcely average height herself and looked skinny, but her lean frame hid muscles developed from years of sports. She was round the counter and had the boy by the arm before he could react. Holding him in a wrestling hold she forced him to his knees and pressed the palm of her free hand onto his, exerting a steady pressure on his splayed fingers.

'Shit, stop, you're breaking my hand!' he cried.

'Apologise,' said Alex.

'Okay, I'm sorry. I'm sorry! It was just a joke. We all do it . . . aah!' The pressure increased and he was forced down further until he was huddled on the carpet at her feet.

'Alex, stop, please!' Lauren hurried towards her and pulled at her elbow. Alex lifted her hand but leaned on the boy's shoulder to stop him rising.

'It is not a joke and it will not be tolerated. Tell everyone – your friends and cronies – because if I ever hear that again I'm coming after you – understand?'

The boy nodded, cradling his hand to his chest.

'Good. Now, who have you come to see? And you can get up now.'

The young man struggled to his feet and slunk back to his chair.

'Girt bitch,' he muttered.

Alex swung round to face him again. 'You have something else to say?'

The boy sneered at her. 'You'm in trouble. I'm going to tell my probation officer on you. You'm can't do that – 'tis not right.'

Lauren laughed and held up a buff folder. 'Good luck with that Brian. Alex is your new P.O.'

Brian stared at Alex. 'That's not it. I always get Mr Malcolm. I don't want you!'

Alex reached over and took the folder, flipping through a sorry catalogue of petty crime and minor misdemeanours. Brian had been a very busy boy for the past few years. She snapped the file shut and beckoned to him.

'Well Brian, you had the misfortune to turn seventeen last month,' she said. 'Mr Malcolm looks after the juveniles but you, alas, are no longer numbered amongst them.'

There was a pause as Brian struggled to make out what had happened. Alex waited for a moment then said softly, 'You're a youth now, Brian. You get me, not Mr Malcolm. Now come on, we've got work to do.'

'So what exactly is an elver?' asked Alex later that day, as she and Lauren sat in the lunch room. It was a glorious day, the sun streaming through the open windows accompanied by the gentle cooing of doves from the eaves of the converted

27

schoolhouse they now occupied. Lauren took a bite of her sandwich and chewed thoughtfully.

'It's a baby eel,' she said. 'They swarm up the rivers and the locals set up nets and haul them out in their thousands. But it's not legal unless you have a licence.'

Alex sipped her tea. 'So Kevin was poaching?'

Lauren nodded. 'Yep. All of them's poaching I suppose. That's why they sell to the Elver Man. He comes down here just for a few weeks. Buys up everything the lads catch and disappears again. All cash, no questions. Is big business down here, is elvering.'

'Why did Kevin have all that money on him then? The police say he had over £200 in his pockets. That's an absolute fortune for a lad like him, surely.'

Lauren shrugged and took another bite. 'His mother says 'twas his subs for the Watermen. Seems like Kevin didn't trust the banks so he carried it around with him.'

'Okay, who or what's the "Watermen",' asked Alex wearily.

'Now that don't make sense,' said Lauren. 'Watermen's a Carnival club. Big one too, one of the oldest and most important. No way would they let someone like Kevin join, not if he had a thousand pounds. I reckon they was just fobbing him off, asking for such a big sub. They never expected him to raise it.'

'Well, it's given the police a motive,' said Alex sadly. 'They told me he was charged with robbery with violence as well as murder.'

Lauren shook her head, 'Whole thing's just stupid,' she said. 'I know Kevin's several sandwiches short of a picnic but even he's not dumb enough to rob the Elver Man, kill him and then fall asleep in the van. Something's wrong there I reckon.'

'I must say I don't have Kevin down as a murderer,' Alex agreed. 'The police seem happy enough though. What do they say – method, opportunity and motive? They've got two of the three and they reckon the poor man was stabbed with some sort of curved blade, like a fishing knife. Kevin's got one of those so it doesn't look too good for him.'

Lauren screwed up her sandwich paper and lobbed it into the bin. 'Well, I don't think he did it and if the police can't see that maybe we should try to find out ourselves. We can't just abandon the lad. He won't stand a chance in prison.'

Alex peered at her second sandwich, sniffed it and decided not to bother.

'I don't know. It's not exactly my job. I wouldn't know where to start.'

Lauren slid off the chair, excited at the prospect of a new challenge.

'Come on, we've got to try. Someone probably saw him out on the riverbank for a start. We could ask around. What harm can it do?'

'That may be how they do things in London,' said Garry Wilkins, putting a sneer into the name of the capital city, 'but it is not acceptable behaviour in Somerset.'

Alex sat in front of her Senior's desk and nodded. She had long ago decided silence was the best response with Garry. He worked himself up into quite a state if contradicted and tended to take his anger out on the team at random.

'Brawling in the waiting room! We're lucky you're not being accused of assault. What were you thinking?'

Alex tried to look contrite and waited until Garry started again. It was obvious he had no interest at all in what she might have been thinking.

'God, the people we appoint. You don't know the area, you don't know the job, the way you dress – and that terrible old car of yours.'

Alex struggled with the temptation to point out she couldn't afford a better car after five years at university and she always wore a skirt (reluctantly) into court. Besides which, as she said to Lauren later, taking a new car into some of the areas she had to visit was just asking for trouble.

She wandered down to the front office, still smarting with

29

the injustice of it all. To her surprise, Pauline, the senior administrator, opened the door and invited her in to the back office tea-room, a rare honour. Lauren and Pauline brewed fresh coffee and sat her down whilst the other office women smiled and greeted her like an old friend. When Garry rang down demanding to know where she was, she heard Pauline offering a vague story relating to an emergency call-out necessitating her absence for the afternoon.

'Don't worry about him,' said Lauren. 'He's been losing it for a while now. That's why there's so many new staff coming in. No-one wants to stay for long and he moved half the experienced people out into other offices. He thought they were undermining his authority.'

'Glad it's not just me then,' mumbled Alex. The remark about not knowing the job had stung her. She'd left a secure job in the civil service to follow her dream of becoming a probation officer. After three years at university she'd got a degree in social science and she'd spent two more years getting her qualification. A whole year of that had been working on placement in hostels, offices and court buildings. Lauren shook her head at her.

'It's our job to teach you what you really need to know,' she said. 'You may know the book stuff but no-one comes here able to organize a case-load. You got no idea how to address the local court when you need to breach someone, your paperwork is a terrible mess and half of you don't keep proper records. The first year we take one officer each and try to beat you into shape.'

Alex was rendered speechless for a moment, but if she was being honest she suspected there was considerable truth in Lauren's words. The administrators were overworked, undervalued and poorly paid compared to the probation officers but they knew everyone, always had the correct files to hand and seemed to handle the sad and sometimes aggressive procession of clients with tact, humour and considerable skill. Without Lauren, she reflected, she would have crashed and burned in her first week.

She looked around the office with more attention, noting the speed and efficiency of the activity. The women rarely stopped for a chat yet they were good humoured and relaxed in their competence. Lauren was watching her and suddenly grinned.

'Yep, you get it. Lots of you don't, however long you're here. Just don't let Garry see you behaving towards us as if we're real people. Seems it offends his sense of importance.'

'And, off the record now,' added Pauline, 'you watch him. He's been known to make rather strange decisions, especially if he thinks someone's a bit of a challenge. So you check with Lauren or me if you're not sure of anything. Now, you go off and get that old car of yours out of the car park before he spots it.'

'What about work?'

Lauren held up a form. 'Is already being logged. You've been very busy this afternoon, doing your job somewhere else. Why don't you go see Ada Mallory, see if Kevin was teamed up with anyone else that night? I reckon he must've seen someone else on the river. Maybe someone can give him an alibi.'

On the way out she passed Gordon, damp cloth in hand, scrubbing at the back seat of his car and received a vague wave in acknowledgment of her greeting. Stung by his attitude she drove off feeling almost surplus to requirements once more.

It was abominably hot in the Mallory's front room. The windows were closed against the fresh spring air, the fire was roaring in the hearth and the whole room was crowded with furniture, ornaments and dogs. Clothes were scattered across most surfaces and there was a layer of animal hair on the sofa where Alex perched after Mrs Mallory had swept a pile of grey underclothes on to the floor to make space. One large and overly affectionate dog of indeterminate breed lay across the rest of the couch, inching its head towards her as she reluctantly accepted a biscuit to go with her dark, stewed tea. She declined the offer of sugar after seeing the bowl with its

31

mix of lumpy white granules and unidentified black specks. Ada Mallory settled her ample self in an armchair, pulled her bright pink cardigan around her shoulders and sighed heavily.

'My poor boy, he's no killer. Half the time he don't even kill them fish proper. They was still moving around when they police gets there. I ask yer, how comes there's no blood on him then 'cepting that bit on his shoes? They said he's washed it off but I know they can tell now even after washing. And to be honest, he's not a great one for that is Kev. He was still all muddy from that fishing.'

Alex nodded sympathetically and nibbled at her biscuit. It was very old and very stale. She tried a sip of tea to wash away the taste and wished she hadn't. Clearing her throat as she tried to marshal a suitable response she glanced at Ada and suddenly realized she was crying. Great fat tears rolled down her face and fell into her tea cup. Alex put her own cup on the floor and reached out to steady the woman's shaking hands.

''Tis not right! My poor little lad, they knows it's not him but they've got him now. Don't reckon we'll stand no chance of getting him back. He hates bein' inside. Always out in all weathers he is. He's not got no chance locked up with them evil men.' She sobbed, sniffed loudly and sobbed again.

'And I can't even go see him. 'Tis so far, Bristol. There's no bus nor nothing!' She finished with a wail.

Alex fumbled in her case and pulled out one rather crumpled tissue. Mrs Mallory took this feeble offering, soaking it with one huge blast from her nose. Note to self, thought Alex, get better tissues. She felt something nudge her leg and flinched as another dog, a long haired lurcher speckled in grey and tan leaned on her foot, mouth open to steal the biscuit she had left on her saucer.

'So I ended up offering her a lift when I go up to see him,' she admitted to Lauren the next morning. Lauren threw her a look of withering scorn.

'Now how do you suppose she's going to get in without a visiting order? Kevin can't read you know, so he don't send them out.'

'Oh shit, I didn't think of that. How does she usually manage?'

Lauren sighed and pointed to a row of folders on a shelf by the window.

'The tacky green one on the right,' she said.

Alex reached up and took the folder. It was labelled 'KM: VO', and inside was a bundle of form letters, neatly typed and signed, requesting a visit with Kevin. Lauren held out her hand and took a blank form.

'He's in Bristol isn't he – right. What day you planning to go?' She typed in the details, addressed an envelope and flipped the finished letter into the post tray.

'Now you have to go back and tell her to expect the order,' she instructed. 'The Mallorys have a nasty habit of burning anything official looking as soon as it lands through their door.'

Alex groaned. She was already heartily sick of the Levels and still could not find her way out from that eerie, flat landscape. She knew one road – and it was only wide enough for one car. Once again she had driven straight on from her visit to Mrs Mallory, emerging somewhere near Glastonbury.

'Isn't there a map or something,' she asked. Pauline looked up and laughed at this.

'There's a map, sure. We call it the "Edgar", but you're welcome to a copy if you want.'

'Edgar?'

'For Edgar Allan Poe,' said Lauren. 'You know, "Tales of Mystery and Imagination".'

'More like "The House of Usher", out there,' commented Paul Malcolm, leaning over the counter. 'Hi Alex, how's it going with Brian?'

Alex was working frantically, trying to finish up her notes from her day in court when a call came through summoning

33

her to Garry's office. He gave her an approving glance as she knocked and entered.

'That's much better,' he commented taking in her skirt, blouse and jacket. 'That's how a probation officer should dress.'

'Just the women though,' said Alex, and regretted it the instant the words left her mouth. Garry frowned.

'Of course, just the women. What are you implying?'

'Sorry, nothing. Nothing – it was just a bit of a joke Garry.'

Her Senior did not seem to find it very funny and continued to frown in her direction.

'Well, I suppose you have different ideas, coming from London.' Again the sneer in his voice. 'But I hope you will settle down soon and start to do things our way.'

He reached into his desk and pulled out a pile of folders, thrusting them over the desk at her.

'You've been here six months now, seven I think it is, so we will be increasing your case-load until you reach the norm. As you know, we try to break new officers in gently.'

Alex took the files and tried to hide her dismay. She was already struggling to cope with the twenty or so probationers allotted to her, especially as she was now on the court rota and expected to attend, suitably dressed of course, for one full day a week.

'There are a few old hands in there – see what you can do with them but don't get your hopes up,' said Garry, waving his hand in dismissal. 'Oh yes, and a transfer from Exeter office. We've no details yet but there's an address. I'd like you to make contact with him at once. Thank you.'

He had turned his attention back to his desk before she reached the door leaving her to struggle with the folders and the handle, which was sticking as usual. One of the joys of an old and poorly converted building she had decided.

Well, that was not one of his best pep-talks she thought as she hurried back to her room. He really should work on his motivational skills. She dropped the folders on her desk, sank into her chair and surrendered to the misery that flooded over her. Lauren found her, damp eyed and hunched behind the desk, having failed to get an answer on the internal phone.

'It's too soon to expect you to carry a full case-load,' she said. 'You're supposed to have a year before you build up to that. What's he given you?' She rummaged through the files sorting them into three piles as she went.

'Hopeless cases,' said Lauren tapping the first stack. 'Give them a month with weekly calls and take 'em back to court. No point in wasting time 'cos they're not going to attend and they've probably already breached their parole. They've just not been caught yet.'

She turned to the second pile. 'These are your real work. Mainly young lads on first or second offence, a few come up from Social Service nannying like Brian.' She caught sight of Alex's face. 'They not all like Brian, you know. And actually I do think you're doing him some good. He's been quite polite since you had a little word with him and he's actually come in almost sober a couple of times.'

She turned her attention to the last folder. 'This 'ent right,' she said, opening it to show a single piece of paper with a note attached. 'This is supposed to be a transfer, some bloke from Exeter out on licence from Dartmoor, but there's nothing but a name, address and this scrawly old signature. It's not even on proper paper so I can't tell which office it's from.'

Alex took the page and examined it. There was a name – Andrew Michael Hinton – and an address she did not recognize. Someone had scribbled something at the bottom which looked like 'Agg B. P/L?' She couldn't make it out properly as there was a bold, clear stamp across it saying 'TRANSFER TO: with 'Highpoint' written in pencil.

'I'm not sure you should just go out there,' said Lauren. ''Tis out on the Levels, way past the Mallorys' place. Used to be Ada's family home, way back. I thought it'd fallen down years back. Maybe you should get him to visit first. We don't even know what he was in for, nor how long he got.'

Alex knew she was right, but Garry had practically ordered

her to see this Andrew Hinton as soon as possible and she was reluctant to question his instructions any further.

'I'll be okay,' she said. 'I worked shifts in some of the nastiest hostels in London. I know how to take care of myself and how to avoid trouble.'

Lauren looked unconvinced. 'Well you go during the day and let us know when so we can check you's back safe,' she said. 'I don't like it. I don't think he should be sending a woman out there alone at all.'

The assumption that she was somehow weaker, more vulnerable than her male colleagues, coming straight after Garry's comments on her 'unsuitable appearance', drove all the sense from Alex's head. She was sick of people telling her this was not a job for a woman. She'd had enough of that whilst training and still heard it from her family when she phoned home every week.

'Rubbish,' she said angrily. 'I'll pop out this evening. I've got my map and I want to get this sorted at once. Thank you Lauren.'

Lauren stood up, stung by her tone, and walked to the door. She stopped and turned but Alex glared at her and said, 'Thank you Lauren. Good night.'

Lauren shrugged and left, leaving Alex feeling more miserable than ever, guilty and slightly apprehensive. She looked out of the window and saw clouds gathering in the distance. Well, there was nothing for it, she had to go or lose face entirely. She would apologize in the morning, she thought, as she watched Lauren climb into her specially modified car and drive away into the gathering gloom. There was no time to go home and change either, she realized, cursing her own temper. Stamping on the clutch and banging the gear stick she set off to meet this mysterious new parolee as the rain began to fall around her.

Chapter Three

He wasn't sure why he'd come back to this place. Sure, he
had some good memories – holidays and sunny times when
he'd been a kid, the early years with the warmth of a family
and times spent with his sweetheart in this front room or the
little garden out the back. Still, it was not a good idea going
back to places where he was known. It was just he didn't
have many choices in his life now. This was the only place he
could think of where he might get some news, call in a few
favours. He was supposed to be Andrew Michael Hinton, but
as soon as he got the bad news about his health he knew he
had to be Kevin's dad, at least this once in his life.

He stared out of the window and scowled at the clouds
mounting into grey, sullen hills on the horizon. He hated the
rain, hated being cold and he'd been cold a lot of the time
recently. Dartmoor was a dour and bleak place for those
confined within the walls of the Victorian prison. He turned
from the window and searched the ceiling, trying to locate
the source of a steady dripping sound. The cottage was in
a poor state of repair and the roof was leaking. There was

a movement outside and his attention fixed on the muddy track leading to the cottage's front door. A battered blue motorcar turned in and wallowed slowly over the potholes towards him. He knew who it was before she got out of the car. Alex's eccentric Citroën was already a standing joke in local criminal circles.

Alex slid to a halt some way from the front door and leaned back into the seat cushions. Despite being only too familiar there was still something slightly unsettling about the slow descent of the car body as the suspension deflated. For months she had fought the urge to get out and check the car was clear of the wheels before moving off and several younger probationers had taken to hanging around the car park first thing in the morning or in the evening to watch her arrive or drive off. That showed you how little there was to keep them entertained she thought grimly as she opened the door and stepped out into the rain. Her left foot landed in a pothole, the water oozing into her impractical 'court' shoes.

'Bugger, bugger, bugger!' she muttered to herself as she tried to twist free of the clinging mud without falling face first into the surrounding ooze. She pulled herself upright, slammed the car door shut and staggered up to the cottage door. Actually 'cottage' was a rather flattering description, she decided. Several windows were boarded up, the roof sagged alarmingly on one side and the brickwork surrounding the front door was crumbling away. One good shove, she thought, and the whole front would cave in. She tapped on the filthy glass, one eye on the porch balanced precariously over her head. There was no response and as she stepped back she noted there was no smoke from the chimney or light inside any of the rooms. She really ought to check the back, just in case, she thought, as the rain trickled down her neck, but the brambles and nettles crowding the old wooden gate off to the side decided her. The first call was made, there was no-one there and she could come back later when she was dressed for the task.

Inside the house, standing back from the filthy windows, his eyes followed her every move. There was a tense moment when her car misfired, stuttering in the heavy rain, but finally she bumped and rolled her way out of sight and he felt himself relax. Turning to the hearth he considered lighting a fire, balancing his yearning for comfort against his need for secrecy, when the front door opened and it all became academic.

'Hello Frank,' said a familiar voice. 'Fancy seeing you back here.'

He turned to face his old neighbour, the person he least wanted to see in the whole world.

'Derek, now look, let's just sit down and talk about things, right?'

Derek Johns shook his head as he reached behind him. 'I don't think there's much to talk about d'you? You're a grass, Frank Mallory. You got out by selling my lads to the police and now you think you can come back here and pick up where you left off, just like that. Not going to happen, boy. My youngest, he hung himself. You know 'bout that? All on his own, locked up at night in the cells, they didn't keep no eye on him like they're meant to. By the time they found him he was gone. My Iris, she had to go identify him, look at him with his face all bruised and his eyes near popping out of his head. Do you know about *that* then Frankie-boy?'

Frank backed away, his hands raised as if pleading. Derek pulled a knife from his pocket and moved towards him, slow, smooth steps like a cat stalking its prey.

'So now your boy'll know what it's like. He's in Bristol ain't he? Nasty lock-up, Bristol. Reckon they might take to a little lad like Kevin – know what I mean?'

Derek aimed a vicious blow, the knife ripping through Frank Mallory's raised hand and into his soft stomach. Frank gasped, jerking on the knife as Derek twisted and pulled upwards, gutting him like a fish. Frank collapsed making low, keening sounds as his chest and throat filled with blood. Derek turned away and stared out of the window until the sounds stopped. Walking over to the hearth he aimed a final kick to the head.

'Two down, three to go,' muttered Derek as he rummaged through Frank's pockets. Then he cleaned up the mess in the fireplace.

Alex was spared having to face Lauren the next morning. Driving out to the Mallorys' place she mused on her wasted trip the night before, but the sight of Ada Mallory dressed for visiting the prison shook her out of her sombre mood. Like a galleon in full sail, she swept down the muddy path resplendent in vivid pink polyester. The whole outfit, complete with matching gloves and hat, was only marred by her sensible brown boots. Alex opened the passenger door and helped to prod and tuck her into the front seat. Closing the door carefully she reflected the ensemble was likely to generate enough static electricity to constitute a fire hazard.

'Have you got the visiting order?' she asked, as she squeezed into the space left behind the wheel.

Mrs Mallory opened her pink vinyl handbag and rummaged through it. There was a significant delay as she emptied most of the contents onto her lap before flourishing the brown envelope in triumph.

Alex looked carefully at the array of objects as they were packed back into the bag.

'Um, I don't think you can take some of those in with you,' she said.

Mrs Mallory stopped and stared at her, the brim of her hat quivering with indignation. 'What you mean then? 'Tis nothing bad I got. Just a few things I reckon Kev might need. Anyway, no *gennlemun* would go looking through a lady's handbag.'

Privately Alex agreed, but the guards were not likely to be gentlemen, though they would need to be very brave to delve into Mrs Mallory's handbag.

'We want to see Kevin don't we? So maybe we should just – be very sensible until we know how things work. He's

40

in a proper prison now, on remand. It's not like the Young Offenders places he was in last time. So maybe, well, I'd leave the penknife in the car. And the lighters.'

Mrs Mallory glared at her but removed the offending items and shoved them into the door pocket.

'Anything else?' she asked.

'Well, he's not allowed to take a packet of cigarettes, just smoke one with us . . . .'

Mrs Mallory pulled out more items and added them to the door.

'So I suppose he can't have no sweets neither?'

'They might be okay – we'll ask as we go in.' Alex glanced at her passenger, who was turning an angry shade of red, and hurried on. 'And maybe you should leave the scissors behind.'

'Now you'm just being daft! They's nail scissors, for his toes. Kevin suffers terrible with his toes.'

This was too much detail for Alex, who turned her full attention to the bumpy road. There was a moment's silence before Ada Mallory burst out, 'And why're we goin' this way anyway? 'Tis miles out of the way. You just take this left here, see, and follow Sedgemoor for a bit 'til you get to the proper road.'

Alex turned left as instructed and found herself bumping along beside the huge canal cut over the years to help reclaim the rich peat lands of the Levels. The rest of the journey passed in silence as Ada Mallory brooded on her son's plight and Alex, mindful of Lauren's warnings, mused on hers.

There is a particular, peculiar smell to a prison which is quite unlike anywhere else. The first big hit is cheap, strong carbolic soap, used day after day on walls and floors until it seeps into every pore of the building's fabric. Under this is the counterpoint of the transient beings, the sad and lonely men housed within this pungent environment. The smell of feet, sweat and a whiff of stale tobacco smoke hangs in the air, gradually gaining strength as the visitor moves further into the institution. Alex hated visiting prisons but then she doubted many people enjoyed it very much. She parked in the official visitor spaces below the walls and had her warrant card out before she left the car. Within seconds an attendant pounced, ready to send them away to find a place in nearby streets or more distant car parks. His face fell when he saw her official status.

'She's with me,' said Alex firmly, as she took Ada Mallory's arm and hustled her away. The attendant hesitated but forgot all about them as another car pulled in to try its luck. Alex closed her ears to the raised voices behind her and guided her charge towards the gatehouse.

'Remember, they may take some things from your bag but you get them back when we leave. Don't make a fuss or they can refuse to let you in. You don't want to disappoint Kevin, do you?' She glanced at Ada whose face was wearing what she had come to think of as her 'mutinous' look.

'Why do they all have to be so nasty?' she demanded. 'Having a lad in prison's bad enough. Don't cost nothing to be polite, show a bit of respect. 'Tis not necessary, all this pushing people about.'

There wasn't enough time left in the day to try to explain the psychology of the prison service to Ada Mallory and anyway, sometimes Alex suspected pushing people about was one of the few perks of the job for some officers.

Alex presented her card and emptied her pockets, calmly waiting with her arms out as a female officer patted her down. She nodded as the guard warned her against passing anything to the prisoners but was allowed to take the packet of cigarettes and a small disposable lighter after being reminded she could only give Kevin one at a time, after the last one had been smoked right down to the butt. She stepped through the metal detector and watched anxiously as Ada plonked her bag on the counter. She had hoped her example would be reassuring but from the look on her face this was probably wishful thinking. Despite Alex's warnings there were still several packets of cigarettes in the pink handbag as well as a few boxes of matches. These went into a metal drawer along with the nail scissors, a nail file (what *had* she been thinking, Alex asked herself), a girlie magazine, two pairs of rather moth-eaten socks and the sweets. The guard shook his head at the haul as he handed it to his assistant. It was a struggle to get the drawer in the rack and closed, Alex noted with some amusement. The female attendant stepped forward and began patting at her coat rather cautiously. Ada drew herself up to her full height and stood rigid as the check was completed.

'Could you, er, remove your hat?' the attendant asked. She received the full force of Mrs Mallory's fury directed through a single glare. Alex leaned round so she could be seen and made encouraging gestures, nodding hopefully. With a huge sigh Ada reached up and withdrew a long, lethal hatpin, a good six inches in length. The hat came off and was laid on the counter, the pin by its side as the guards looked at it in horror for a moment.

'You'd better keep that safe too. Takes ages to fix it does and I'm wanting to see my boy now.' With that she stepped through the metal detector and looked pointedly at the door barring her way. Alex caught the eye of the female officer as she turned to unlock the entrance and both of them struggled not to smile. As she set off down the corridor to the visitors' room she heard, 'Bloody hell – never seen that before . . .' as the Gatehouse officers contemplated how close they had come to letting the pin, a truly deadly object in a prison, get past.

The visitors' room was almost as unwelcoming as the Gatehouse. Despite attempts to make it seem less like part of the prison there was no disguising the blank walls, the furniture fixed to the floor or the all-pervading smell. Metal doors admitted visitors at one end and a trickle of prisoners at the other. The windows were covered with some sort of heavy plastic, designed to be shatterproof, and it had faded over the years so the little light that made it over the encircling wall was filtered and polluted to a sickly yellow. The refreshment bar offered grey tea or equally grey coffee dispensed by an unsmiling volunteer in thin, squashy plastic beakers. It did little to lighten the mood. Every time the door opened the sounds of keys and chains echoed around the room, rendering normal conversation impossible. Alex sat next to Ada, waiting patiently for Kevin's arrival whilst around them families settled to their meetings with questions, pleading, a few angry words, more questions until the sounds became one huge, desperate babble. Alex glanced at Ada and realized she was on the verge of tears. Hurriedly breaking in to the pack of emergency tissues she always carried in her pocket, she thrust several into the crying woman's hand and was startled when Ada squeezed her hand in thanks. Then the door opened and Kevin sloped in, head down.

Ada rose to her feet and moved to embrace her wayward son but Kevin pulled away, dropping into a chair opposite and slumping over the table.

'Oh, oh Kev. . .' she began, tears flowing. Kevin turned his head away and stared at Alex.

'Got a fag?'

She passed him a cigarette from the packet and lit it for him, leaning back slightly to avoid the cloud of smoke. Kevin puffed away for a moment, then pinched out the glowing end and tucked the butt behind his ear where it was hidden by his hair. He glanced at Alex hopefully and she handed him another, lit it and pointedly pulled the packet back to her side of the table.

'Don't make a fuss now,' he muttered to his mother. 'This ain't like Young Offenders. There's real hard'ns in here. Can't have no woman crying over us like I'm a kid.'

Alex glanced around, casually thinking he wasn't much more than a kid, especially compared to most of the men sitting at the other tables. Some, like Kevin, wore their own clothes but most were dressed in the prison uniform of blue shirts, dark trousers and grey jumpers. Her eye was caught by one young man resplendent in yellow and blue harlequin trousers and she stared for a moment before Kevin's voice said, 'Escaper, he is. Won't get far in them now will he?'

She turned back to the young man in front of her.

'This isn't an official probation visit Kevin, so we can talk properly next time. Still, if there's anything you need let me know and I'll do what I can to get it sent.'

Kevin took a final puff of his cigarette and placed the filter in the ashtray.

'Could use some more clothes. These is damp in the morning from washing 'um. Any chance of some cash for the commissary?' he asked his mother. She began to rummage in her bag before realizing her purse was back at the gatehouse. Alex laid a hand on her shoulder in an attempt to reassure her.

'We'll sort that out,' she said. 'Now, you've got a solicitor haven't you?'

Kevin shook his head, 'Not yet I've not. I'm makin' do with the duty muppet. You was going to sort that out Mum!'

Ada shook her head, her mouth working, though she seemed unable to say anything. Alex pushed her chair back from the table and stood up.

'I'll go out now,' she said. 'You can have a chat in private'. As she walked to the back of the room, she decided that this was probably the least private place in the whole City of Bristol.

On the way home, Ada was uncharacteristically silent. After a few attempts at conversation Alex abandoned all pretence of sociability and they drove through the gloom of the overcast afternoon, both occupied with their own thoughts. Alex was concerned about Kevin. He had seemed so young, almost fragile seen next to so many muscular older men. She had long been of the opinion that the much celebrated 'short sharp shock' programme did nothing except take weedy, wheezy lads and turn them into strong, fit hooligans who could fight back and run away. Her encounter with the inmates of Bristol Prison had done nothing to change her mind. The silence was finally broken as they turned off the main road and began to bump along the track towards the Mallory place.

45

'I don't reckon he's safe in that place,' said Ada fiercely.

Alex's job was to uphold the orders of the court but privately she agreed with her. She didn't think Kevin was safe there either. Despite his tough talk he had looked lonely and scared.

'You try an' get him moved.'

Alex almost swerved into the ditch running next to the track.

'I can't do that. It's down to the court and the police. They just allocate them after the hearing.'

'I don't care. He's not safe there. I'll not rest.'

Alex waited for a moment before saying, 'Maybe if you get him a solicitor . . .'

Ada rounded on her, 'I'm trying! Think I don't know he needs one? But how do I choose one, eh? And how can I pay for one. Real solicitors, they cost a sight more than legal aid, and Smythe – he's got my boy's papers anyway. So what'm I supposed to do?'

Her anger swirled around the car, heavy and rank like the stale tobacco smoke seeping out of Alex's clothes.

'Anyway, I went looking last week but I'm not sure some of them as I talked to was solicitors. A couple, they looked so young I think they was just grammar school boys, as made up a certificate for their walls.' Ada nodded her head as she stared out of the windscreen leaving Alex at a loss for words. Just when she began to feel some empathy with the Mallorys she ran up hard against their own special view of the world . . .

It was just gone four o'clock when she dropped Ada Mallory at her house and set off to find the road back to town. She felt she really ought to go into the office, just in case anything had come up. Be honest, she told herself, she should go in and see Lauren. Despite the stresses of the day she was still squirming at the memory of her behaviour the night before. She had been rude, arrogant and childish and the sooner she put it right the better she would feel. At the turning onto the town road she hesitated – town or home, she wondered. She could no longer stand the smell of herself, the odour of the prison that rose from her clothes and hair. Feeling guilty, but also slightly relieved, she turned right and headed for the calm of her clean, tidy home.

The next morning there was a note on her desk from Garry demanding her immediate attendance. It was dated the day before and she read it with a sinking feeling in the pit of her stomach. She flipped through her diary and realized she'd not entered the Bristol visit – she'd not been sure whether it was 'official' and she doubted whether driving prisoner's relatives around the country counted as part of her duties. She hesitated before picking up the phone. Lauren would know, she thought, only Lauren was not in the office – she had rung in the day before and taken a few days off, Pauline informed her rather briskly. Alex replaced the phone, picked up the note and headed upstairs feeling utterly alone.

Garry was reading a file and waved her to a chair without looking up. She sat for a few minutes as he continued to ignore her, the silence broken by the rustling of turned pages and the frantic buzzing of a fly trapped behind the half-drawn blinds. The windows were tightly closed against the warm spring air and the room was stuffy. Garry was wearing a particularly strong aftershave lotion and the pungent smell began to make her feel quite dizzy. Finally he laid the report down on his desk and looked at her.

'So, you've not made contact with Mr Hinton yet?'

She felt a rush of relief – this wasn't about her absence yesterday after all.

'I went out the same evening,' she said, 'but there was no-one home. I thought I might try again today.' She heard her ingratiating tones and despised herself for this show of weakness. Garry, on the other hand, looked rather pleased. He nodded approvingly and tapped the file in front of him.

'We've got a few more details come through,' he said, and then lowered his voice forcing her to lean forwards. The aftershave became almost overwhelming as he continued.

'Mr Hinton is a special case. The police will be looking after him for a while, whilst he's with us. You should not mention him to anyone. Do you understand?'

Her confusion must have shown on her face and Garry gave a deep sigh sending a wave of peppermint mouthwash in her direction.

'He is a special case, an early release for – *co-operation* shall we say. He'll only be in the area for a short while and then he'll move on somewhere where he's not going to be recognized. Now do you understand?'

'What do I do about his case then?' Alex asked.

Garry waved a hand at her. 'Oh, go and see him, make sure he doesn't need anything and make it look like a normal release order in your notes,' he said. 'Obviously there are some issues of confidentiality here and I expect you to be discreet. The fewer people know about him the better really.'

Alex nodded and rose from the chair. 'Of course.'

'Let me know when he's moving on,' said Garry, as she walked to the door. 'Oh and by the way, where were you for the whole of yesterday?' he added.

She didn't think the day could get much worse but she was wrong. Hurrying down the stairs to the office, her head humming in white-hot fury at Garry's latest scathing estimate of her worth as a probation officer, she bounced off Paul Malcolm labouring up to her office.

'Oh, gosh, sorry Alex,' he said, leaning back against the wall. 'Ah, let me catch my breath.'

Alex stepped back, stumbling as her foot caught the riser behind her but managed to grab the rail in time.

'No Paul, really, it was my fault,' she said, trying to slip past him around the corner but Paul was not to be deterred.

'Well, now I've got you I wonder if I might have a quick word about Brian.'

It was late by the time she escaped Paul's well-intentioned attempts to assist Brian, and Alex still had to finish her work for the court later in the week. She sat at her desk struggling to make sense of her notes, desperately trying to force them into something the magistrates (and more importantly Lauren) might recognize as a competent social enquiry report. Finally she abandoned the whole mess as the light faded from the sky outside her window. The car park was empty and she climbed into her car, cursing the parking restrictions on her road that forced her to drive in each day just to avoid a ticket. The memory of her interview with Garry and her grovelling assurance she was on her way to see the mysterious client mocked her as, teeth grinding in frustration, she turned the ignition key. Flinging the Citroën into reverse she swooped round the empty space, turning towards the exit when she spotted a movement in the rear-view mirror. She slammed on her brakes and tried to swerve, an impossible manoeuvre when going backwards. The heavy car slid sideways, skidding 180 degrees and came to rest in the midst of the dustbins. Shaken but unhurt she scrambled out and hurried round the vehicle. A skinny figure in ragged jeans and a floppy T-shirt was sprawled amidst the scattered rubbish. His feet, she noticed, were bare and filthy. No matter how hard they tried no-one could get Simon the Lorry Boy to wear shoes.

'Bloody hell! Are you hurt?' She reached out a hand but Simon shook himself, scattering bits of shredded paper and the contents of ashtrays around him.

'I'm sorry,' he said, 'The warning sensor doesn't work on my truck. I've been meaning to get it fixed but I can't afford it. You wouldn't have heard me coming.' He mimed turning the ignition, looked over his shoulder and began to drive his imaginary lorry out of the bin store making soft engine noises as he went.

'Don't tell my Boss, will you? I could be fired for that,' he said anxiously as he shunted what appeared to be a fantasy trailer back and forth before lining himself up with the gate. Then with a wave of his hand he was gone, out onto the road to 'drive' the three miles home. Alex opened her mouth to call after him but it was too late, and, anyway, Simon couldn't hear her above the noise of his engine. She hoped he would stick to the pavements on the way out to Petherton. Simon was a familiar figure to the locals, who tended to look out for him, but there were already a lot of tourists around, strangers who hooted and swore as they swerved around the barefoot boy. Clambering back into her car she turned the key and knew at once something was wrong. The suspension on the driver's side was fine but the other side remained firmly enmeshed in the bins. Several expensive looking warning lights came on and stayed on until she removed the key. She clambered out and rested her head wearily on the roof of the car, closing her eyes as she wondered how she'd ended up here, in this strange place amongst these strange people.

She managed to get the car back into her parking space with the help of Bert, the janitor, and together they tidied up the worst of the rubbish. Bert flipped the most damaged bins around to hide the dents and nodded in approval at their handiwork.

'You just get off now,' he said. 'You look just worn out. Mebbe you'm due a bit of a holiday?'

Alex felt a lump rise in her throat at his kindness. 'I'm fine Bert, really. We're so short staffed at the moment I can't just go off and leave everyone else in the lurch.'

Bert raised his eyebrows. 'Well, you look after yerself. You'm here late too much. Won't do you no good, getting so tired and, well . . . .' Here he lowered his voice and glanced up at the windows behind him. ''Tis not like it's appreciated much, now is it?'

Alex followed his gaze up to her Senior's window. Things must be bad, she thought, if even Bert knew how Garry felt about her.

The next day she arrived on foot, before anyone else and spent several hours catching up with her case notes. She had a number of social enquiry reports to prepare for the court but was at a loss without a car. She needed to visit two of the households before she could finish the background sections but they were both out in the countryside and the only buses ran to factory hours, collecting workers for the giant plastics complex in town and delivering them home again after their shifts. She gazed out of the window, chewing a pencil and punching the keys to her calculator. She could either pay for the taxis to go and do her work visits or pay to get the car fixed. Her budget was not big enough for both.

'Shit!' she exclaimed, throwing the pencil across the room just as the door opened and an unfamiliar face peered round.

'Whoa, bloody hell!' said a woman's voice, the owner ducking back out of harm's way.

Alex leaned to one side and peered at the doorway, 'Can I help you?' The woman looked in, poised for flight.

'Yes?' asked Alex. She knew she was being less than gracious but she didn't feel very welcoming. The woman entered and held out her hand.

'Hi, I'm Susan but everyone calls me Sue,' she said with a smile.

Alex blinked at her, her tired brain running through the possibilities — client, client's girlfriend, probably not old enough to be client's mother . . . .

'I'm the new probation officer,' said Sue. 'I'm in the next office. Mind if I sit down?' She plonked herself into the easy chair by the window and kicked off her shoes, gold coloured sandals with light soles and thin straps.

'You've got a fabulous view. That bike shed thingy is in the way from my room.'

Alex knew all about the 'bike shed thingy' as on her arrival she's been offered a choice and opted for this room precisely because of the uninterrupted view of the river. Things had been so much rosier then, almost welcoming in fact.

'Ah, I'm Alex,' she said, realizing she had been staring in silence ever since Sue's entrance.

Sue flicked her hair back, long blonde hair that flowed down her back almost to her waist and gave Alex a glittering smile. 'I know. I've been looking forward to meeting you. We both went for the same job in the summer and you got it, but last month they rang me up and said they had a post after all and would I like it, so – here I am.'

Alex nodded, rather at a loss.

'Are you, ah . . .,' she searched for a polite way to ask whether Sue had any experience, settling for, 'transferring from another office?'

Sue shook her head. 'No, I qualified last August but I've had to make do with Social Services work until now. I was running an Intermediate Treatment group in Devon for a while. That was fun.'

Alex wasn't sure 'fun' quite encapsulated the experimental and occasionally risky nature of most I.T. work. Combining the social work approach of offering alternative interests to juvenile criminals with a client group drawn mainly from the super-fit 'short sharp shockers', it was frequently ridiculed in the press, and the more spectacular failures ('Hooligans on free trips abroad burn down beach huts – we foot the bill!') were career killers. She looked at Sue with new respect.

'What is that shed thing anyway?' Sue asked. Alex joined her at the window.

'It was going to be a vehicle maintenance project before the government decided our emphasis should be on "control" rather than "rehabilitation",' she said. 'We lost the funding for our instructor and no-one here wants to take it up. We're all too busy writing reports.'

Sue wrinkled her nose and stared at the building.

'Well, maybe we can do something about that. They're planning a day centre, aren't they? So there's one activity straight away. Anyway, I'm really pleased to meet you. I do hope we can be friends – I don't really know anyone here so maybe you could show me what you do in the evenings round here'.

Before Alex could reply, the phone rang in Sue's office and she headed out of the door, waving goodbye and leaving her sandals by Alex's window. Just as well really, Alex thought. She struggled to remember a decent night out since her arrival. The social life of the town revolved around the Carnival, the Carnival concerts and fundraising for the clubs and gangs. The area was awash with pubs, each the home for one group or club and each wary of strangers and less than welcoming to women. In London the most common offence committed by Alex's charges had been 'Touching the Dog's Arse' – car theft or 'taking and driving away' in official language. Here it was ABH, actual bodily harm, which made the area sound rather more dangerous than the capital. Examining the figures showed a slightly different picture, however – lots of men went out at night, got drunk and hit each other. There was a tap on the door and Sue reappeared.

'Sorry, forgot my shoes. I'm always doing that.' She retrieved her sandals and stopped at the door, looking back at Alex.

'I'm staying with Margaret at the moment and to be honest it's driving me a bit crazy. Do you know anywhere decent going? Going cheap if possible.'

Alex waved her towards the chair again. 'Sit down if you've got a moment. What sort of place do you want?'

Sue shrugged. 'Oh, maybe a little country cottage, a few roses, not far from work but quiet . . .' She grinned at Alex's expression of disbelief. 'Only kidding. Anywhere off a main road but not way out in the wilds. And not too cold either. I hate the cold.'

Alex sympathized, her experiences in the forge still clear in her mind.

'You don't really want to settle on anywhere until around September or October,' she advised. 'That way you can feel how draughty a place is. The ropiest old shack looks nice in the summer. There's a lot more around to choose from in the winter too. All the summer labourers leave, all the people who come down here for the weather and stuff. They rush back to cities and you can get a much better price in the winter.'

Sue nodded. 'Thanks. I'll take your advice, though I'm not sure I can stand a whole summer at Margaret's place. Here,' she twisted round and much to Alex's alarm began to unbutton her dress, 'what do you think these are?' She pulled the whole front down and displayed a series of red dots running across her chest and over one shoulder. 'I've got some on my bum too . . .'

'That's okay, I can see fine,' said Alex raising her hands to ward off any further disrobing. Unconcerned, Sue pulled her dress back up and flopped into Alex's easy chair.

'I thought they might be fleas but they fade away every day. They seem to come out at night. Maybe I'm allergic to the factory fumes . . .'

'If you were anywhere else I'm probably say they were bedbugs,' said Alex.

Sue pulled a face and rubbed her back against the chair. 'Surely not. I mean, Margaret's *posh*.'

Alex nodded in agreement. 'Still, you did think they might be fleas. So she can't be that posh,' she said.

Sue sighed and gestured vaguely in the direction of Margaret's office down the hall. 'Yes but she has cats. Note, cats plural and the place has a rather odd smell when you go in. Haven't you noticed?'

Alex had to confess she's never been invited to Margaret's house, though she had been treated to several pictures of the garden in full bloom. Sue snorted. 'Yes the bloody garden. Not only do I pay rent and have to feed myself, I'm expected to pull up weeds and clip things outside in the evening. Look!' She held out her hands, resplendent with pearly pink nails. 'Do these look as if they're comfortable digging around in the dirt? Then, by the time I'm finished I'm starving and there's not a single take-away in the whole village. I'm practically living on toast. Thank God for the chippy round the corner here.'

'Don't you get use of the kitchen?' Alex asked.

Sue gave her a hard stare.

'Kitchen. Yes, that implies cooking. I sort of – don't.'

'Don't or can't?' Alex asked, intrigued by the thought of a woman who preferred to eat like a single man.

'Both,' said Sue. 'Tried it a few times and hated it. And if you've got a boyfriend in tow they suddenly start appearing at mealtimes looking hopeful. Honestly, it's virtually slavery. Do you cook?' she added hopefully.

Alex burst out laughing. There was something really quite attractive about this woman.

'Sorry,' said Sue, grinning up at her, 'I guess that was a bit cheeky.'

'It was worth it,' said Alex. 'I could do with a good laugh at the moment. And yes, I do cook. I enjoy it even if it's just for me. Do you fancy dinner one evening – say Friday? You could stay over if you want to drink . . .'

Sue bounded to her feet, sandals in hand.

'Friday sounds great. I'll bring some wine. Oh – address?'

Alex pulled out one of her official cards and scribbled on the back.

'Don't lose it,' she warned. 'There are several clients I'd rather not know exactly where I live.'

Sue sauntered towards the door and then turned back.

'Is that your car outside, the Citroën?'

Alex nodded wearily. 'Yep. And I am so screwed unless I can get it fixed in the next week or so. I've got a load of visits to make and no way of getting out to them.'

Sue tilted her head to one side and pursed her lips. 'Maybe I can help. I need some experience writing the reports and running an interview. Why don't I drive you out and observe?'

Alex felt a rush of hope – maybe this was a way round her problems. Then she thought of Garry and his 'value for money' cost-cutting framework and her shoulders slumped despondently.

'I'd love that but I'm not sure how we'd arrange it. I don't expect Garry will consider me – experienced enough.' She had almost said 'suitable'. Sue waved her hand, swatting away such feeble obstacles.

'I'll sort it out with my admin support,' she said. 'She'll rustle up some paperwork for us, I'm sure. She's just wonderful – well, you would know. You had Lauren when you started too didn't you?'

Chapter Four

Alex frowned at the forms in front of her trying to make sense of the latest entries. With just a cursory glance she detected several spelling errors, the margins didn't line up properly and the last lines were smudged and faded as if they had been typed using an old carbon sheet. The whole page was a mess and looked thoroughly unprofessional. She reached for the phone to ring the office, then remembered her recent behaviour towards Lauren. With a rush of shame she put the receiver back and gathered the offending papers together, intending to go down and have a quiet word in person. At that moment there was a knock on her door and Alison, one of the clerical staff, entered clutching more folders and juggling a cup of coffee.

'Here you are,' she said cheerfully, plonking the cup on the desk and flopping into a chair. The coffee slopped into the saucer and dribbled across the desk before Alex managed to blot it with some tissues from the ever-present box. Alison glanced around her, taking in the bookshelves crammed with Alex's textbooks and official manuals, the swathe of papers surrounding a small, clear patch on the desk and the gallery of modern art postcards stuck up in the corner. She was a pale woman, almost anaemic with washed-out grey eyes and wispy straw-coloured hair. On special occasions, such as office socials or a day in court to record details, she applied enough make-up to her bland features to make her look like an anxious panda or (as Alex had once confided to Lauren) a weevil that hadn't slept for days. Although she was only in her mid-twenties she acted like a middle-aged secretary, or maybe the way she thought a middle-aged secretary should act. She was recently married and had spent the first month of Alex's tenure drifting dreamily around the office, placing her ring hand casually in front of anyone who came to the counter. It was difficult to imagine anyone in the office less compatible with Alex than Alison.

'Ah, thanks,' said Alex, trying to hide her confusion. 'Er, why are you . . .' she searched for a polite way to ask *here*. Finally she raised her eyebrows and tried an encouraging smile.

'I thought we'd better get stuff sorted,' said Alison, 'so we both know how it's going to work.'

There was a sinking feeling in Alex's stomach.

'How what's going to work?' she asked though she was already fairly sure she knew the answer.

'I'm taking you over, from Lauren. I've already brought your case notes up to date so we should start off all square and ready to go,' Alison said smugly, 'and I can bring you coffee if you like.'

Alex glanced at the cup in front of her as the implication of this artless remark hit her. She opened her mouth to snap at this mean little person and then realized she was going to be stuck with Alison for some time. It was her own fault and she needed to avoid making matters worse if possible.

'I don't expect anyone to get my coffee thank you,' she said forcing a smile. 'And I was looking at the files – is there a problem with the carbons? It's just they're a bit fuzzy in places . . .' She came to a halt as Alison's face turned sulky at the first hint of criticism.

'We're supposed to be economizing,' she snapped. 'We have to turn all the ribbons around and use them twice. That's why they're a *bit fuzzy*.'

Alex raised a hand, despising her own weakness, 'I'm sure you are doing your best in a difficult situation,' she said. Alison fixed her with those pale, washed-out eyes and finally nodded, mollified by the conciliatory tone.

'Well, okay. Now, let me have your diary.' She held out her hand as Alex sat back in horror. The diary was the single most important item a probation officer used. It was both an indispensable tool for planning and scheduling the many tasks that made up the job and a legal document providing evidence admissible in court for breaching non-attendees. Alex had studied cases where the diary had been used to save an officer's career and been called in evidence at the Coroner's Court. With notes, meetings and appointments the diary showed what work was done with and for each client. A probation officer was expected to 'advise, assist and befriend' but it didn't always work like that. Most officers lost at least one client in the course of their careers and it was natural for the families to blame someone. Sometimes the diary was the only thing standing between an officer and a career-ending disciplinary meeting. Alex was not about to hand hers over to an unknown and deeply suspect guardian such as Alison.

She was saved by Sue who made her usual entrance, flinging the door wide and announcing, 'Let's go then. You promised to take me on a home visit and it's going to rain later – oh, sorry Alison. Have you just finished?'

Alison rose from the chair, gathering the fuzzy files to her almost non-existent bosom before leaving with a poor grace. Alex breathed a sigh of relief when the door slammed behind her retreating back.

'Thank you so much. Your timing is impeccable – you

know she wants to keep my diary? God knows what sort of a mess she's make of it.'

Sue plonked herself down by the desk and pulled Alex's diary out from under a pile of forms and scribbled notes. Flicking through it she pulled a face before shoving it back onto the desk.

'Almost as much of a mess as you've made, from the look of it. Half your meetings are put in pencil. Any court would throw it out as inadmissible.'

Alex groaned in frustration. 'There's just so much to do and I can never find anything. Still, at least I know what's missing. Look – I'll fill it in this evening so it's all up to date but I'm not handing it over to that airhead. I might just as well resign right now and save what's left of my reputation.'

Sue made a rude noise. 'Thoroughly tiresome. Everyone here thinks you work far too hard but you really care about your clients. Paul's bowled over with the changes in Brian.'

'Well, not everyone's so impressed,' Alex muttered as she attempted to force her diary in an already over-stuffed drawer.

'Are you going to sit there feeling sorry for yourself all day?' demanded Sue, rising to her feet. 'You promised me a ride out onto the Levels. My car's downstairs so let's go and meet this infamous Ada Mallory.'

As they made their way across the car-park they passed Gordon cleaning his car again, the mats drying in the sunlight but still emitting a strong odour of dog vomit.

Spring was already casting its spell over the Levels and Alex felt her spirits rise as they whizzed merrily along the road to Lowpoint.

'How's your car doing?' asked Sue, as she navigated the narrow twists and turns of the road.

'I should have it back by the end of the week. Just as well really – I don't think even Lauren could disguise a lift to Dartmoor to see a prisoner and I need to get up to Bristol to see Kevin as well.'

Sue glanced at her. 'Look, are you okay with me having Lauren?' she asked.

Alex shrugged, eyes fixed to the road as she searched for the correct turning.

'It's not up to us,' she mumbled. 'Garry and Pauline sort out the admin allocations.'

'Well, Garry's a dick,' said Sue. Alex turned her head and then burst out laughing.

'Oh, say what you really mean,' she giggled. 'Don't hold back.'

Sue joined in and together they bounced over the rough track that ran along side the main drainage channel. The water was high, Alex noted, as they climbed out of the car by Ada Mallory's house. The winter rains and spring melt had seeped through the peat and bog lands surrounding the ditches and rivers, gathering until the water reached saturation point. Then, as a trickle and later a flood, it poured into the waterways to make a thick, slow mass of water flowing into ever larger ditches. Kings Sedgemoor was the last line of defence against inundation, both a massive safety valve and a vital source of freshwater for industry and farming. To their right, on past the road bridge was Greylake Sluice, its gates barely raised as the flow of water downstream to the River Parrett was held back by the heavy shutters.

'Ugh,' said Sue, peering at the murky waters. 'Surely nothing's alive in that!'

Alex remembered the boxes of elvers taken from Kevin's pram on his arrest.

'You'd be surprised,' she said. 'This is good fishing country apparently. Just ask Eddie.'

'No thanks,' said Sue. 'I don't want to encourage him. He's already suggested I might like to try one of the shorter walks with his lads. I mean – do I look like a hiking sort of girl?'

She gestured to her feet, still clad in thin gold sandals despite the brisk wind and spring damp. Her flowery skirt and pale cardigan added to her air of sweet innocence – a deceptive look, Alex was beginning to realize. Still, she definitely did

60

not look like someone prepared to tramp over muddy fields and high hills for pleasure.

The Mallory house looked even more dilapidated than it had in the autumn. The remains of the front gate shrieked in protest as Alex pushed it open and the surrounding fence wobbled in sympathy. Grass grew between the cracked slabs of the path and the lawn was a muddy backdrop to the decaying motor vehicles. Sue picked her way towards the peeling front door trying to keep her feet out of the surrounding swamp. Alex knocked on the door several times but they were greeted by silence. Reluctantly she stepped off the relative safety of the porch and squelched her way over to the front window, rapping on the panes and calling Ada's name. She turned round just in time to see Sue stoop down to peer through the letterbox.

'No!' she yelled, hurling herself towards the door and grabbing Sue's shoulder, pulling her away just as the blade of a wickedly long kitchen knife poked out. They stepped back and watched as the knife rattled back and forth several times before disappearing inside once more.

'Bloody hell,' muttered Sue. 'I thought we were supposed to be on their side. What do they do when the police turn up?'

Alex reached out and knocked again, taking care to keep clear of the letterbox.

'Ada? Ada, it's Alex. I've come to see if there's anything you want me to take Kevin next week.'

There was a pause and then a rattling, the sound of a bolt, another bolt and finally the door creaked open and Ada peered out at them.

'Where's she to then?' she asked, jerking her head towards Sue.

'This is Sue,' said Alex, delighted to show off her hard-won knowledge of the local dialect. 'She's just started in the office and wanted to come out and get a look at the Levels.'

Ada grunted and turned away. 'Well, don't stand there lettin' all my heat out. 'Tis perishing still.'

They followed her into the tiny living room and perched on the sticky couch. Alex declined Ada's offer of tea and nudged Sue in an attempt to warn her but Sue was in Social Worker mode.

'I'd love a cup. Thank you so much,' she said brightly.

'Why did you refuse?' she asked when Ada was safely in the kitchen. 'It builds rapport and . . .'

'I know all that stuff,' Alex hissed. 'I did the same courses remember? But there's a whole world of difference between the ideas and the reality and, believe me, if you drink much of Ada Mallory's tea you'll not live long enough to . . .' She fell silent as Ada returned with two cups on mismatched saucers and the too-familiar tin under her arm.

'Well,' she said, handing the less chipped cup to Sue, 'you'll have a biscuit I hope.'

Alex gave a rather sickly grin and took her biscuit, glancing at Sue who was staring glassy eyed at the scummy liquid in her cup. There was no sign of the dogs and after a moment's hesitation she asked where they were.

'Oh, them's outside, watching the back. I likes to be sure no' un's comin' in that way. ''Sides, I've Frankie out and he gets 'un all riled up.'

'Frankie – your cat?' asked Alex, her eyes sliding around the room in search of this new, elusive animal. Ada shook her head.

'No, wouldn't have no *cat*,' she said. 'Nasty, dirty things, always nesting in the clean clothes and bringing in dead stuff. No, Frankie's my Kev's rat.' She took a slurp of her tea before continuing. 'I named him after that no good dead beat of a husband of mine. Don't seem fair really now. Frankie's been a good friend to Kev – more than I can say for Frank bloody Mallory!' She set her cup down with a bang and turned her head abruptly, looking out of the window as she recovered her composure.

'Well now, you was saying about my Kevin?' Her voice was steady but there were traces of tears in her eyes and for the first time Alex saw Ada Mallory as a person, not just a client's relative or an eccentric and embarrassing woman. She looked around the mean, shabby living room and saw the tiny signs of care, the attempts to make this lonely life a little more homely. The cushions were wrapped in brightly coloured crochet covers, a bit lumpy in places from washing but arranged in matching pairs on each chair. A collection of photographs in a wide range of frames crowded one side of an occasional table whilst an assortment of pottery animals faced off against them from another. Ada followed her gaze and a soft smile crept over her features.

'Them's is all from Kevin,' she said. 'He knows I like animals. 'Cept for cats, of course.'

Alex nodded, wondering how to bring the conversation back to Kevin's plight. It was not looking good for the lad, with him being caught in the van, a few feet away from the body and no witness to confirm his activities for the earlier part of the night. Alex was sure Kevin was innocent but how to convince the authorities was beyond her.

Sue put her cup down rather abruptly, breaking the silence.

'Why did you do that with the letterbox?' she asked. Ada glared at her and addressed her answer to Alex.

'I didn't recognize her, see. There's been some noises, creeping around and such like, specially in the last few days. I don' like being here all by myself. 'Tis lonely and I don't feel safe no more. I thought you was the creeper so I figured I'd scare yer off.'

In Ada's world this was perfectly logical, even a sensible way of going about things. Alex was more concerned about the consequences should Ada stab someone by mistake and somehow the story of the mysterious creeper failed to register beyond the probable imaginings of a woman who saw all strangers as a threat. Ada, however, refused to give up her knife.

'How'm I supposed to cut the bread then?' she demanded. ''Tis not like I bought it special. Is just my kitchen knife.'

In the end Alex gave up and turned her attention to the

details she needed for her records. She wasn't supposed to complete the social enquiry report until after Kevin's trial but she hoped she might get some information she could feed to his solicitor, something to help him. Finally she left with a plastic bag filled with spare clothes and several loving messages for Kevin.

'Well, what do you think of the Mallorys?' Alex asked, as she buckled herself into Sue's car. Sue began an attempt to turn the vehicle on the narrow road.

'How are we supposed to get out of here?' she demanded after several minutes of futile manoeuvring. Alex pointed down the stony track.

'The only way is further in and then a loop left on to the A38,' she said. They bumped along in silence for a few minutes before Sue said, 'I hate rats.'

Alex grinned. 'Lots of the lads keep them as pets. I had one in last week and he had a rat in his jacket pocket. He wanted to let it out on the desk while we talked.'

'God, that's horrible! What did you do?'

Alex shrugged. 'Told him no. Rats have no sphincter muscles so they just wee and stuff as they walk.'

'Yuck!' Sue pulled a face then added, 'There was something really vile in the bottom of my tea. Sort of green and lumpy.'

Alex looked at her in horror, 'Oh what – that sounds like . . .'

Sue cut her off. 'I know what it sounds like and I don't want to even think about it okay?'

Alex's car arrived back in the car park that Friday, as promised. Unfortunately so did the bill, excessive in spite of the fact she'd refused the offer of cosmetic repairs and limited her expenditure to the mechanically necessary. Alex sat at her desk, punching her calculator as she tried to work out whether she should try to claim on the insurance and lose her no-claims bonus or try to squeeze the money out of her dwindling bank account. After five years of studying and existing on part-time jobs her salary had looked almost lavish but now she had a house, a car and bills, seemingly from nowhere, pouring through her letterbox every week. Prices were rising every week and she was barely able to make her money stretch to the end of the month even without insanely high garage bills. But the one item she had to have to do her job was a car. She went through her bank statement for the third time trying to find a mistake, some area where she could economize. She didn't even have a post office account with a few pounds tucked away for a rainy day, and in financial terms it was pouring outside. With a sigh she picked up her phone and called Sue.

'It's not much,' she said, as they stepped into the front room.

Sue took a deep breath and sniffed appreciatively. 'No cats! I love it already.'

Alex grinned as she turned on the light and drew the curtains at the front window. 'We're about six inches from the pavement,' she said, 'so I always pull the curtains at night. I can't believe the number of people sitting in a lit room in full view.'

Sue tilted her head to one side. 'What's the problem with that?' she asked.

'Where did you do your training?' asked Alex.

'Exeter. I'm almost local though they're very different round here. Much more . . . different than I expected.'

'I trained in London,' said Alex, 'as Garry is always pointing out. But one thing I did learn is that a lot of the nasty weirdoes are opportunistic and they like to watch. They wander the street until they see something they like, then they watch. When they go home at night they fantasize about what they've seen. And then they come back and they come inside and act it all out. So you should always close your curtains after dark, especially if you're a woman on your own.'

Derek Johns stared at the window, the frown on his dark face reflected in the ebbing twilight. The curtains were closed tight – not a glimmer of light seeped out around the heavy material. From outside, the house looked unoccupied. Good. He nodded to himself and walked back along the muddy path, letting himself in through the creaking door. It was dim inside the cottage, the front room lit only by the flames of the fire in the hearth. Some light seeped in round the warped doorframe to the kitchen, but not enough to show outside, from the road. There were few cars out this far anyway, he thought, but he checked the back windows, just in case. All was dark and still as he opened the cupboards and prepared for his next task. He had a busy night ahead and he didn't want to be disturbed.

Sue stood by Alex in the narrow kitchen, frowning as she watched her new friend. Alex flipped a chicken on to the chopping board and gestured to Sue with the other hand.

'Now, here we have a chicken,' she began, picking up a heavy knife with her left hand.

'I know it's a chicken,' said Sue. 'I'm not a total idiot.'

Alex put the knife down again and looked at her.

'Okay, how would you cook it then?'

Sue thought for a moment and smiled disarmingly.

'I'd give it to someone else,' she said.

Alex sighed and picked up the knife again. 'Well here's the first lesson,' she said, as she bent over the board, '. . . how to get eight meals – or four meals for the two of us – from one chicken.'

'Does it involve dieting,' asked Sue suspiciously.

Alex snorted in disgust. 'I don't think so. Now, first you take off the legs. Pull them back at the joint, here where they meet the body – see?' She cut deftly through the skin, exposing the hip joints. 'Now, hold the body and pull back until you hear the joint snap, then cut around here. Let the knife follow the natural line of the meat.'

Derek leaned on the table, using all his strength. There was a sharp cracking sound but the leg refused to separate.

'Bugger,' he muttered, hefting his heavy cook's knife. He

worked it around the joint, wiggling the blade and feeling for the line with the point and tried again but it refused to give any more. Sighing heavily he reached across the table for the meat-saw. A few hearty strokes and the whole leg wobbled and splayed outwards, finally tearing free and falling to the floor. It lay on the spread newspaper, oozing slightly as it began to defrost. Muttering to himself, Derek picked it up, hoisted it over his shoulder and went out to the old scullery. He opened the lid to the large chest freezer that stood humming softly in the centre of the floor. Derek threw the leg in, slammed the lid and hurried back to the kitchen. With a bit of luck he'd get Frank's other leg off before it defrosted too much.

'Now,' said Alex, placing the neatly trimmed legs in a baking tin, 'we roast up the legs tonight. That's one meal.'

Sue watched as she added herbs, lemon juice and a sprinkle of salt before putting the loosely covered meat in the oven. The chicken stood on the board looking rather forlorn, shorn of its lower limbs. Alex rinsed her hands under the tap and returned to her task.

'Now, we get the wings and upper joints off,' she said. 'They're very like the legs actually, smaller but there's a lot of meat here.' She pointed as she cut around the carcass, cleaning down to the bone with deft strokes. There was a bit of a tussle as the tendons stretched and refused to snap but Alex twisted the knife round to cut them and separate their next meal.

'Get me a plastic bag from the drawer there will you?' she asked as she pulled the smaller wings back and sliced through the thin bones making up the joint. Sue rummaged around, emerging with a plastic carrier.

'No, one of the clear ones, on that roll there.'

Alex slid the pieces into the bag and tied the top, expelling all the air as she did so.

'We can have these in a bit of a casserole or fry them up with garlic and have them with potatoes,' she said. 'So that's two meals.'

Derek was in a hurry and the second leg wouldn't come free despite hacking at it with the cook's knife, so he had to resort to the saw again. It was messy and little gobbets of flesh stuck in the teeth and spattered on to the floor around him. The saw snagged on the bone and he felt his feet slip but the leg came free at last as he hacked at the hip joint. Reluctantly he decided he's better finish up for tonight and wait for everything to freeze again.

Alex turned the legless carcass towards her on the board and took out a thinner knife. 'This is a filleting knife,' she said, 'good for fish and stuff like this. You can use a boning knife but I like the flexibility of the blade to do this bit.'

She slid the point of the knife along the breastbone and carefully cut through the meat, peeling it free and lifting it off in one piece. There was a slight grating as the edge of the knife hit the ribcage and Sue flinched.

'Sorry,' said Alex. 'Still, you can't be a good cook if you're too squeamish.' She flipped the breast over and carefully separated the edge of the fillet, making a neat pocket in each. 'There you go,' she said proudly. 'We pack these up and they'll make Chicken Kiev. Three meals.'

Sue took the bags of meat and followed Alex out into the back porch where an old freezer stood in the corner. Alex opened the door and took the bags, laying them neatly with other similar bundles. Sue peered in at the rows of neatly labelled packets.

'This is a bit creepy. It looks like some serial killer's fridge,' she said. Alex slammed the door shut. 'Only if he's a cannibal too,' she countered.

They went back inside to the warm kitchen, the rich smell of roasting chicken greeting them.

'How about opening that bottle of wine while I clear up and do the vegetables?' asked Alex.

Sue rummaged in a drawer and drew out a corkscrew. 'That's three meals,' she said, as she sliced through the lead foil and uncoiled it carefully. 'That's impressive but you did say four.'

Alex picked up the carcass and dropped it into a large pot,

covered it in water and set it to simmer. 'And this will make a thick, hearty Italian soup with some pasta and a few veg,' she said.

'I'm rather glad you didn't get the head too,' said Sue as she poured the wine. 'I dread to think what you could have made from that!'

Derek turned the severed leg over and stripped some of the meat from the calf before returning everything to the freezer. It was starting to bleed and he worked quickly, his filleting knife grating on the bone as he cut. The leg was an awkward shape and the freezer lid wouldn't close so, cursing as he worked, he hacked through the knee, flinging the two pieces in before slamming it shut. He decided to clean up the worst of the mess before making the fillets and poured a bucket full of hot water from the kettles set ready on the stove. The newspapers went on the fire and he scrubbed around the table and across the floor several times before he was satisfied. He knew he couldn't disguise all the blood from a professional but he wasn't expecting visitors and he planned to destroy the cottage in a well planned accident when he was finished.

He cleaned his knives carefully and put them back in the pockets of his butcher's roll. The saw he hung up in the scullery out of sight. Then he took the filleting knife and began to slice the meat from the leg into short, narrow lengths. Too long and they'd be rejected, he thought, just wide enough and thick enough and they'd be gobbled up. It was full dark when he laid his knife to one side. He was tempted to try out his idea at once but it was beginning to rain and he was tired, cold and surprisingly hungry. Wrapping the strips carefully in newspaper, he placed them in the fridge before rummaging through his meagre supplies for some supper. After a few moments' thought he took down an iron frying pan, black with age and use, and rinsed his hands off in the sink before putting a couple of eggs on to fry. He propped some bread up in front of the fire to toast and stood in the glow of the fire, humming contentedly as he considered a good evening's work.

Chapter Five

The prison gate at Bristol was as unwelcoming as ever and Alex felt her spirits sag beneath the shadows of the high walls. She glanced back down the street leading to the car park gates and wondered what it might be like to live always in sight of such an intrusive and uncompromising building. Did you get used to it, she wondered. Did you leave for work in the morning and nod absently at the trickle of pale figures drifting past in their unfashionable clothes or did you watch through barely opened curtains until they had turned the corner and moved on to become someone else's problem? Reaching in to collect her briefcase and warrant card she slammed the car door and locked it carefully. The car was running very well, even better than before her unfortunate encounter with the office bins, but the locks were a bit tricky on the passenger side.

One of the officers at the reception desk was the same as her last visit and he nudged his companion as Alex entered, case open ready for the search.

'Oh ho – here comes trouble,' he said grinning at her. His

partner took the proffered briefcase and poked through it rather gingerly.

'Just you today then?'

Alex nodded, relieved they'd taken last time's events so well. Warrant card notwithstanding, she'd half expected to be led into a small windowless room for the dreaded full body search.

'Yes, this is a professional visit,' she said. 'I was doing a favour for his mother last time.'

'She's the talk of the canteen,' said the first officer. 'In fact, we've had new guidelines come down about searching following your last visit so I guess you done us a favour really.'

Alex gathered up her belongings and headed for the side door into the visitors area. As an official visitor she could bypass the main visitors' entrance with its queues and groups of relatives haggling over what they could and could not take in with them. Today she was glad of the short cut that let her into the visiting room ahead of everyone else. She chose a seat off to the left, in the corner nearest the door to the prison. She figured they were less likely to be disturbed, at least for a short while, and it gave a modicum of privacy.

When Kevin shuffled in to the empty visiting room Alex was shocked at the decline in his appearance. It had only been two weeks since her last visit but he seemed to have aged years in that time. He slumped into the seat opposite her and stared at the table, his hands clasped together as if to disguise the faint trembling that ran through his whole body. She glanced at his head, half expecting to see the first grey hairs but he was as resolutely mousy as ever. Without thinking she reached out and laid her hand over his. His fingers were icy cold.

'Kevin. Kevin? Are you okay?'

He snatched his arms back and tucked his hands out of sight under the table.

'Kevin! Look at me. I've come to see if there's anything you need. Can I help?'

His head jerked up and she saw his eyes were red-rimmed,

as if he'd been crying. He opened his mouth, about to speak, then shook his head and stared at the table again. Alex was at a loss how to get through to him.

'I've brought you some clean clothes from home,' she said, 'and I've been to see you mother. She sends her love . . . .'

Kevin raised his head and glared at her. 'Girt load of good *that* is,' he snapped. 'What's she doin' 'bout me, eh? Nothing, that's what.'

Alex took a deep breath before replying, 'It's not that easy Kevin. There's hearing dates to wait for and disclosure from the police—'

Kevin cut her off. 'Don't make no difference do it? I'm in here and if I don't get out soon I'm not never going to. So you go and tell her to get me a decent solicitor and get him to talk to bloody Brian and get me *out*.'

His voice had risen to a shout and the officer next to the door stepped forwards hurriedly, ready to intervene. Alex waved to show she was fine and he retreated somewhat reluctantly.

'Brian?' she asked gently, 'Is that Brian Morris?'

Kevin was slumped forwards on the table but he moved his head in what looked like a nod.

'Why Brian Morris?' Alex asked. Bloody little Brian, Brian the curse of her professional life – don't let him be mixed up in this too, she thought.

Kevin kept his head down on the table but gave a shrug, muttering something incomprehensible. Alex leaned over him and poked him hard.

'Cut this out Kevin! Sit up and talk to me or you can go back to your cell and fester.'

Kevin sat up abruptly and blinked at her in surprise.

'That's not nice. You'm supposed to be on my side.'

Alex felt a brief flash of guilt at her harsh words but she refused to back down.

'I'm supposed to advise you and assist you,' she told him, 'but that doesn't mean I have to put up with all this silly game playing. And I don't think it's helping to hold your hand and tell you everything's going to be just fine when it probably isn't.'

There was a pause as they eyed one another warily. Alex continued. 'So tell me about Brian. What's he got to do with all this?'

Kevin pulled a face, still sulking, but he did answer her question.

'He seen me, that night. On the other bank just as I was heading off to see the Elver Man. He was getting ready to pack up on account of it bein' so wet and there not being much running on his side. That's not much of a spot, over there. Only a divvy would bother, so Brian gets to use it 'cos no-one else wants it, see? Reckon his nets was pretty much empty, so he waved at I and next time I looked over he were gone.'

Alex felt her heart beat faster but tried to keep her voice steady. She didn't want to give Kevin any false hope, not when he was so fragile. She made a note to talk to the guards before she left, for she was seriously worried about him.

'Are you sure it was Brian Morris?' she said. Kevin nodded. He was looking better now someone was listening to him. He sat up straight in the chair and there was a tiny glimmer of his old cockiness. 'And you're certain of the time – just as you were heading down to the bridge?'

'Yep,' said Kevin, 'Only time I see anyone, that night. I'm walking maybe just past the sluice gate, near where the old canal joins, see?'

Alex did a quick mental calculation. If Brian had seen him that night he'd been about half a mile from the bridge where the Elver Man was parked. Even on such a foul night, pushing his pram full of elvers, Kevin was no more than 20 minutes away. The police had said the Elver Man had been dead for at least four hours so Kevin couldn't be the killer! She nodded, trying to keep her face calm, making cryptic little scribbles in the folder of notes on the table. She was in dangerous territory here she knew, discussing a crime for which Kevin had not been committed. If he gave her any information that could be used as evidence she would have to report it to the police and that would make her a witness for the prosecution. Not exactly the role she wanted and not likely to endear her to her colleagues or her probationers, but she was sure Kevin was innocent and no-one else in authority seemed willing to look at the case twice. If she didn't stand up for him then who would?

A door opened, this time on the left of the visiting room, and a line of prisoners shuffled in, spreading themselves around the room to receive their visitors. Kevin stiffened and his face paled as he caught sight of one man at the back of the group. Alex glanced over casually but caught the eye of the cause of Kevin's concern. A tall, well-built man with dark eyes stared at her for an instant and bared his teeth in a smile that was almost feral. He has a mouth full of gold teeth and he flicked his tongue at her before she could look away. The guard behind Kevin moved swiftly to stand between the man and Alex, manhandling him roughly into a seat away from Kevin's table and muttering something in his ear. He gave Alex a nod as he resumed his post and she responded with a quick smile, trying to disguise how much the incident had shaken her. Kevin looked ghastly, she realized. He'd turned a horrible grey colour and seemed to be struggling for breath. Glancing down she saw his hands were clenched tightly together on the table in an effort to stop them shaking. She reached out to touch him, hoping to offer some comfort, but he jerked away and twisted round in his seat to signal to the guard.

'I'm done here,' Kevin said, rising to his feet. The officer looked at Alex and shrugged before taking Kevin by the shoulder and leading him out into the Remand area.

Alex looked around, careful to avoid the gaze of the dark-haired man. At that moment the door to the visitors' area opened and the day's procession of visitors flooded in, a rag-tag mix of old and very young, happy and fearful. She slipped past and out of the door amidst the confusion of greetings and raised voices stepping thankfully into the relative calm of the waiting room. On the other side of the room beside the exit to the gate was the female guard from her visit with Ada Mallory who flashed a quick grin of recognition.

'Just you today then?' she asked, as she unlocked the door through to the main reception area. Alex shook her head at her as she rummaged in her briefcase for the all-important warrant card.

'Yeah, I've not brought the pantomime this time. Say, do you ever work on the Remand wing?'

The woman pulled a face. 'Sometimes, though I'm mainly here for the female visitors. They don't like us mixing with the cons – seem to think we can't handle it. I do a couple of shifts a week at the moment because we're so overcrowded, they need every officer they can get some days.'

Alex smiled at her. 'I wonder where they get their ideas from sometimes. I used to work in a probation hostel at night before I qualified and there was always trouble if I had to work the shift with a man. Two women – no trouble at all.'

'Right. I tell you, there's some here I hate working with. They just have to walk through the door and all the inmates start to square up to them. Maybe it's the testosterone or something. Anyway, you were asking about the Remand wing?'

Alex outlined her concerns about Kevin as quickly as she could. The waiting room was empty and a lull in the comings and goings of visitors was rare. The woman pursed her lips as Alex described the dark-haired man.

'Sounds like he's run foul of the didicoys,' she said.

Alex tried to hide her shock at this statement. She'd heard the term around the office, a disparaging reference to the travellers and groups of gypsies who followed the horse markets and fun fairs that rotated through the West Country from April to early November. It was not considered polite, the local equivalent of 'pikey' from her native Essex.

'Don't look at me like that,' said the officer. 'Them's not proper gypsies most of them. They's just lazy bastards that don't want to do a decent day's work. Just fly-by-night con-men looking for something to steal.' Her tone was bitter as if the 'didicoys' represented a personal insult. She turned back to the door, unlocking it with a great rattle of keys.

'They conned my Nan out of most of her savings,' she added as she pulled at the heavy iron door. 'Told her they'd fix her roof after the storms last year. Course, they just grabbed the money, splashed a bit of cement on and took all the lead flashing off with them.'

Alex opened her mouth to speak but found herself lost for words.

'Well, anyway, don't you worry. I'll keep an eye out for your lad. There's a couple of decent blokes on the Remand an' all, so I'll let them know.'

'Thanks,' said Alex as she stepped through to the reception hall.

'I'm Margie, by the way,' added the woman as she closed the door behind her.

'I'm Alex—' the door closed with a clang, but she saw Margie nod and smile in acknowledgement through the tiny barred window.

There was no getting round it, Alex thought as she bowled merrily through the lanes towards the office, she needed to talk to Brian. She was not surprised he'd said nothing about seeing Kevin that night. Elvering was almost a way of life for the local men, but it was poaching and the river wardens were coming down very hard on everyone they caught. There was a lot of talk about the dwindling stocks of eels and the need to protect the baby elvers as they made their long and arduous journey up the rivers and over the fields to the eel equivalent of their ancestral home. Elvers were a delicacy in some parts of the world and they represented a short-lived but rich stream of income for those willing to brave the elements and the wardens. Getting Brian to talk to her, let alone make a statement to the police, would not be easy.

Derek stood on the footbridge over the canal, just up from the sluice gate that closed the huge drainage system off from the river, and peered around him. It was early morning and the mist was rising from the surrounding land as the spring sunlight began to suck the winter moisture from the sodden earth. The air was still and around him came the sounds of wildlife waking to greet the warmer weather. Birds called from the bushes, seeking mates or claiming their territory, croaks and clucks from small groups of waterfowl echoed eerily up the canal and there was a nervous rustling from the reeds along the bank as the smaller mammals peered out into the daylight. The barges that had once made this a busy port had long departed and nature had returned to claim the river and the shallower canals. Derek coughed, hawked and spat into the water below the bridge and there was an instant's stillness at this, the only human sound on the Levels. After a moment one bird called, then another and gradually the morning song of the wild resumed around him. Derek was oblivious to it all. Once he was sure he was alone he focussed his attention on the river below, peering down at the murky waters seeking signs of life.

'He's a lazy bastard is Mr Pike,' his father had told him. 'Look, down there, see?'

The young Derek had stared into the muddy stream, desperate to see something, but all he had been able to make out was the sunlight reflecting off the water.

'No boy, there – look, just there by them reeds – see him now?'

Young Derek trembled, opening his eyes wide and searching frantically for the elusive fish. He was rocked forwards by a slap on the back of his head.

'You'm not trying you goddam little fool. Plain as day he is!'

A tiny bubble rose to the surface, several feet behind where Derek had been looking and suddenly he spotted the pike.

'I see him,' he shouted. 'There – just down there sort of hidden.' With a flick of its tail the fish was gone. This time Derek saw stars as the blow nearly toppled him into the stream.

'Shut up you idjut! We want them fish here, not the bastard river wardens. Get up now, we've best be off though I'm minded to leave you here.' Young Derek staggered after his father, head still spinning as he tripped and stumbled along a path so faint only his father could see it.

'Quiet now. Can't you do nothin' right? You're a bloody liability you are boy. Don't know why I bother with you, I really don't.'

Derek cringed away, dreading what was to come next. They continued down the path away from the water as his father muttered, 'I dunno, seems to me I lost the wrong son. You're not a patch on your brother and you never will be . . .'

However often he'd heard them, those words always made Young Derek want to cry.

'So Mr Pike, you lazy bastard, you down there then?' whispered Derek as he leaned over the rickety bridge. The reeds were thick and luxurious around the old wooden pilings and the canal ran a little shallower a few yards in each direction. Sunlight cut through the murk lighting up the water on each side but it was dark in the shadow of the bridge. It was the perfect hunting ground for pike, the arch-predator of the river. Floating almost motionless in the deep shade, superbly camouflaged amongst the dappled water and armed with size, strength and fearsome teeth, this was the most hated and feared inhabitant of the river. Fishermen yearned for the glory of a big catch but shied away from the pike's vicious bite. Many of the locals wouldn't touch the flesh swearing it was unclean. Pike were, after all, notoriously unfussy about what they ate. Lurking in the shadows with ever-open mouths they would grab whatever came close – fish, bird or amphibian, dead or alive, they weren't picky. They seized their prey in an almost unbreakable grasp because their teeth aligned in opposite directions. They would wait until the catch weakened before using their hard, rough tongues to twist the meal round lengthways, stripping flesh from bones as they did so. Smaller victims could be swallowed whole.

Derek opened the newspaper parcel he was holding and

lifted out one of the strips of meat he'd prepared the previous evening. It glistened pink in the morning sun and he felt a brief spasm of nausea, ruthlessly suppressed. Leaning carefully over the flimsy rail he dropped it into the water just by the reeds. Nothing. He waited for a moment and then tried another piece. The water flowed smoothly on, undisturbed.

'Shit,' he muttered. It had been a great idea, one of his best. Hell, he'd dreamed about chopping up his father and feeding him to the pike when he'd been a boy. So much for childhood ambition. Suddenly there was a tiny ripple, against the flow of the river. He moved slowly, careful to avoid casting a shadow on the water. A single bubble rose to the surface and a great grin stretched Derek Johns' face as he peeled the next titbit from the parcel and tossed it into the reeds. There was no mistaking it this time. He glimpsed the sharp snout and dorsal fin of a pike as it snatched at the meat, pulling it out of sight in a second. Derek was cautious, not wanting to startle the fish away and he took it gently, dropping the pieces one at a time and always a little away from one another. There were several pike down there he reckoned and good news spread fast along the river. Such a rich source of easy food would bring more of them in the coming days. Yes, he was a right lazy bastard was Mr Pike and he'd wait under the bridge for his dinner to fall into his mouth rather than go elsewhere and hunt if he had a choice. Derek screwed up the empty paper and hurried back to the cottage where a lot more preparation was waiting, for tomorrow. Below the bridge the water frothed and churned for a few minutes and then all was still as the pike waited, their rapacious eyes glittering in the darkness.

'Fuck off!'

'Brian, come on . . .'

'I don't know nothing.'

Alex took a deep breath and struggled to control her temper. Brian was in one of his more challenging moods and not inclined towards altruism. She stared at him as he sat hunched up in a chair below the top window. He was almost curled up, arms around his knees and with his head down. His hair hung over to one side, unwashed and greasy with just a hint of the red dye he had used a couple of weeks ago. Then he'd had it up in a Mohican and his whole demeanour had been strong, positive and surprisingly receptive. She wondered if there might be some correlation between the hair and Brian's mood. Which influenced the other? she mused. Did he take more care of his appearance when he was feeling good or, like a juvenile Samson, did his personality wither away if his hair drooped?

'I 'ent saying nothing to no-one. Don't know nothing,' he repeated.

'Look, I know you're worried about the river wardens but maybe we can sort something out. This is a big thing, Brian. Kevin could be charged with murder and you could be the only person who can save him.'

Brian snorted, but finally lifted his head a little. She could just see his eyes as they caught the light in the shadows.

'Maybe's no good. Maybe's weasel talk, just to get me to give myself up. Well, you just forget it 'cos I don't know nothing and I'm not saying nothing'.

Alex was almost overcome by a wave of absolute fury. For an instant she felt dizzy and she was aware of the sound of her heart beating thunderously in her ears. She wanted to fling herself over the desk, grab Brian by the throat and choke the selfish, stupid little . . . She was saved by the sound of phone ringing on her desk and she snatched at it, nearly knocking the receiver off the side of her desk.

'Yes?' she demanded. There was a moment's silence before Alison's hurt voice answered.

'I'm sorry if I'm interrupting something *important*.'

Alex took a deep breath and forced herself to speak more calmly. 'No, sorry Alison. What can I do for you?'

'I've a message from Garry, about your meeting at three this afternoon.'

Alex opened her mouth to protest her ignorance. Surely she wouldn't forget something like that – meetings with Garry weighed heavy on her consciousness, sometimes to the extent of generating surreal and disturbing dreams.

'I put it in your diary,' came Alison's smug voice. 'Anyway, he has another meeting so he wants to move you up to 2.45. In his office,' she added unnecessarily.

In the diary. Alex groaned as she rummaged through the debris strewn across her desk. The diary, her 'shared' document and the only one she allowed Alison to touch, was under a pile of unfinished case notes. So was her dictaphone, she noted with surprise. Well, she'd been looking for that for a few days now. She glanced up and realized Brian was still watching her from the chair.

'Oh, go on, bugger off.' She waved her hand at him dismissively.

Brian got up and made for the door, his feet dragging as if the effort was just too much for him.

'Same time next week,' she called as he lugged the door open and shuffled into the corridor.

'Don't see why. Don't seem worth the effort,' he muttered. Alex was on her feet and had him by the collar before the door could close behind him.

'Now you listen to me,' she said, resisting the temptation to shake him like a rat, 'I can file the papers today and have you up in court by Monday. Do you want to go back to Pucklechurch? Because that's where you're going if you don't start working with me.'

Brian flopped forwards in her grasp, his mouth open in surprise. She caught a faint odour on his breath, sweetish and slightly acidic, and as she turned him round to face the light she saw a faint rash, a smattering of tiny red sores around his mouth and nose.

'Oh you bloody little fool,' she said, dropping him back into his chair. Brian slumped back, his head lolling to the left as if seeking support from the wall. No wonder he was so unresponsive, Alex thought, as she stared at him. He was probably still 'glued'.

'Well can I go then or what?' muttered Brian.

There was no point in talking to him when he was in this state and there was always the danger of an aggressive response, especially when 'glueys' were on the way down. Alex stepped back and gestured to the door.

'Go on. But . . . Brian?' He stopped and looked at her, suspicion in every line of his face. 'I want you to come back tomorrow, about 11am. And I want you to be sober, understand? No natch, no glue, no nothing. Or I'll breach you tomorrow afternoon.'

He slammed the door behind him and she heard his steps thump down the main staircase, slightly unsteady as he lurched under the influence of the solvent. Shit, she thought, glue! That's all we need down here. She turned to her bookshelf seeking guidance and caught sight of the clock. Five minutes to the meeting with Garry, she thought, and she still had no idea what it was about. Which could be considered the lesser of two evils, she wondered, going in unprepared or spending five minutes with Alison trying to get something useful out of her? It was a close call but after a moment she sighed and pushed the door open, heading down the stairs after Brian.

'Have you made any progress with Mr Hinton yet?' asked Garry. It was clearly a rhetorical question. Garry made it his business to know where his officers were at all times and without the sterling, and occasionally devious, support of Lauren, Alex found herself increasingly under scrutiny. She sat up straight in the chair and clicked her pen as she opened her diary. A few minutes before, she'd reached the reception area to find Alison gone – out on some nebulous errand no-one could quite recall. She had stood for an instant, feeling like a complete fool, but just as she was turning away she'd heard Lauren's voice from the side office.

'Don't forget your diary. You might want to show the appointment you've booked in for Hinton. The one you made for this afternoon . . . after Brian.'

Alex had leant as far over the counter as she could but Lauren was out of sight, tucked away safely in her new room.

'Thanks,' Alex had called. There had been no reply, and the rest of the office staff had been busy, heads bent over files or typewriters. It was only when she was half-way up the stairs again that she had stopped and wondered how Lauren came to be so closely acquainted with her schedule. Now she gave silent thanks to Lauren, the amazing ever-vigilant Lauren and her timely hint.

'He's been very elusive when I've gone out on my evening visits,' she said, flipping through the diary and stopping at several points as if consulting the document for exact times and days. 'I thought I'd try him this afternoon. I had some clients in earlier and also this meeting, but hopefully I'll be early enough to meet up with him this time.'

Garry stared at her, his eyes sharp with suspicion. For a moment she thought he was going to reach out to check the diary and she forced herself to relax, letting the book flop open on to her lap. He couldn't resist a quick glance at the upside-down page, now with her appointments set out in neat print, in ink: '3.30pm – A.M. Hinton (home visit)' he read.

'Very well. It is most important we make contact with this man, you do understand this don't you?' She felt herself nodding like a fool.

'It would be most unfortunate, *most* unfortunate if we found ourselves in a position of having to breach this particular gentleman. I have instructions from head office to ensure he is able to complete any business he has in the area as soon as possible so he can be safely on his way.'

Alex was privately of the opinion it would be close to impossible to breach him, seeing as Andrew Michael Hinton didn't exist outside of the probation file bearing his name; he probably had no matching criminal record anymore, and no-one seemed to have seen him since his somewhat insubstantial materialization onto her case-load two weeks ago. Mr Hinton, she suspected, could probably get away with murder at this point, providing he took minimal precautions and wore gloves. It was not a comforting thought.

'He may be a little elusive,' continued Garry, 'but this sort of case is just one of the many challenges of our work. Real probation work.' He warmed to his theme and Alex sat with a sinking heart, recognizing the opening paragraph of his 'inspire and encourage' lecture. She'd sat through a bit of it at her interview, she'd had the whole thing at induction, and she'd dozed through several versions in various meetings over the past eight months.

'I'm sorry, Garry, but I really need to go if I'm to make contact with Mr Hinton,' she said, trying to inject just the right amount of regret into her voice. Garry stopped in mid-sentence, blinking at her. He was not used to being interrupted so abruptly, but he could hardly reprimand her for doing what she'd been told to do.

'Of course. Yes, go on. Let me know how you get on,' he added as the door closed behind her. He sat for an instant staring at the door, his eyes half closed as he pondered the problem that was Alex Hastings. He stood, unfolding his long length from behind his desk and stepped over to the window, a beautiful mullioned relic from the original building. He could see the whole car park from here, across to the sheds, where he hoped to establish workshops and a day centre for the clients, and down on to the front door. Here he could observe the comings and goings of staff and clients, mentally ticking them off on a long list and noting any irregularities. He had already spotted Alison's premature departure and had a note in his diary to talk to her about it. As he watched, Alex appeared, coat flying and bag slung carelessly over her shoulder. She turned to latch the door behind her, dropped her keys, snatched them up, dropped them again and finally managed to get down the steps without tripping. Really, he thought as she fumbled with the lock to her car, she was an absolute shambles sometimes. Yet there was a good mind in there somewhere, insightful, smart and even occasional flashes of brilliance. It would be a shame if she failed *her* probationary year.

Chapter Six

The evenings were getting longer as spring moved towards summer, and Derek Johns sat in his bleak front room fretting over the wasted time. It was true that passers-by were rare this far out into the Levels and he wasn't expecting visitors. No-one knew he was here and he doubted anyone knew that Frank Mallory had taken up residence in the tumbledown cottage on his release from Dartmoor. There was no reason to be worried but every reason to be careful and he decided to wait until full dusk before drawing the curtains and continuing his preparations for the next morning's feeding. The cottage was gloomy with thick walls and tiny windows set far back to protect them from the winter storms. Once a crofter's home, it had been used by a family of peat-cutters for several generations, the family living off the summer vegetables and whatever they could trade for the rich peat sliced and stacked by the whole family over the warmer months. The hearth set into the end wall was blackened with the smoke of generations of fires, started in late autumn and banked carefully each night, a spark of warmth and light to carry them through the endless dark days of winter. Ada had finally abandoned it in favour of Frank's marginally more modern home up the road when she married, and none of the family had bothered to return and reclaim it.

It was cool in the cottage even in high summer and Derek was tempted to light a fire, but he hesitated, concerned the smoke from the chimney might attract unwelcome attention. When night fell he could cover the windows, light a lantern in the back room and get back to work. In the meantime he propped himself up in the one remaining armchair, draped his jacket over his shoulders and fell into a doze. By the time he heard the car draw up it was too late.

Alex pulled off the road and bumped over the muddy yard of the cottage. The silence seemed to flow into the car as she turned the engine off and she was suddenly very aware she was completely alone and about to meet someone she could not even identify properly. She recalled the warning from Pauline, so blithely disregarded a few weeks earlier, and felt a momentary shiver run through her body. She took several slow, deep breaths and rolled her head round to loosen her neck muscles before reaching over to the back seat to collect her case.

'Don't let them get to you,' she told herself. 'If you lose confidence in your own ability how can you expect anyone else to believe in you?' Feeling slightly better she opened the door and stepped out of the car.

'Oh bloody hell!' muttered Derek, as he glimpsed Alex through the grimy window. He stepped back out of sight as she looked in his direction, glancing around the room to see if there was anything suspicious in view. There was nothing in the room except the chair, his jacket and himself. He risked another look and gritted his teeth as he saw her approaching the front door. Something in her demeanour told him she knew he was there. It would arouse too much suspicion if he ignored her, so he composed himself, ready to bluff his way out of the situation if he could. There was a sharp knock on the door.

Alex studied the cottage for an instant. No smoke, but it was still early evening and mild. No lights either, but she was sure she'd caught a flicker of movement behind the dirt-encrusted window on the ground floor. Summoning her 'brisk and efficient' demeanour she stepped up to the front door and knocked. It opened with a soft creak as the rarely-used hinges grated together. The doorway was deep and the setting sun behind the house cast a shadow across her field of vision. Blinking her eyes she focussed on the figure in the doorway. Big, tall, dark-haired – there was something slightly familiar about him. There was also something – off was the best way she could describe it – something off and a bit menacing about him just standing there, a great lump in the doorway. She tightened her grip on her case as she looked up at him.

'Mr Hinton? I'm Alex Hastings, from Highpoint Probation Office.'

The figure paused and for a moment she thought he was going to refuse her entry, but then he moved back a step and jerked his head at her.

'Better come in then,' he said. Etiquette demanded she offer to shake hands, make a friendly gesture and smile but every ounce of instinct Alex possessed was shouting at her to make an excuse and leave. Instead she nodded, stepping into the dim, cold room, wanting to keep some distance between them.

Hell, she was tiny, Derek thought. He could pick her up in one hand and throw her . . . He stopped abruptly, aware she was surveying the room with a cool, professional eye. Bloody fearless this one, he thought, as he stepped towards the solitary armchair and gestured towards it.

'Sit down then. I'll get a stool from the kitchen.'

Alex perched herself on the edge of the chair and instinctively glanced behind her, checking the route to the door was clear. Even though he was a big man, he could probably move fast, very fast and almost silently, she thought. She pulled his file – such as it was – from her case and took out a pen ready to add her notes. Derek returned with his chair and placed it by the kitchen door, which he had closed behind him. He was close, she noted, but not close enough to appear obviously threatening. They glanced at one another and for a second their eyes met. The flat, almost reptilian look he gave her made Alex want to shiver. There was something very wrong here; she just couldn't work out what it was.

As their eyes met, Derek was taken aback by her directness, the hard, bold stare that seemed to be weighing him up and finding him wanting. He'd have to be careful, he thought. She was physically small but that didn't make her any less of a threat. He'd met women like this before – they were as help-less as a bag of adders.

He turned towards the empty hearth and said, 'Do you want the fire on? It's still a bit cold.'

Alex shook her head and attempted a smile.

'No, don't put it on just for me. I'm fine thank you and I'll not keep you long.'

He nodded absently but kept his attention on the fireplace. She waited a moment and decided she's better get on with it. It was dark in the room now, the sun to the back of the cot-tage offering no light to the east-facing windows. She peered at the notes in front of her and gave up. She'd just ask the most important questions and get out of there.

'Sorry there's no light,' he said. 'Can't seem to get the cir-cuit working properly, see. I'm using a couple of lamps but they're out back.'

Before she could stop herself she asked, 'Why did you choose this place? It can't be very comfortable. Surely they could have arranged something a bit better for you.' She knew it was the wrong thing to say the moment she started. Hinton's body tensed and his head swung round towards her, his features set into a glare.

'That's my business. I'm happy here for my own reasons and I'm a free man now.'

Technically that wasn't strictly true. Hinton was still on licence and as his supervising probation officer she was sup-posed to report to the police if she found him living in unsuitable conditions, but this was definitely not the time or the place to argue the point. She allowed her attention to wander back to the page in front of her as if unaware of his anger, a show of unconcern as she tried to step back from the little trap she had dug for herself. It was almost impossible to see the paper in front of her but she made some meaningless scribbles, her eyes focused on the movement of the pen.

Derek cursed himself for being a clumsy, loudmouthed fool. He'd come close to losing his temper at the very first question. He watched Alex as she sat, so calm and composed making her notes. Damn the woman, did she have X-ray eyes or something? It was near pitch dark, yet she was still writing away. He took a deep breath and tried to let it out softly, gripping the edge of the wooden chair as he strove to calm himself.

Alex stalled, making soft meaningless sounds of the 'um, a-ha' variety as she tried to formulate a strategy that would get her out in one piece. He was sitting very still, watchful and tense she thought, like an animal ready to pounce. Play dumb, she decided. Play the 'just a routine and I don't really care' role and take the first opportunity to leave.

'As you say,' she said as casually as she could. 'Anyway, I just need to put something in to show we've made contact. Keep the forms up to date and the courts happy – you know how it is.' She was becoming increasingly aware of an odour, faint but pungent, seeping round the room. She cleared her throat and tried a bright smile in his direction, all the while wondering just what it was making that smell.

Derek was not fooled by the smile but he seized on the chance to cut the meeting short. He felt himself beginning to sweat and knew that in the light his face would be turning a tell-tale red with the strain. He played along – anything to get away from her. He sniffed, sure he could smell something from the kitchen, a wisp of ripe meat awaiting his knife.

'Yeah, well I'm not plannin' on staying long, see. Just stopping by then off to – well, you know. Fewer people hear that the better eh?'

Alex nodded, scribbled again and said, 'So you'll be calling in to the office next week?'

He'd not expected that. All parolees had to report to their probation officers for the length of their licence but he'd not been released on licence – Frank Mallory had. And now he was Frank Mallory, aka Andrew Hinton, until someone recognized him and then there'd be hell to pay. Well, what was the alternative? He couldn't offer to pop into the police station – he was known to every copper within fifty miles. Yet he certainly didn't want her back here again, poking around and looking in every corner with her sharp, bright eyes. When in doubt, lie.

'I'm hoping to pick up a car the end of next week,' he said. 'Maybe I can call you and come in the week after?' Three weeks should be enough time, he thought. He'd need to move on anyway once he'd finished his business here. He had a couple more meetings planned but he couldn't hang around here too long, not knowing the coppers might pop by to see how dear old Frank was getting on.

Alex nodded, secure in the knowledge he had no intention of reporting. Whoever he really was, whatever he'd done to get his release, he was about to skip.

'Fine,' she said, holding out an official card. 'Here's my number. Give me a call in the next few weeks and let me know how you're getting on. If you could just sign here please.' She held out the form, indicating the bottom of the page. Derek took the pen, signed and pushed the papers back towards her before leaning back with his arms folded. Alex bundled the whole lot into her case, rose and bumped into the chair as she turned to go. She stumbled and almost fell and her case fell open, papers and folders slipping on to the floor. She grabbed at the pile, ignoring the sardonic grin on Hinton's face as he enjoyed her embarrassment. He made no move to help her, just sat there smirking as she flung the door open and stepped out into the cold, clean air. She'd not realized how close it had been in the cottage and she took several deep breaths as she hurried to her car. Flinging everything inside she flopped into the driver's seat and turned the key just as the cottage door opened and Hinton barrelled across the yard towards her. She was overcome by panic, an unreasoning fear that threatened to overwhelm her. Desperately she tried the ignition, cursing the ingenious and eccentric suspension as she did so. Nothing happened of course. It took her aging model almost thirty seconds to inflate and free the safety system – plenty of time for him to reach the car and knock on the window. She stared at him through the glass, only too aware of her vulnerability, the dodgy locks on the passenger side and the fact she was about to make an utter fool of herself. His face was expressionless as he knocked again and she reluctantly wound the window down a fraction. She realized she could smell him, a thick, musky smell of sweat, dirt and – something else, something ripe and slightly rancid. He pushed an object through the gap at the top of the door and stepped back.

'Here, you forgot your pen,' he said, and then he smiled. It was a mocking smile, the grin of a hunter who scents their prey. The engine fired and she swung the car round, screeching off back down the road and off the Levels. Her hands shook as she gripped the wheel in a tense grasp. Now she realized why he seemed familiar. When he gave that smile he looked disturbingly like the 'didicoy' from Bristol.

'Well that's the thing, you see,' said Alex. 'He didn't actually do anything'.

Sitting at the dining table, safe in her own house, she began to feel rather foolish. What had Andrew Hinton done after all? He'd not refused her entry, he'd been polite and he'd even offered to put the fire on.

'Maybe my family are right,' she mumbled, 'maybe I'm losing my nerve. It's just . . .' She struggled to describe exactly what had made her so uneasy – no, if she were honest, what had made her so afraid. She's never been scared by a client before and she's met some thoroughly unpleasant characters in the past few years but there was a sense of menace about this man that made her skin crawl. Most clients played along with the system. They might not really think it was helping or even want anything she could offer but it was better than the alternatives. The fact Alex could take them back to court and have them shipped off to prison was a great incentive to co-operation but she knew instinctively that was not the case here. There was something, something broken in this one. The only reason he'd not picked her up and snapped her in two was because he couldn't be bothered. Had she pushed a bit harder she suspected she wouldn't have escaped so easily.

'Here,' said Sue, pushing a glass towards her.

Alex shook her head. 'I don't drink during the week,' she said. 'You know that.'

Sue snorted and picked up an open bottle. 'The week you're having, it's about time you started,' she said, pouring a generous glass of wine.

Alex managed a wry grin and took a sip. The wine slid down, soothing her fear and sending a gentle warmth outwards through her body. She drank again and leaned back in her chair with a sigh.

'I know he's a danger,' she said. 'He'll skip, for sure and then he'll be on the loose, free to do any damn horrible thing he wants but there's nothing I can do about it. Can you imagine the police if I went along now. "Well, he looked at me in a funny way, his house smelt and he ran after me to give my pen back". They'd laugh me out of station and with good reason.'

Sue nodded, took a slug of her wine and put the glass down with a bang. 'Well, while you were out socializing you missed another of Garry's delightful surprise meetings,' she said.

'Oh? How the hell did he manage to fit that in? He was heading off somewhere else about three this afternoon. I know because he changed the time of *my* meeting. Not that I knew about the wretched thing in the first place,' she added bitterly.

'Alison?' asked Sue.

'Alison. So tell me, what was this get-together about?' Alex drained her glass and did not protest when Sue filled it again.

'He had a couple of Head Office bods round just after you left. Then a few minutes to five he had Pauline herd us all upstairs and launched into this presentation.'

Alex waited but there was there was nothing more forthcoming.

'Presentation about what?' she asked finally.

Sue shrugged. 'I don't know. He started on about stopping snot or something. It sounded disgusting so I just sort of tuned out for a lot of it.'

'The new priorities,' Alex said. 'SNOP, SLOP and STOP.'

'That's it,' said Sue. 'I remember now. Anyway, I wasn't paying much attention until he got on to the stuff about the away-day.' Sue picked up the bottle, upended it with a frown and rose from the table.

'Away-day? What do you mean, away-day?' said Alex.

'Next month, in some hall somewhere. We're all going, clerical and everyone,' called Sue from the kitchen. 'Ah, here we are.' She appeared in the doorway flourishing a fresh bottle of wine and a corkscrew.

'You're a fount of information today,' grumbled Alex. 'A meeting for an indeterminate purpose, on an unspecified date, at an unspecified location and for an unspecified length of time. Oh please don't let it be a residential!'

Sue was wrestling with the cork but glanced up at the anguish in her friend's voice.

'Oh, yes there is that. It's two days so we're all staying overnight.' The cork popped out of the bottle and Alex reached for her glass, holding it out for another refill.

'Are you sure? You don't normally drink this much in a whole evening.'

'Shut up and fill it, you bringer of doom. Like you said, I'm having a pretty terrible week.'

When Margie looked into Kevin's cell that evening he was sitting on his bunk, scrunched up in the corner with his arms around his legs and his knees drawn up tight against his body.

'Hey,' she said softly.

Kevin peeked out at her through his greasy hair but did not reply. Margie waited for a moment on the threshold and then stepped into the cell. Like most of the prison it smelt of feet, sweat and cheap aftershave, probably splashed around to cover the scent of illegal alcohol fermenting in a warm corner somewhere. It was amazing what they could produce from orange juice, sugar and any potato peelings they could smuggle out of the kitchen, Margie thought as she approached the figure huddled on the bed.

'Just checking you're alright,' said Margie. She was careful to keep her voice level and neutral, as much to avoid undue attention from other prisoners as to keep the young man calm. Kevin tucked his head into his arms and muttered something she couldn't make out. Giving a glance behind her to make sure it was safe, she stepped further into the room and was disturbed to see Kevin flinch.

'Kevin – it is Kevin, right?' She waited but there was no response. 'Well, your P.O. asked me to drop by, see if there's anything you need.' There was still no reaction from Kevin but at least he'd stopped cowering away from her. Alex was right, thought Margie, there was something nasty going on here and she wasn't letting it go. Not on her watch. Margie prided herself on doing the best job she could. She'd never lost a prisoner whist on duty, not from violence or suicide, but she recognized the signs and this was a very vulnerable inmate. In theory there was nothing she could do. He was on remand and should be safe, separated from the convicted criminals in the main population. He certainly didn't belong with the 'veeps' – the 'vulnerable prisoners' who had their own wing. That elite group was a mix of drug dealers, sex offenders and members of the justice system – bent coppers, judges or ex prison officers, all of whom were at risk in the main population, or, in the case of the drug dealers, constituted a threat to others. Anyway, he was still not convicted, presumed innocent despite the fact he was locked up. There was nowhere for him to go except . . . she hesitated, knowing

94

she was setting herself up for days of derision from the male officers. She looked at Kevin for a moment and sighed heavily as she reached out and took his elbow.

'Up you get. You're coming with me.'

'The hospital? Why's he in the hospital? Has something happened to him?' Alex demanded when she got a call from the prison in the morning. She felt dreadful – pounding head, red eyes, sick and slightly dizzy, the classic symptoms of a monster hangover for which she held Garry personally responsible. Too much wine last night, the pending 'away-day' and now this. She hoped she didn't have to go back to Bristol because she suspected she was in no state to drive.

'He's all right, not injured or anything like that,' said Margie's voice on the other end of the phone. 'I checked up on him and you're right, I think he's being picked on. He looked pretty dreadful and was in no state to watch out for himself, so I had a word with the duty doctor on the phone and got him signed into the hospital for a week. Give him a chance to rest a bit, maybe. Can't be more though – he'll have to go back on the wing in seven days and the best I can do then is put him on suicide watch. That'll not improve his popularity with his cell mates neither.'

Alex knew just how effective suicide watch was sometimes. Regular checks on prisoners thought to be leaning towards self-harm were designed to dissuade them as well as ensuring the officers knew what they were up to. Unfortunately the constant clanging of the hatch, every half-hour through the night, tended to result in broken sleep and frayed tempers, particularly amongst the non-suicidal cellmates. No, Kevin wasn't necessarily suicidal but he was in danger from someone in the jail and they could bide their time and get to him during the day.

Margie echoed her thoughts as she added, 'Better try getting him out on bail. Maybe a hostel or something down near your way?'

Alex thanked her profusely. She knew Margie would have

to put up with all kind of snide, sexist remarks about 'soft-hearted women' and 'mothering the criminals'. As she hung up she wondered why any woman would choose to work in such a place. Still, it was a good thing for Kevin she did and, on reflection, wasn't that exactly the sort of knee-jerk reaction she had to put up from her own family?

Desperate for a coffee, she made her way downstairs to the communal lounge. To her relief it was empty and she filled the kettle and began spooning coffee (only instant but better than nothing) and sugar into a relatively clean mug. She was rooting through the fridge for milk when she heard the main door open behind her and Alison walked in. Alex turned to face her and knew something was wrong. Alison wore her usual sulky face but this morning it was embellished with a scowl.

'Ah, morning Alison,' said Alex, trying to inject some enthusiasm into her tone. 'How are you today?'

Alison blinked at her with watery eyes and gave a sniff, another of her delightful mannerisms, the product of a low-grade but seemingly eternal cold.

'Fine, thank you, just fine. Are you finished with that?' She held out her hand for the milk bottle and Alex tipped milk into her beaker and handed it over. Alison turned her back and began to pick through the sink searching for a cup that didn't have green crusty mould in the bottom. She was muttering to herself, Alex realized.

'I'm sorry Alison, is there a problem?' she asked. For a moment she thought the woman would back down, but her hopes were dashed when she launched into a tirade about 'snooty, overpaid officers thinking they were too good to clear up after themselves'. She was almost crying, Alex noticed with some alarm. She was no psychologist but she was pretty sure this wasn't about who did the washing up. Struggling with a cowardly impulse to flee the scene and nurse her hangover upstairs, she put down her own beaker and guided Alison gently towards the window seats.

'Here, sit down for a moment. I'll get you a drink. Oh – do you prefer tea or coffee?' She felt a flash of guilt. She'd taken so little interest in Alison she didn't even know which she preferred. Maybe there was some truth in her view of 'snooty officers' thinking they were better than everyone else. Deep down inside, Alex had to admit to herself she did think she was better than Alison, but she certainly didn't consider herself in any way superior to Lauren, so what did that say about her? She hastily made tea, picked up her own mug and walked over to join Alison at the table. Alison took the cup and muttered 'Ta' before resuming her moody contemplation of the sky through the window.

'So, what is it Alison? I can see you're upset about something.' Alison gave a shrug worthy of Brian at his sulky best – or worst. Fighting an almost overwhelming urge to reach over and slap her very hard, Alex ploughed on. 'Has someone upset you or perhaps there's a problem in the office?'

Alison swivelled her head round on her long, skinny neck and stared at her. 'As if you don't know,' she said.

Alex waited, but Alison just sat, in silence, staring at her until she gave another watery sniff and turned back to the window. Alex's patience was exhausted. She had enough of this type of behaviour from the clients – she was damned if she'd put up with it from the staff as well.

'Fine, if you don't want to talk there's nothing I can do. I've got work to be getting on with,' she said as she rose to her feet.

'You know what you did,' muttered Alison, the sulky child fully in evidence as she screwed up her face and pouted.

'No, I don't. I don't know what you think I've done and unless you tell me I can't do anything about it.'

'Yesterday, when you were with Garry. You didn't have to tell him I'd had to go out. Now he's put a note on my file. He was really horrible this morning.'

Alex was aghast. 'You think I told Garry you'd gone out yesterday? What on earth gave you that idea?'

Alison snuffled into a soggy tissue. 'You were up there in the afternoon, at the meeting just after we spoke. Someone said you came down to find me.'

Alex gave a deep sigh. 'Alison, stand up. Now, where's Garry's office from here?'

Alison pointed out of the window, up another floor to the imposing centrepiece of the block at right angles to them.

'Right. Now, look down into the yard – see? He's got a perfect view of the entrance. He spends half his time at that window, watching who goes in and out. Haven't you ever noticed him up there?'

Alison looked so stricken Alex wondered what else she'd been up to recently.

'So it wasn't you?' she asked in a tiny voice.

'No, it wasn't me. I don't do things like that. If I'm annoyed because I can't find you I'll ask you about it, not tattle away to Pauline or Garry. So, is there anything else?'

Alison shook her head. She looked close to tears as she reached over and tried to give Alex a hug. Her hands were damp and fortunately the table was in the way. Alex patted her shoulder and gave a rather sickly smile.

'Well, I'm glad that's sorted out. I'll be upstairs if you need me.'

She extricated herself as gently as possible and hurried out, wondering how anyone could possibly think she'd toady up to Garry, of all people.

Back in her office she mused on the problem of Kevin. It was highly unlikely she'd be able to get Brian to make a statement and he was neither the most reliable nor the most believable of witnesses at the best of times. There had to be something else she could point to. The police case seemed weak, relying on circumstantial evidence – Kevin's presence in the van and the money in his pockets. There was no sign of the knife used, Kevin had no blood on him or his clothes, except for his shoes, and, crucially, he had no reason to murder the Elver Man. Kevin was obsessed with the Carnival gangs and he needed his income from elvering to meet the hefty subscription demanded by the town clubs. Even if he had robbed him that night, he'd needed more – quite a lot more according to Lauren. The Elver Man had been the best source of income Kevin had. Besides, Kevin was a nervous specimen. He was going to pieces in the prison, not the sort of character to kill someone in cold blood, take their money and calmly settle down at the scene for a snooze until the rain stopped. . . . She was struck by a sudden memory. Kevin's clothes were still wet when he was arrested. He'd been out in the rain just a few minutes before the police arrived. And the elvers – the elvers were still alive! She realized she didn't know anything about elvers. How long did they live out of water, for example? Maybe Eddie would know. He was the outdoorsy type, after all, and he was a local boy, raised near Glastonbury. He'd probably sneaked out to go elvering himself when young. She picked up the phone and buzzed his office.

'Well now, it really depends on so many things,' said Eddie. Alex smothered a sigh. She just wanted a simple yes or no answer, but like most things in her life at the moment it looked as if she was going to get a lecture on the difficulties inherent in her question.

'They travel overland if the way is blocked,' Eddie continued, warming to his theme. 'It's an extraordinary sight, hundreds and hundreds of tiny eels glittering in the sunlight as they wriggle their way over river banks and across fields. They're almost transparent, you know, so some books call them glass eels.'

Alex did know that but she nodded anyway, hoping he'd get to the point more quickly. Eddie frowned as he considered the likely fate of Kevin's haul.

'Well, I'm not 100 per cent certain,' he said finally, 'but I wouldn't expect the elvers at the bottom of the crates to last too long, especially if they were stacked up on one another. Silly boy, he could have lost a lot of money like that. They really need to be alive when they're delivered to the wholesaler. They're so fragile, you see, they can go off really fast once they're dead.'

Privately, Alex thought this was a suspiciously high level of knowledge concerning the marketability of the elver.

'So how long is not long do you think?' she asked.

Eddie shook his head. 'Couldn't say really. Probably only a matter of minutes if they were crushed, of course. I don't suppose anyone photographed the elvers at the scene?'

Alex considered this to be highly unlikely. It looked as if Kevin's alibi was evaporating before her eyes. She thanked Eddie and went back to her room. Even if she could get Brian to testify she needed something more. His clothes had been wet but it was hardly definitive. Anyone who knew Kevin would assume he'd been wading in the river or splashed himself getting his elvers out of the net. She sat at her desk trying not to stare at the calendar. It was Thursday already and Kevin had been in the hospital since Tuesday evening. She was running out of time and had no idea what to do next.

Derek found himself in a quandary and he knew who was to blame. That interfering bitch of a probation officer – it was all her fault. He'd never intended to live in the cottage, just drop by to do his work and be off to somewhere a bit more comfortable. No-one in their right mind would want to stay in this poky little hovel, not if they had a choice anyway. It was cold, it was dark and it leaked when the rain fell. Derek sat in his armchair, feet up on an old crate he'd fished out of the canal at the back. He sniffed the air and pulled a face, convinced he could smell something in the kitchen. Just the smell of the river, he told himself. Just a bit of mould and rot coming up from the surrounding peat that's all. Nothing to do with his work. He dismissed the thought as he concentrated on the problem posed by Alex-bloody- probation. He had to check back on Iris, see if she was pulling herself together a bit. He had business to attend to elsewhere and the whole organization needed a firm hand and he needed to check each day, see who had come by. He'd bought himself a couple of weeks with the story about the car, but she'd be back after that, unless he went into the office in town and that was out of the question, especially during the day. Too many people knew him, knew who he really was. He had to get a move on, finish up and get out of there before someone dropped by and started nosing about. With a sigh, he pushed himself up out of the chair and went into the kitchen to prepare the next meal for the pike.

Newt lay on his bunk and stared at the ceiling. Although he was one of the youngest on the wing, his position had been enhanced by the support of Big Bill and his escape attempt. His cell mate, a wizened little safe-breaker who smoked the thinnest roll-up cigarettes Newt had ever seen, had insisted he should have the top bunk, and Newt was happy to accept. From his elevated position Newt was partially hidden from the eyes that peered in at odd intervals, and as the days ground on he was able to read by the security floodlight shining through the high barred window. The prison library had a reasonable selection of thrillers and war stories and he was content to pass the time and rebuild his reputation as a steady prisoner, his jog into the village appearing to be just a moment of recklessness. He was not likely to get an outside work-place for a long, long time, but at least his exploits had earned him a measure of respect amongst his fellow inmates.

There was a knock on the door and Big Bill looked in, beaming all over his battered face.

'Watcha Newt,' he said.

Newt sat up and swung his legs over the side of the bunk.

'You're looking right cheerful,' he said.

Bill stepped into the cell, his head almost level with Newt's as he grinned at him happily. 'Heading for the great outdoors tomorrow,' he said. 'Time's up and you're on your own for a bit.'

Newt nodded, unconcerned by the news. He was more confident now, secure in his position as the heir to the Johns gang empire. Big Bill had been useful but he was not really needed any more. He held out his hand for Bill to shake.

'Well, good luck then and thanks for the help. I made sure Dad got the message, about our one-time friend.'

Bill grunted. 'Wouldn't like to be in his shoes. Well, I'll be dropping in to see your family, so any messages I can take?'

Newt considered for a moment and then shook his head. 'Just let Mum know I'm doin' alright. Don't want her fussing, what with Biff gone and all . . .'

There was a moment's silence between them, which was broken as the door opened and Mack, Newt's cellmate, strolled in. He stopped, turned abruptly and scooted out again mumbling an apology. Totally ignoring him, the two men shook hands again. Bill hesitated before turning to leave but Newt was already settling down to catch the last of the quiet spell before dinner.

'Tell Mack he can come in again, will you,' he said without looking up from his book.

'Right, Boss,' Bill replied before he realized what he'd said.

Up on his bunk Newt hid the traces of a smile behind his book.

Chapter Seven

Ada Mallory had been born on the Levels, arriving unaided in the front room of her parents' small cottage over by the sluice gate on the main drain. Her father, a hard-drinking man with a tendency to spread his affections far and wide, had scraped a living from seasonal work – peat cutting, apple picking and poaching mainly. Her mother was tied to the family home by the needs of four young children and by the time she was ten Ada was working alongside her. Washing, cleaning and cooking took precedent over schoolwork, especially when her father was away 'working', as her mother put it, though he rarely brought much of his earnings home with him when he did come back.

Ada had quite enjoyed her time at school. It had offered a break from the endless demands of her younger siblings, a period of quiet away from the chatter and cries of the family. She was a good student too, picking up the basics of reading and writing ahead of many of her classmates. Only numbers defeated her. Try as she might, as soon as she ran out of fingers for counting, all the numbers mixed up together in her head and she was left confused and angry by her inability to complete all but the simplest sum.

When she stopped going one November, the school sent a truancy officer, but it was to no avail as the Levels were still poorly drained and the roads mainly unmetalled and virtually impassable in winter. By the time the summer came they had pretty much written her off, just another child of uneducated and illiterate parents and not worth the effort. All except one teacher, that is, a student from the college in Taunton who believed every child was important and every one had potential.

Miss Nichols had been impressed by Ada's ability, the quickness of her mind and her almost painful enthusiasm for any and all knowledge. So, in due course, she arrived at Ada's home one evening on her bicycle with a basket full of books gleaned from the depths of the library store cupboards. For the first time in her life Ada cried in front of an outsider as she turned the pages of the old, worn textbooks and outdated dictionary. In some ways it made it worse, this unspoken acknowledgement that her formal education was over. She took the books inside and hid them under a loose floorboard beneath the big bed she shared with her two sisters, safe from her father's periodic raids on the family's possessions. On the rare occasions when she had time to herself and the house was empty she would take out a book and read, slowly and laboriously but with a sense of triumph in her heart.

The books, Ada's only books, were now lined up neatly on a little shelf Kevin had made for her one Mother's Day. She had read to Kevin from them when he was a baby, sharing tales of explorers in foreign lands, kings and battles, folk wisdom and ancient legend. She'd tried to help him learn to read himself but somehow he'd never managed it. Letters to Kevin were like numbers to her – unintelligible squiggles that taunted from the page as they refused to give up their meaning. She'd fought each day to get him to school and fought to keep him there, ignoring all his efforts to get himself expelled,

104

but despite everything he had left school at 16 with no formal qualifications – hardly surprising as he still could not read. He was good with his hands, though, as the bookshelf and many other little projects around the house demonstrated, and he was an absolute wizard with numbers. He would be sorting out the right coins to pay for something whilst she was still struggling to read a price and often he had stood beside the till in a shop and challenged the total. Somehow he was never wrong and it grieved her to know he could easily have passed his maths exams – if only he could have read the questions. She had heard on the radio that some children got help with their exams and she'd written to the school to ask about this but it seems it wasn't for the likes of Kevin. The help was expensive and he'd needed a good attendance record and a willingness to work. The school didn't even expect him to turn up for his exams so what was the point? And now he was in prison, locked up miles away and facing a possible life sentence. Ada stared out of her back window and tried not to weep.

The best way to cope with life was to just get on with it, she told herself. Enough moping around – that won't help anyone. She took a deep breath and stood up straight, forcing her mind towards the mundane concerns of everyday life. She opened the back door and stepped out into her garden, her own little kingdom. Bordered by willows to the sides, it ran down gently to a stream that bubbled and frothed through the reeds until curving away towards the big drain to the front of the house. As she closed the door behind her the dogs materialized, moving in silence on their wide, soft paws. Mickey, the older of the pair, turned and walked back to the side gate where he stretched out in a sheltered spot, away from the wind that swept the Levels in the spring. Mouse, the younger dog, moved up and nuzzled her hand hopefully.

'Get away you big daft thing,' she said, and gave him a gentle shove. Mouse took up his post behind her, following as Ada walked down the cinder path peering at her rows of vegetables in search of something ready to eat. Late April was a lean time of year: the last of the cabbages had turned yellow on their stalks and the early greens needed an extra week before they were large enough to eat. She carried on past the newly sown beds of salad leaves in their home-made cloches and on to a ramshackle greenhouse composed partly of a garden shed with plastic sheets for a roof and partly a variety of old windows nailed together into larger frames. Opening the door a fraction she ran her eye over the rows of seed trays, each labelled and sprouting a soft feathery green. She smiled to herself as she sniffed the rich, earthy smell of the peat, dug at night by Kevin from the surrounding bog. Who had the right to say she couldn't have just a bit of peat she thought. This was her home and her family had been making their living from the land for generations. As far as Ada was concerned, everything inside her boundary (and most things she could see from the garden, if the truth be told) belonged to her and no busy-body, ignorant, bossy government man was going to tell her what she could or could not use.

Resuming her stroll she reached the banks of the stream and peered through the reed beds, searching for movement in the funnel shaped nets set at intervals under the water. A lean time indeed – nothing stirred and she sighed to herself as she pictured her potato and soup supper. A splash of brighter green caught her eye, nestling behind the lower willows, and she clambered over the fence to investigate. A patch of new nettles waved with the wind and she smiled as she bent to gather the crisp, sharp-scented leaves. She did not flinch away for her hands were roughened by a lifetime of hard work and it took more than a nettle sting to interrupt Ada's foraging. When nettles were this young they were tender right through and if picked carefully they'd come back over and over again through the summer. She still had some useable onions in the shed and enough potatoes to thicken it without leaving herself short. Nettle soup would do fine for a starter. As she stood up she caught a flicker of movement in the field across from the stream.

Standing so still that she faded into the shadows, she

waited until she saw the grass sway and the tips of two grey ears poked up. Damn and damnation, she thought. Hell with the nettle soup when there's a chance of a sweet little coney and there's me with the wrong dog by my side. Mouse was hopeless as a hunter but Mickey – he was fast, could run down a hare if need be, but he was asleep over by the gate and there was no way of waking him without disturbing the rabbits. She turned her head slowly and looked towards the cottage, but it was too far to the back door. By the time she'd got in, loaded the shotgun and got out again they'd be gone for sure. She looked back over the field, marking in her memory the location of those tempting little ears. It was a waste anyway, using a shotgun shell on a little'un, she thought, as she trudged back up the path with her nettles and a couple of onions. She'd go out early and look for the tracks in the dew, rig up a snare maybe. No point in scaring the whole lot of them off and, besides, she didn't want to draw attention to the fact she had a gun in the house. Oh, where was Kevin when she needed him so much? Her head dropped again as she fell to worrying about her son.

Big Bill pulled up outside the Johns' house and sat for a moment, relishing the quiet, the unfamiliar feeling that comes from being unobserved. It had been over a year since his arrest, just two days since his release and he was still in the 'I'm never going back' phase. Life, he thought, as he opened the car door and stepped out into the soft spring day, life was too sweet to waste any more of it behind bars. He glanced down at his feet, rubbing the toes of his shoes on his trouser leg and pulling his jacket straight before stepping up to the front door. It opened at the first knock and for an instant he didn't recognize the woman in front of him. Big Bill had always had a secret crush on Iris, the stately and beautiful woman who had been swept off her feet by Derek just as Bill was summoning up the courage to ask her out. He'd shrugged it off, said the best man won, but although he'd had a string of women over the years he'd never married. The sight of this pathetic, bowed figure awakened all his pity and roused a deep, burning anger.

'Hello Bill,' muttered Iris, her voice as flat as her empty green eyes.

She turned away without waiting for a reply, shuffling in to the front room where a fire roared in the grate. Bill closed the door, wiped his feet on the mat and followed her. The room was almost intolerably hot, stuffy with stale air. Iris sat down in a chair as close to the grate as she could get and gathered a knitted shawl around her shoulders.

'Sorry,' she said, still in that eerie monotone. 'I can't seem to get warm. All winter, I've been . . . just been . . .' She trailed off, staring into the flames. Bill felt the sweat break out all over his body and he dropped his jacket on to the couch farthest from the source of heat.

'How about I get us a cup of tea?' he said.

Iris nodded, her gaze fixed on the fire, making no move to assist him. Bill hesitated for a moment and then went through the door into the kitchen. The place was a tip. The sink was piled high with dirty plates and cutlery, water with a layer of grease covering the items at the bottom. The worktop was covered in crumbs, suspicious looking splashes and vegetable peelings and used knives lay around, abandoned with their blades uppermost. The bin was full, he noticed, and there was a buzzing sound from within. He knew better than to open it inside the house in case an opportunist fly has got in and laid their eggs. It smelt bad enough for maggots, if not worse. Billy was truly appalled, not just by the evidence of neglect but by the contrast to the Iris he had known for so long. She had prided herself on the state of the house. Everything was washed and put away as soon as it was finished with, floors were swept every day and even the cushions on the big, plush couch stood to attention. This sort of mess would have been inconceivable before Biff's death.

Gritting his teeth he plunged his hand into the cold, scummy water and pulled the sink plug. As it drained away he filled the kettle, setting it to boil, and then searched for something to wipe his hands with. The only tea towel on the rail was stiff with dirt and he picked it up gingerly and placed it on the buzzing refuse bin before rummaging through the drawers in search of something a little more wholesome. Finally, armed with hot water and a clean cloth he tackled the sink, stacking the washed pots and crocks on the draining board he had wiped clean. There was no sound from the lounge and he peeked round the door: Iris was still sitting in exactly the same position, frozen in her despair before the fire. He took a deep breath and opened the back door, heaving the bin through and placing it next to the dustbin. Standing well back he flipped the lid open and was rewarded by a stream of flies that poured out and flew off into the wild to wreak more havoc. Trying not to breathe through his nose, Bill jiggled the plastic liner up and heaved the whole stinking mess into the dustbin. There was an outside tap set into the wall and he rinsed the bin out before setting it to drain by the door. After scrubbing his hands under the tap he made a pot of tea and set it out on a tray. Carrying it into the front room, he placed it on the low table next to Iris's chair. He poured them some tea, adding milk and sugar and stirring it round before he held out the cup. For the first time Iris looked at him directly.

'Thank you,' she said softly.

Big Bill felt a rush of emotion, tears threatening to overwhelm him as he saw the depth of her anguish reflected in her eyes.

'So,' he said, coughing to disguise his reaction, 'when is Derek out then?'

Iris turned her attention back to the fire, sipping at her hot tea. 'Oh, he's back. He should be home tonight, I hope. He's out a lot at the moment.'

Bill couldn't believe a husband would leave his wife in this state. If it were him, he'd be by her side, looking after her, trying to cheer her up, keeping the place tidy – but, of course it wasn't him. It was Derek and even he, the loyal and trusted lieutenant, dare not criticize Derek.

'Well, maybe I could pop back this evening then. Catch him then.'

Iris put down her cup and rose unsteadily to her feet, reaching out to the mantelpiece to pull an envelope from behind the clock.

'Here,' she said, holding it out to him, 'he left you this.'

Despite the heat thrown out from the fire, Bill felt himself shiver as he took the envelope. Derek had known he'd come here. Of course he did – he'd expect him to pay his respects. But did he know how he felt about Iris? Bill made his apologies, suddenly desperate to get out of the choking misery of the house.

His heart was pounding as he drove away along the main road, the letter seeming to burn through his pocket. Once outside the village he pulled over and ripped the envelope open. There was a single sheet of paper inside with a brief note scribbled in pencil: 'Meet me by the second place we fished as boys, tomorrow morning at 8.30. D.J.' Bill's hand was shaking as he shoved the letter back into the envelope. How the hell had Derek known he was going to see Iris today?

Alex had planned her day very carefully, moving appointments and creating space to ensure she had a clear day, but her hopes were dashed as she walked through the front door on Monday. Passing Gordon, who was rummaging in the boot of his car, packing items into black bin bags, she hurried to the foot of the stairs.

'Ah, Alex, good, here you go,' said Alison, who had been lurking at the front desk. Alex took the proffered folders and realized with a sinking heart that it was the court pack.

'No – no, I'm down for Friday,' she said, trying to push it back over the counter.

Alison shoved it back at her. 'Oh, Garry was looking for a volunteer this morning as Margaret's called in sick. I checked your diary and you're free all day'.

Alex stopped and looked at her, taking in the greasy hair, the pink nose and the ingratiating smile that trembled on those thin, pale lips. At that moment she wanted to jump over the counter, grab her assistant by her scrawny little neck and bash her head repeatedly on the counter, preferably until she died. There was a faint buzzing in her ears but apart from that all was silent in the room. She took a step towards the desk but Alison suddenly turned and fled, slamming the door behind her. Ignoring the raised voices from the main office, Alex reached out and picked up the court papers, her hands shaking as she opened the dreaded buff folder. She realized she was holding her breath and gave a gasp as the door opened and Lauren appeared over the lip of the counter.

'Are you alright then?' she asked.

Alex took another deep breath and nodded.

'Yeah. Yeah, I guess. It's just . . .' she gestured to the full day's work in the folder. She'd be in court at least until 4.30, maybe later. That was the end of her chance to see Kevin's solicitor. She had done her best but failed dismally and this defeat really hurt. Lauren leaned on the counter and laced her stubby fingers together.

'So, what was you was planning to do with the day you've so carefully left free, I'm wondering.'

Alex glanced over her shoulder but the room was still empty. She leaned forward and said softly, 'I was hoping to meet Smythe. I've not got a lot but maybe I can get Kevin out on bail, staying at the hostel or something. He's having a really hard time inside and he's got to move back out of the hospital tomorrow. I'm so worried about him.'

Lauren nodded. 'I was thinking it was probably something to do with Kevin. Well, you've got a full day in court to get ready so maybe you should go and do that. If you happened to drop a note off to me on the way back out, perhaps saying what you'm hoping to say to Smythe that might be a good thing. Then you can go and be today's hero, earn a bit of good will and all without worrying about anything else.'

Alex closed the folder and sighed. 'Lauren – I'm so sorry about how I behaved, you know . . .'

Lauren waved her hand at her dismissively. 'I know that,'

she said. 'I'm small, I'm not stupid. You was worried about the job and people's getting at you all the time, 'course you're going to be a bit – well not short, maybe grumpy.' She grinned and Alex found herself smiling in response.

'Seriously though, I really do need to see Smythe.'

Lauren looked at her and shook her head. 'Now that's your problem, right there. *You* don't need to see him so long as *someone* sees him. And maybe that someone could be a long-standing acquaintance with a favour or two to call in.'

Alex hefted the court pack and moved towards the door. 'Thank you,' she said softly.

'Welcome. You can't do it all on your own, you know,' said Lauren. 'Job's too big; it'll break your heart.'

Alex turned back, meaning to ask her why Gordon was emptying his car and scrubbing it yet again, but Lauren was gone, the office door closing behind her. As she reached the stairs she spotted Garry on the first landing, anxiety creasing his face.

'Ah, yes, Alex – have you seen Alison this morning?'

Alex waved the folder at him as she climbed the stairs.

'All under control Garry,' she said, trying to sound cheerful.

A look of surprise flitted over her senior's face. 'Oh, right, well – jolly good. Thanks – that's a great help.'

Alex nodded politely as she walked past and up the second flight of stairs. She was really smiling despite the prospect of a grindingly boring day in court. Garry had sounded almost disappointed at her willingness to be a 'team player'. That, along with her friendship with Lauren, made it all worthwhile.

Derek woke early the next morning, just as the light from the rising sun crept over the sill and round the curtains into his front room. It was quiet in the house, with Iris upstairs sleeping deeply and no sons to disturb the silence. He'd managed to get Iris to take a pill last night, as much for his own sake as hers and she probably wouldn't stir much before midday. That gave him plenty of time, he thought, time to get to the cottage and prepare before he met Big Bill. He stretched out on the couch where he'd spent the night. Better not to risk waking his wife so early, he thought. She'd only ask awkward questions and he needed to be sharp today. Softly he padded into the kitchen, noting with approval the tidy draining board and empty sink. Well, maybe she was pulling herself together a bit after all this time. It was very hard on him, all this grieving. He was a man of action and he was working through the loss of his son in his own way. He had plans, important plans months in the making, and he needed to focus on what was important, especially on a day like today.

The sun was over the Levels and beginning to burn off the morning mist as Derek tramped along the Sedgemoor Drove. It was going to be a warm day, the sort of May day that might result in a storm from the look of the sky in the distance. Skirting the old earthworks he kept well clear of the disused airfield, deserted at this time of day but a magnet for kids on motorbikes at the weekends. He carried a small army pack on his back, the rough webbing chafing his shoulder as he marched towards the footbridge over Kings Sedgemoor Drain. His breath was coming in ragged gasps and he was sweating heavily by the time he crossed the canal and headed into the water meadows on the other side. He was out of condition, he thought, unfit, a bit overweight – he'd let himself get soft in prison. Gritting his teeth he ploughed on, jumping the smaller cuts in the land where the water trickled down to ever-wider drains until joining the larger canals on the journey out to sea. In the distance he spotted his destination, a bird hide of reeds and witheys overlooking Shapwich Right Rhyne. He walked more slowly, casting his eyes about him, but there was no-one else around. Gratefully he slumped down into the hide to catch his breath. He was going to have to do something about this, he decided. He'd always been strong, able to walk for hours without stopping. It didn't occur to him he was getting old.

He heard Big Bill before he saw him, his habitually cheerful whistling reaching his ears as it disturbed the waterfowl around the hide. Derek gritted his teeth but a part of him welcomed the annoyance. He was very fond of Bill: he had been a trusted and loyal companion since they were boys running wild through the Levels. He'd been tall even as a junior, he recalled, his size a boon for climbing trees and getting a boost over a farm hedge. Big Bill had served him well and he would be difficult to replace. He reached into the rucksack and drew out his old fishing knife in its leather case. He clipped it to his belt at the back out of sight and stood up to wave.

'Wotcha, Derek,' called Bill as he ambled across the muddy track, a broad grin splitting his face.

'Shut up you girt fool! Bloody hell, might as well send up a flare, the racket you'm kicking up.'

Bill flopped down next to him in the hide, not at all put out by Derek's temper.

'Sorry Boss. Just – it's good to be out again, walking around in the sun. Good to see you too.'

Derek looked him over before moving to stand by the entrance.

'See you went to visit my Iris,' he said casually. Bill blinked up at him, screwing his eyes half closed to cut out the first rays of sun as they sliced through the loosely woven walls.

'Yeah, well I wanted to give her my condolences on account of Biff - and see when you was out of course.'

Derek nodded, half silhouetted against the light. 'Yeah, she's taking this real hard. Not herself at all she ain't. So, I was wondering if you had any thoughts about it all then, seeing as you was banged up with the bastard that grassed up my two lads?'

Bill felt himself go cold all over. Somehow he'd walked into a trap but he had no idea why or how. His mouth was dry as he struggled to respond.

'I don't get you, Boss. Don't know nothing about that – hell, I've been locked up most of the past year.' He tried to peer through the glare, judging his chance of getting past Derek and out of the door. It didn't look good, but he was stronger than his old friend and he'd kept himself in shape whilst in Dartmoor. If he could get out of here he might be able to talk some sense into Derek later, when he was more himself.

'You have been, right enough. Strange though, first thing you do when you get out, you come sniffing round my wife. Got anything to say about that then?'

All his confidence, all his good humour and high spirits were knocked clear out of him as he looked up at the man hovering over him. Big Bill was in a whole world of trouble and he hadn't a clue how it had happened.

'I promised Newt,' he said. 'Saw him just before I left and he said to go see his Mam. There's nothing to it, Derek, honest – I was just payin' my respects.'

Derek turned away slightly and looked through the window to the hide.

'I heard you was looking after Billy, keeping an eye out for him and helping him find a place inside.'

Big Bill seized on the chance. 'Course I did,' he said. 'Only right, watching out for the lad. Helping him along a bit . . .'

'Don't get up,' said Derek, without moving his head. 'You just stay down there for a while longer.'

Bill slumped back onto the floor. Now he knew it was hopeless – Derek was going to hurt him, probably really, really badly.

'Why, Derek?' he asked abandoning all pretence. 'I did my best by Newt, I've always been loyal – you know that. What've I done wrong?'

Derek glanced at the figure sitting at his feet.

'Twas Frank Mallory that told the screws about my boys and the post office. Lots of detail he gave, enough so they was waiting for them. Now Frank, he was banged up too, all on his own inside and no visitors so I hear, so how's he know so much, eh? Unless someone's been blabbing, been buying their own status using me and my boys to make themselves look like a big man. Word gets around, see. People talk and even the little runt at the bottom of the pile gets to hear and then – well, we both know what happened then, don't we?'

Big Bill struggled to his feet but Derek punched him behind his ear and knocked him face-down in the dirt.

'No, you stay there,' he said dispassionately. 'I'll say if you can get up.'

Bill lifted his head just clear of the mud and took a deep breath. His head was spinning from the force of the blow and he had black spots dancing in front of his eyes. After a moment he realized Derek was still talking.

'I reckon that person's just as responsible for my lad's death as the lazy copper that never looked in on him and the bastard that grassed him up in the first place. What do you think then? You reckon they should get off easy?'

He waited but Bill had no answer. His head ringing and his mouth full of dust, he lay slumped on the floor of the hide. His last thought as Derek pulled his head back and drew the curved blade of the fishing knife across his throat was of Iris, a young, beautiful laughing Iris – the only woman he had ever loved.

Derek stepped back and bounced off the rough walls of the hide as he tried to avoid the gush of blood. Damn it, he'd sliced too far across and now Bill was bleeding all over the floor. He'd meant to slit his throat neatly, leave him gasping and choking for a minute until he drowned. Derek looked at the mess all over the hide in disgust. Now he'd need to clean it up a bit and getting the body away to chuck it in the river meant he'd likely be covered too. He was definitely losing his touch and the messier things were the more chance there was of getting caught. He grabbed Bill's feet and began to pull him towards the door but his eye caught a flicker of movement in the distance.

Peering out of the window he gave a low growl compounded of fury and despair. A group of cagoule-clad adults bearing rucksacks and binoculars was weaving its way towards the hide. Bloody nature loving freaks! They were about half a mile away but he needed to get out at once or they'd spot him. He let go of Bill's legs, grabbed his own pack and dropping to his knees crawled from the hide and into the surrounding reeds. Keeping low he wriggled as fast as he could, heading away from the cottage and the route he'd taken to the hide. He ducked down between two low humps in the land, the only areas above sea level in the entire area and bent over, trying to catch his breath. Then he sat facing the Rhyne and looked himself over, searching for tell-tale splashes of blood. His hands were grazed from crawling over the rough earth but apart from that he seemed unharmed. His jeans were a mess of course and his boots were badly marked but overall he reckoned he didn't look too bad.

From the distance came a scream and the sounds of panic as the birdwatchers reached the hide and made their grim discovery. Derek waited for a few minutes knowing they would run around a bit and stare out over the Levels, frantically searching for the perpetrator. When the noise died down again he risked a quick look and spotted them beating a hasty retreat along the footpath. He tried to count heads but they were too far away to be sure they'd not left someone behind. He decided it was too risky trying to get back the way he'd come. They'd stop at the first building they got to and ring for the police, so it was time to get as far away as possible. He rose to his feet and began to lope over the land, careful to keep the mounds between him and the hide. The Shapwick Rhyne was between him and the other footpath but it wasn't far to the footbridge and on to the main road. He reckoned he'd be halfway back to his cottage to change his clothes before the coppers got there.

The first policemen to arrive peered round the door and recoiled in horror at the scene. Two of the birdwatchers had stayed behind and they were taken off to one side to be questioned as witnesses. The police worked quickly to preserve the scene and waited for the crime techs to arrive with the police doctor but they were hampered by the remoteness of the hide. They'd left their car on the drove, unable to get beyond the tiny bridge except on foot and they had been in a hurry to get to the scene, leaving even the minimum amount of equipment they carried back in the patrol car. Standing outside the hide they tried in vain to get a clear signal on their radios, the occasional squawks and clicks only increasing their frustration.

'Looks like it's clouding over,' remarked the senior officer, eying the sky. 'Better get the plastic sheet out of the car before it starts to rain.'

The junior PC opened his mouth to protest but thought better of it and set off at a jog across the water meadows.

'Put some effort in! Go on, you can do better'n that,' shouted the senior after him, before turning his attention to the two birdwatchers who were hunched together miserably a few yards away.

The main party arrived along the Moorlinch road and were able to get their flotilla of vehicles within a few hundred yards of the crime scene. The doctor entered the hide, pronounced the victim dead and left very quickly, looking a lot more pale than when he'd arrived. The cause of death was obvious and the time wasn't in much doubt – as the pathologist pointed out, the body was still slightly warm and the pool of blood surrounding the corpse hadn't even congealed.

'Single knife slash across the throat, from behind I'd say. Almost certainly right-handed from the angle. It looks as if the victim was kneeling at the time. No bindings on the wrists or ankles but there are signs of a blow to the side of the head – here, see – delivered a few minutes before death. There's more bruising on the forehead at the front, possibly from falling.'

The dry, analytical tones of the pathologist painted a chilling picture of Big Bill's last few minutes and the officers from the newly formed Special Action Group from Taunton stood in a semi-circle outside the hide, glancing at one another and occasionally out over the Levels in case the perpetrator of this horror still lurked amongst the witheys.

'Any idea who he is?' the pathologist asked.

'I know him,' said an older PC standing on the fringes. The Taunton officers turned to look at him. 'It's William Boyd. Big Bill he's called.'

This information was greeted by silence.

'Go on,' prompted the Special Action Group Sergeant.

'He's Derek Johns' right-hand man. Just released from Dartmoor – on Friday I think. There's going to be hell on about this, if someone's going after the Johns gang.'

'We don't know that yet,' said the Sergeant,' so let's just do it by the book. Right, whoever did this arrived and left on foot – no-one heard a motor vehicle so he must have been close by when they arrived.' He jerked his thumb at the birdwatchers.

'Lucky they weren't five minutes earlier then,' said the young PC who'd returned from the car with his now-redundant piece of sheeting.

'Lucky for who, lad?' asked the Sergeant. 'Not lucky for Mr Boyd here, that's for sure. Five minutes might have saved his life.'

The junior PC ducked his head, wishing the ground would suck him down into it, away from the stares of his colleagues.

As the clouds closed in, the specialists moved quickly to photograph and record as much of the scene as they could. An Inspector arrived to take charge and the PCs were dispatched in pairs to scour the immediate vicinity, looking for anything that might show where the killer had made his escape. Meanwhile, the birdwatchers were finally allowed to leave, having given their initial statements. Just as a fine drizzle began to fall there was a shout from the team out by the two humps.

'What have you got?' demanded the Sergeant, peering at the ground.

One PC was hunched over a patch of mud and crushed grass trying to shelter it from the rain.

'Looks like a footprint sir,' his companion said.

'Well, go and get a photographer will you? We can't cast it in this and it'll be gone it in a minute. And you . . . 'He pointed to the hovering PC. 'Don't you dare move an inch.'

'Right Sarge,' came the muffled reply.

Back at the hide the junior PC shuffled around the outside

of the structure trying to keep out of everyone's way. His partner spotted him and, taking pity on him, called him over to the door.

'Here,' he said, 'look around here, see if there's anything useful.'

The junior scanned the ground but there was nothing to be seen. Besides, he thought, there's been a whole party of birdwatchers and a load of specialists, police and doctors, not to mention the staff from the mortuary waiting off to one side with their gurney. The area around the hut was hopelessly compromised and he was just wasting time, especially as the drizzle continued to fall. Still, at least he could hear what was being said inside. Eager to learn, he looked round the entrance.

'Smooth, single edged blade, extremely sharp from the look of the wound. Possibly a curved blade, at least five inches long I'd say,' said the pathologist.

'Like a fishing knife,' said the PC. The group around the body turned to stare at him.

'A filleting knife,' he went on, 'and I think it was a Normark.'

'How the bloody hell do you come to that conclusion,' snapped the Inspector. The young PC swallowed nervously and pointed to a scrap of leather shaped like a fish tail caught on the rough wall near the door.

'That's off the sheath to a Normark knife,' he said.

'Could have been dropped by anyone,' said the Inspector gruffly.

'With respect sir, it's got no blood on it but the wall behind has so it got here after the murder. Of course, we can check but I can't see any birdwatcher carrying that sort of fishing knife.'

The ensuing silence was broken by the pathologist.

'Well done, I think you may be right. The wound certainly seems to fit.' He nodded at the PC as the Inspector ordered a member of the team to photograph and bag the little emblem.

'Yes, well spotted, Constable . . .'

'Constable Brown, sir.'

'Constable Brown – well, good work. I think we're almost ready to get Mr Boyd out of here. Tell the chaps from the mortuary to come in will you?'

Brown stepped out of the hide, grateful to be away from the glare of unwanted attention and the thick, metallic stink of the body. His hands were shaking and he was desperate for a cigarette. It was his first murder, for serious violent crime was rare out on the Levels and he was relieved to have survived this far without throwing up or disgracing himself. He jumped as his partner appeared from round the side of the hut.

'Reckon we should be going now,' he said. 'We're not needed and there's so many coppers here the villains'll think it's Christmas in town.'

Together they made their way back across the fields, now sticky with mud as the rain began to fall in earnest.

'What do you think then?' Brown asked. 'Some sort of vendetta against the Johns gang?'

'Who knows. Maybe they'll all kill each other, make our lives a bit easier. Come on, I'll buy you a sandwich when we get back to town.'

The search began to wind down as the rain persisted and even the most optimistic of officers acknowledged their quarry was miles away. The hut was scoured one last time for trace evidence before it was cordoned off in an attempt to keep the idly curious and the vicarious thrill-seeker away. The mortal remains of Big Bill Boyd made the journey back to the mortuary at Taunton as the Special Action Group headed off to their new headquarters to draw diagrams and flow-charts and type up their notes on their new computer terminals. Out on the Levels, Derek Johns stripped off his dirty clothes, cut them into pieces and fed them into the fire one bit at a time. When he'd finished he boiled a tub full of scalding water and scrubbed himself to remove any trace of Big Bill or the bird hide. When he'd done he sat brooding in front of the dying embers of the fire, a glass in his hand as he tried to erase the memory of Bill's face as he pitched forward in a fountain of blood. Finally, half way down the bottle, the glass fell from his hand and rolled away into a corner and Derek slept.

Chapter Eight

Alex opened her eyes on Wednesday morning and lay for a moment in her warm bed, puzzling over the sinking feeling in the pit of her stomach. For several blissful moments she searched her memory in vain before she realized it was *that* Wednesday, the day she had been dreading for a month.

She struggled out of bed trying not to groan as she looked around her room and realized she was not ready. Despite all her intentions, she'd managed to avoid packing her overnight bag and from the look of the laundry bin that overflowed onto the floor in the corner she was probably going in shorts and T-shirt. There was a knock on the door and Sue peered in, up uncharacteristically early and bearing a cup of coffee.

'Here you go. I thought you might need this.'

'You're a life-saver.' Alex took the beaker and sank back onto the bed sipping the caffeine-laced drink with gratitude.

'You're not packed, are you?' said Sue. Alex shook her head, her attention on the hot coffee.

Sue sighed heavily. 'Avoidance is not a coping strategy you know.' Alex glared at her but did not reply.

'Do you want me to sort out your papers and stuff while you're in the shower?' she said.

Alex put down her empty mug and groaned. 'What I want is not to have to go,' she snapped.

An hour or so later and they were on their way. Sue had elected to drive, partly as Alex was 'not really a morning person', as she so delicately put it, and partly as her car was both more comfortable and more reliable. It was a beautiful day as they bowled through the Somerset countryside. Alex, though, appeared a picture of misery as she stared out at the fields and trees.

'Come on, it might not be that bad,' said Sue. 'We may just have a couple of days of crashing boredom interspersed with someone else's cooking.'

'I like cooking,' Alex grumbled. 'And if we're unlucky we'll have two days of crashing boredom interspersed with Garry ranting about team players and the need for objective professionalism. Or blatant indifference as I call it.'

'You really are a miserable cow in the morning,' said Sue. 'It's an away-day not a public execution.'

Alex returned to looking moodily out of the window, wishing she could get out of the car and walk on the grass or sit quietly beside the stream she could see running away into the distance. She was working too hard, she knew.

'Well yes, we all know that,' said Sue.

'Did I say that aloud?' Alex said anxiously.

Sue laughed. 'Better now than half-way through the meeting,' she said as she turned the car off on to a gravel drive and they jolted across the forecourt to park at the Hall.

Inside it was chaotic as people milled around with overnight bags, briefcases and various items of what Alex mentally termed 'comfort luggage'. Her own comfort luggage consisted of her Walkman, six tapes of operas and three novels, just in case she got enough time and privacy to enjoy them. Sue's, she knew, contained two bottles of red wine, a corkscrew and a short-wave radio. Gordon was leaning on the reception desk smiling calmly at the mob as it swirled around the space. He raised a hand in greeting as the two women ploughed across towards him.

'Morning,' he said, 'Glad to see you. I wondered if you'd make it or manage to be mysteriously ill.' He looked at Alex as he said this and she felt herself flush. She hadn't realized how obvious her dislike of the whole idea had been.

'Actually,' she countered, 'I woke up about six and decided I wasn't coming. I was going to get Sue to tell Garry I'd broken my ankle but when I woke up a bit later I realized that probably wasn't the best of plans.'

Gordon burst out laughing. 'Well, if you'd actually broken an ankle just to get out of this then I guess we would have to take your reservations seriously,' he said. 'Oh, hold on, stand to attention everyone.'

The door swung open once more and Garry swept into the lobby dragging a set of matching luggage on wheels – large case, round sports bag and matching shoulder bag, all neatly clipped together with a tartan luggage strap.

'Guess who didn't have to pack his own bags,' Alex murmured to Sue.

'Neither did you,' she retorted.

Garry pulled up at the desk and looked around, holding up his hand for silence. The cheery hubbub died away and the group waited to see what he would say. Somehow everyone knew this little speech would set the tone for the rest of the stay.

'Right, welcome to you all,' he began, almost as if he owned the Hall. 'Now we've a lot to get through so perhaps you could collect your room keys and we could all meet down here in, oh say, 20 minutes? Please remember your Priorities files – I hope no-one has forgotten to bring them.' Here he glanced at Alex. 'And we will begin with coffee and introductions in the Seymour Room – over there on the right.' He pointed to an imposing doorway on the far side of the lobby.

Alex shuffled over to the counter, collected her key and began a long tramp up the grand (but fake) medieval staircase, around an impressive (but also fake) minstrels' gallery, through a rather gloomy smoking room decorated with stuffed animal heads (unfortunately not fake) and finally to the end of a dim corridor where two rooms stood side by side. She wondered who was next door as she jiggled the antique-style brass key in the lock before finally flinging the door open to reveal a slightly disappointing interior decorated in a style best described as 'hotel bland'. She unpacked her case and was peering out of the window at the parkland that stretched away into the misty distance when her door was flung open and Sue burst in and flopped on to the bed.

'Well, it's all right, I suppose, but I was rather hoping for roaring open fires and a four-poster bed after that trek through architectural history,' she said.

Alex smiled at her friend. 'I'm so glad you're next door. I was dreading finding Alison – or even Garry.'

Sue shivered at the thought, 'Don't worry about him,' she said. 'I expect he's got a nice perch, hanging upside down in the attic.'

Giggling like a couple of naughty children they made their way back towards the stairs, stopping in the smoking room to stare at the hunting trophies. 'Just nasty,' was Sue's verdict.

As they emerged onto the balcony of the heavy-beamed entrance hall they heard the sound of voices coming from the training room.

'Better hurry,' said Sue. 'We don't want to be the last ones in. They always get picked on.'

'One thing's bothering me, you know,' mused Alex. 'He was doing quite well until the end of that little speech. We all know each other so why do we need to do 'introductions'?'

After the debacle of the previous day, Derek knew it was only a matter of time before the inevitable man-hunt arrived at the cottage door and there was a lot of stuff to get rid of before that happened. He was tempted to just burn the place down immediately and make his escape, but he'd put a lot of thought into his plans and he wasn't going to let a little run of bad luck destroy it all. Anyway he knew fire was extremely unreliable when it came to hiding evidence, especially where dead bodies were concerned. The police and fire brigade had all sorts of tricks – dental records, measuring skeletons and stuff like that – so even a badly burned corpse could still be identified. He couldn't risk them finding out about Frank, not before he was finished.

There was definitely an odd smell in the kitchen even with the freezer locked tight, and when he lifted the lid the stench increased dramatically. Derek screwed his face up in disgust but he made himself lean over to examine the contents. There was still an awful lot to get rid of, he thought, and there was the problem of the bones, but he'd been thinking about that. More urgent was the need to make it hard to identify the remains. Head and hands, he thought, that's the key to it. Head and hands – without those they had no chance. He dropped the lid and went into the kitchen to fetch his butcher's saw and a block of wood to prop under the neck. The freezer was definitely not doing its job properly and Frank was looking very much the worse for wear. After a moment's hesitation he fetched a plastic bag. Getting it over the lolling head was a difficult and messy task but finally he was ready to cut. The smell was just as bad, but at least he didn't have to look into those watery grey eyes as he worked. Derek had hunted all his life, butchering his own catch without a second thought and laughing at those soft or squeamish folk who turned away from fur coats or stuffed animals, but that cold, empty gaze seemed to stare at him accusingly from the freezer. He shook his head as if to clear it and bent to his task.

'Hello everyone, I'm Sally, Sally Forbes and I'm your facilitator for the next two days.'

'What the bloody hell is a facilitator?' whispered Sue.

'Haven't a clue but I have a ghastly feeling we're about to find out,' replied Alex. Garry turned his head, searching for the person responsible for this insubordination and they both slid a few inches further down in their hard plastic chairs.

'Now,' continued Sally brightly, 'you know who I am so

let's all introduce ourselves shall we?' There was a horrible silence as the whole group stared fixedly at the floor, willing themselves somewhere else.

'Well, I'll pick someone to start, shall I? Let me see, how about you?' She pointed at Sue, who gave a tiny groan before shrugging and saying, 'I'm Sue, I'm a probation officer.' There was a pause before Sally trilled, 'Tell us a bit about yourself and could you stand up please so we can all see you.'

'Okay, my name is Sue . . .'

'And I'm an alcoholic' came a voice from the other side of the room.

'Not yet but soon, probably,' countered Sue as a ripple of laughter swept around the room. Garry scowled and looked as if he wanted to get to his feet but Sally stopped him with a gesture.

'I understand you might all be feeling a bit nervous and humour is an excellent ice-breaker but let's focus on the process shall we.' She turned back to Sue with a patronizing smile. 'Go on.' Sue glanced sideways at Alex. It was going to be a very long day.

Derek waited until it was fully dark before slipping out of the back door, locking up carefully before making his way over the marshy land to the lay-by on the back road where he'd left his car. He dumped the two carrier bags in the back on a tarpaulin that lined the boot, sealing it against accidental spillage. One of the bags was leaking a bit and seeped out onto the tough fabric; Derek muttered a curse, making a mental note to clean it on his return. He drove through the darkening landscape using dipped headlights as he wove his way through a maze of narrow tracks and by-roads with the ease of one native-born. There was no-one else on the road at this hour between people going out for the evening and the pubs throwing them back into their cars at the end of the night. Most cars used full lights to navigate the tiny roads with their screens of earth banks and witheys and it was easy to spot another car from the splash of lights up to a mile away. He pulled over almost into the hedgerow a couple of times, turning off his engine and waiting as the occasional vehicle drove past in the opposite direction, the driver oblivious to his presence.

Finally he reached his destination, out past Edington where the Avalon marsh stretched away in bleak emptiness. Gathering his burden from the boot he tramped over the broken earth until he reached the leading edge of the peat cuttings. Here the rich land was sliced and removed in wedges to make compost for greenhouses and sometimes used to revive exhausted soil. It had been a local industry for centuries but now it was coming to an end as conservationists and wildlife experts raised concerns about the damage to the land, the loss of wildlife and the impact on the flocks of birds who lived there. Operations were being scaled back, planning permission for new digging was routinely denied and the existing cuts were abandoned to lie fallow and recover.

At the edge of one of these Derek stopped and looked around before stepping into the shallow pit left by the diggers. The bottom was already beginning to ooze as the water from the low lying table began to reclaim the area. He pulled out a short handled spade, purchased from the Army and Navy surplus store in Bath, and began to dig. He dropped the hands in the smaller of the two holes and covered them with about nine inches of soil. Peat was notorious for preserving just about anything buried in it but it was very unlikely anyone would disturb this area for a number of years now it was set aside and he doubted the fingerprints would survive long in the moist conditions. Still, he pondered the problem of the head. There had been that body found somewhere, pulled out of a bog after thousands of years. It was all leathery and dried up but the people who found it had been able to tell how he died and even what sort of things he'd eaten by looking at the teeth . . . He really did not want to have to look at the head again but it was too risky just burying it. The world was full of nosy dog walkers – and unexpected birdwatchers, he remembered. He tipped the head out on to the bottom of the cutting and rolled it over with the tip of his boot. The eyes stared at him as he picked up the shovel, set it against the mouth and smashed the teeth. As he felt the tip of the shovel bite into the mouth he was overcome with nausea and turned away, struggling to control himself. After a few moments he turned back to his task and pushed the mutilated head into a deeper hole a few feet away. 'Bye Frank,' he muttered, shovelling the dirt down on to it. It amused him briefly to think of Frank pickled in the bog long after everyone he'd know was gone. When he was finished and had done his best to remove all trace of his presence he made his way shakily back to the car that waited hidden under the trees lining the road. Somehow revenge didn't make him feel better. It was hard work and at the end of it he'd still lost his son.

The Wednesday morning had been the stuff of nightmares for Alex. Naturally reserved and inherently awkward she also reacted to stress by becoming tactless and clumsy. On a day of 'team-building' this was a disastrous combination. Following the introductions they went on to an ice-breaker, 'just to help get rid of some of those stuffy inhibitions,' said Sally. After wringing the last drops of conviviality out of the group she then went on to 'family trees', an exercise where each person placed themselves in relation to everyone else.

'Not so much "family tree" as power play,' muttered Sue as she shuffled Alex into position.

'More like the Circles of Hell, if you ask me,' Alex replied.

She was not the only one suffering or the only rebel. When it came to Lauren she began by setting out the office staff on their knees in a loose semi-circle. Several of the probation officers were placed standing behind them and finally she suggested Garry stand on a chair with one arm forward and the other raised above his head. Garry took his place reluctantly as the puzzled staff looked around and tried to work out what was going on. Suddenly Sue and Alex began to laugh as they recognized the tableau. Garry promptly stepped down and announced it was time for lunch, stalking off as they congratulated Lauren on her 'charioteer'.

'Well, I do feel he's up there cracking the whip and we just all got to keep pulling him along,' she said as they crowded around the buffet tables. Oh! Is that chicken? Get me some of that will you?'

'At least the food's not bad,' said Sue, as they sat on the terrace after lunch. 'It's quite nice getting away for a bit.'

'If this is your idea of a good time you should get out more,' said Alex.

'That's a bit rich, coming from you,' Sue countered. 'You're the most anti-social person I know. When was the last time you went out, just for fun?'

Alex hesitated, searching her recent memory but all she encountered was work, more work and some solitary gardening.

'See? You're a hermit. You don't go anywhere, you've not had a holiday since I've known you and you don't have people round either.'

Not for the first time Alex wished she'd not given up smoking when she became a student. Financially it was a total waste of money and it was really bad for you, of course, but now she longed for the buzz of the nicotine. She took a deep breath, held it for a moment and released it slowly, willing her cravings away as she did so.

'All right,' she said, 'It's my birthday at the end of September. Let's have a party or something.'

'Really? You're on. I'll do the planning and you can cook – unless you'd rather do it the other way round.'

Alex laughed in spite of herself. 'No, let's try and make it a success shall we – no point in playing to our weaknesses.'

There was the sound of voices from the Seymour Room where the windows were open to let in the warm, fresh air of early summer and Alex gazed at the parkland longingly before reluctantly following Sue back inside.

'So the new priority will necessitate an increase in the provision of practical and work-based activities. Planned and purposeful engagement of the client – that is the key.' Garry waved his arms around enthusiastically as he turned back to the flow chart projected on to the back wall.

'How long has he been going on now? Sue whispered.

'Um, forty-seven minutes,' said Alex, checking her watch.

'And he's said . . .?'

'We need to get the day centre running as soon as possible.'

Garry stopped in mid-sentence and glared at the pair.

'Is there something you would like to add?' he demanded.

'Oh shit,' muttered Sue, but Alex rose to her feet and said, 'I was wondering about the implementation of the new orders.' There was silence in the room as she went on. 'Will one person have to hold all the orders with mandatory attendance or will we need to negotiate and monitor this section of a mixed case-load?' She sat down, aware of Sue's admiring grin next to her. Garry blinked at her and turned back to his flow-chart for inspiration.

'Well, I think these types of issues need to be negotiated on an individual basis, as and when they arise within a team framework.'

Eddie stuck up his hand and said, 'Due respect Garry but it is one of the main changes to our work. I think it is a bit more important than whether we allow them a pool table'.

Gordon was next. 'Perhaps it should be a consideration for the SLOP document.'

There was a general nodding of heads around the room. In the corner Sally frowned and beckoned Garry over as she mouthed, 'Slop? What is Slop?' As the murmuring in the room grew louder Garry tried to explain the new priorities to Sally in a few words before swinging round and raising his voice at the noise.

'Team – please – quiet! These are all issues we will examine in due course.'

The hubbub subsided and he continued with his presentation, but it was obvious his enthusiasm had evaporated, and barely ten minutes later he dismissed them all, distributing a depressingly thick document for them to read before the next morning.

Unable to face another night of slicing and dicing, Derek Johns decided to scope out the next of his potential targets. Wednesday evening was always very quiet around town, with most of the pubs half empty as people stayed home and nursed a beer in front of the television. In these difficult times it was hard to stretch the weekly pay packet over a whole week, what with inflation running rampant and the spectre of unemployment looming over the town's industries. Derek chose a remote garage to put petrol in his car, serving himself and muttering at the ridiculous cost of fuel. Paying in cash, he got back in his car and doubled back around past Glastonbury and Street before picking up the main road into town. Lot of shops with sales in Street he noticed, and some closed up in Glastonbury too. At this rate there'd be nothing worth stealing in the whole county.

The police station was sited along the road to Petherton, so he took a rat-run parallel to the river, weaving his way round the cars parked up outside their owners' terraced houses. Just as he was approaching the roundabout he braked and pulled over, scarcely believing his luck. There was no mistaking Alex's car – probably the only Citroën like it in the area with the distinctive curly wing where she always seemed to nudge the bins on her way out of the office. There was a parking ticket on her windscreen, he noted. Good. He looked up and down the road carefully but there was no-one in sight and on an impulse he turned off the engine and got out, retrieving the fishing knife from the glove compartment before making his way over to the vehicle. It was the work of a few seconds to slash the two front tyres and he was back in his own car and driving calmly down the road, a grin on his face, before anyone looked out of a window or spotted him.

He pulled in to the car park of the Iron Beehive, a pub along the river near where the main road bridge crossed on its way out of town. It was skittles night and so the bar was crowded despite the town's economic malaise. The air was thick with smoke and all eyes were on the long wooden alley where men (and the occasional woman) slid and swung their bodies to hurl the heavy balls the length of the room. Amidst the shouting and heckling no-one noticed the big, dark man who sat quietly in the shadows watching the Combined Police and Ambulance team lose to the home squad. After half an hour, and several pints, Derek slipped out to wait in his car until the visitors left. He scribbled down a licence plate before turning and heading back towards the limited home comforts of his wife.

'Come on, the men are buying drinks and you might as well enjoy the evening,' urged Sue from the door. Alex put down the document with a sigh.

'Have you read this?' she asked.

Sue shook her head. 'No and neither has anyone else I suspect . . . except possibly Gordon, hopefully Gordon – I'm going to get him to give me the condensed version. Are you coming or not?'

Alex looked at the papers in her hand, threw them on the bed and followed her down to the bar. 'What about Garry?' she said, hurrying along the corridor and down the stairs.

'Look, if he's there he'll only stay for a while and he'll have to buy a round. It's the done thing, but he won't want to spend the evening rubbing shoulders with the peasants. He's too mean and too snobbish for that. On the other hand, if he's there and you're not he's bound to notice and hold it against you.'

'So you're telling me I have no choice in the matter,' muttered Alex, as they rounded the corner and reached the door to the bar.

'Exactly,' said Sue, flinging the door wide open.

There was a chorus of greetings as they entered.

'Told you,' came a voice from a far corner, as Gordon unfolded his length from a small faux-rustic chair and ambled over to meet them.

'What will you have? Don't worry, Eddie's paying.' He waved his hand vaguely behind him. 'He lost the bet.'

'You were betting on whether we'd come down or not?' asked Alex scandalized.

'No, of course not. We were betting on whether *you* would. I knew you'd make it – you have a strong streak of pragmatism running through that anti-social soul of yours. Now, come and join us. I don't suppose you play dominoes do you?' he added.

Alex grinned at the group around the table. 'Only for money,' she said.

The men shuffled round to make some space and Eddie raised his glass to the newcomers.

'Here's to you both. Good show today Alex – stopped the *Maestro* in his tracks. Almost as good as Lauren's little tableau this morning,' he added with a twinkle in his eye. There was a cheer at this remark and toasts were proposed in the direction of a rather embarrassed Lauren.

There was a slight air of tension amidst the revelry, a glancing over the shoulder each time the door opened until finally Garry made his entrance, the determinedly cheerful Sally trailing in his wake. Sue had been right in her description of his involvement in the evening. After offering to buy a round he made a point of visiting every table to offer a greeting, a touch on the shoulder, and the occasional joke. They were fairly equally distributed, Alex noted cynically, rather as if he were running on a tape loop. She hoped she would escape the touch on the shoulder and found herself counting the remaining people in groups of three, wondering if it would be too obvious if she got up and changed places. When it came to it she got a slightly guarded nod and what sounded suspiciously like a veiled compliment.

'Good questions today, Alex. I should have known you'd see through to the core of the issues.' He moved on, towing Sally behind him, but not before she had leaned over, stared at Alex for a moment and added, 'Ah yes, Alex. Of course . . .'

Alex glowered at her back as she drifted off in Garry's

wake. 'What the bloody hell did all that mean?' she said.

Gordon leaned over and said softly, 'Don't take it to heart. Most people find it threatening to have a subordinate who is cleverer than they are. Now, I believe you were boasting of your prowess at dominoes?' He picked up the box, emptied the dominoes out onto the table with a great clatter and Alex's chance to respond was lost.

Once Garry had left (taking his familiar with him, as Sue rather waspishly put it) it was quite a good night. Alex had learned to play dominoes in the pubs of south London where elderly men from Jamaica, Antigua and Barbados hunched over battered tables fighting to the death for honour and a free pint. These matches were noisy affairs with shouting, laughter and dominoes slammed down at arms' length. Alex had watched, then been invited to play a game for a bet and eventually, after two long years and several sprained fingers, found she could hold her own and even win occasionally. The Somerset game was tame in comparison and after a few whitewashes she felt a bit ashamed of taking their money, but when she tried to leave there was a chorus of disapproval from the men.

'No, now then, you've got to give us a chance to win it back – you can't just clear off when you're winning,' said Eddie.

'I want to work out how you seem to know where the numbers are,' mused Paul Malcolm. 'Is it like counting cards?'

'It's a "tell" of some kind,' mused Gordon. 'You're reading our body language and drawing out the numbers to suit your hand.'

Alex snorted in disgust. 'Set them up you sad losers,' she said. 'I'm just a better player than you are.' She was feeling warm, comfortable and more at ease than she had since leaving London, possibly due to the numerous drinks that kept appearing in front of her.

Some time much later, when Alex, seven colleagues and three boxes of dominoes were involved in a riotous and physically challenging game, Alex heard herself say to Eddie, 'Of course I can. I'm actually a qualified life-saver. Why?'

'Oh, well, it's always good to know. Thank you.'

'You're welcome,' she said, struggling to recall the earlier parts of the conversation, but the pieces had just been dealt and she forgot all about it as she was swept up in the thrill of competition.

It is the norm in prisons that remand and convicted inmates are housed separately. They have different living areas, separate recreation rooms and take their exercise at different times but there are points where the two worlds collide. Although the remand prisoners had their own dining room the food was cooked and served by men from the main population and Kevin came to dread mealtimes. Bristol was the temporary home to a small but cohesive traveller population, victims of the government crackdown on the burgeoning 'New Age' movement that swept up peace activists, tinkers and Romany with a fine lack of discrimination. Relying on income from fringe enterprises, they were united in their hostility to Kevin from the moment they learned what he was charged with. The Elver Man, it seemed, was one of their own, a respected and vital link in their trading network and his loss had hit them hard. Kevin protested his innocence, loud and long, but it made no difference. He tried to survive by slinking around the wing with his head down, ever vigilant and always afraid. His meagre belongings were stolen or broken, his cell was smeared with excrement and he was constantly jostled and tripped in the exercise yard. He was a marked man.

Chapter Nine

The next morning Alex sat at the breakfast table feeling sick, dizzy and with several nasty bruises on her hands. She was puzzling over the fragment of conversation about lifesaving when Lauren popped up beside her.

'You right then?' she asked.

Alex nodded warily, trying to avoid the sight of Lauren's full fried breakfast. She picked at her own piece of toast and sipped at her coffee.

'You was a bit blathered last night,' Lauren went on cheerfully. She sliced through a fried egg, smeared it on to some bread and butter and proceeded to eat it with every sign of enjoyment. Alex suppressed a shudder.

'What makes you say that?'

'Reckon you is normally a bit more careful around Eddie. Not like you, volunteering like that. Bit reckless if you ask me.' She finished the egg, took a slurp of her tea and started on the sausages. Fragments of last night began to float into Alex's memory.

'What exactly did I volunteer for?' she asked.

'Why, making up the numbers on the raft race. You bein' a life-saver and all, you's perfect for it. Now me, I'm no good. Ain't big enough for a start, but anyway I can't swim. Ain't never been able to no matter how hard I tried. My Mum, she used to take me and my brother to the pool every week until the big lads got too much. She gave up in the end – about the only thing she did give up on mind.'

Despite her frail physical condition Alex was drawn to the story. She had wondered sometimes what it had been like to grow up like Lauren, in a world full of giants. Cruel giants from some of the hints she'd picked up over the past year. She risked digging a bit deeper.

'What sort of things did they do then, the big lads?' she asked.

Lauren finished her sausages and looked over at Alex's unfinished toast.

'You eating that? Thanks.' She screwed up her eyes as she munched through the last of the bread. 'They was just stupid most of the time but it was really bad down the pool. They splashed and come close, making waves and pushing. I kept going under and it was really frightening. They'd hang around outside too, sniggering and following us home. They took to calling me "live-bait" and that was when Mum stopped taking me.' Lauren blinked rapidly and looked down at her plate before staring up at Alex defiantly.

'Was the only time I was ever scared. I could live with 'Bridget' but there's something real nasty about "live-bait".'

Before Alex could ask what "live bait" meant there was a call from the doorway and the team began to trudge off dutifully to the second day of their training.

When Derek had arrived back at his house that night he was surprised but pleased to see Iris was still up and moving about the front room, tidying and clearing up. He looked at her approvingly for a moment before she rounded on him, waving the local paper at him.

'What's this then?' she demanded, her face a mask of fury.

He opened his mouth to protest his ignorance of whatever she was shouting about when he spotted the headline. "Body found on the Levels!" it said in inch-high lettering, "Police warn of gangland style vendetta!" His eyes met Iris's over the paper and she snatched it from his hands, screwing it up and flinging the crumpled ball on to the floor. As she advanced on him, Derek took a step back, tripping against a small table set beside the couch. He reached out a hand towards her but she slapped it aside. He'd not seen her this angry since – well, he couldn't properly recall her ever being this angry before.

'Now then,' he said, 'don't you be getting on at me. 'Taint none of my doing. What'd I want to do something like that for – him being my best mate and all?'

Iris stopped, hand raised to deliver another slap. She looked him full in the face and said softly, 'Swear it then. Tell me you had nothing to do with this, that you didn't kill him.'

Derek looked his wife straight in the eyes and said, 'I swear to you, I didn't have nothing to do with it. Not done it, not ordered it.'

She turned away, her shoulders beginning to slump again as she sat down in her familiar place by the fire and Derek felt his heart begin to slow from its frantic pounding. Iris leaned back in the armchair and closed her eyes. He could see the marks of tears on her cheeks and he wondered, not for the first time, why it was she seemed so fond of Big Bill.

'I'll go and change then,' he said 'Reckon 'tis time for bed.'

Without moving she said, 'You'd better not be lying to me Derek Johns. You remember, if I catch you lying you'll live your life in fear. You may be a big strong man but you got to sleep sometime.'

The second day's training was, if anything, worse than the first. In a theoretical exercise masquerading as 'an exploration of the exciting new direction in Criminal Justice', as Garry put it, the entire morning was taken up with mapping the ideas in the SNOP documents on to the SLOP and finally the STOP papers. Basically, Alex and Sue agreed, it was an attempt to take the increasingly redundant ideas of 'advise, assist and befriend' and twist them into a pattern that allowed the government to show it was punishing those who transgressed. The day centre was supposed to be one of the lynch pins of this new approach but the whole plan was fatally flawed, relying as it did on the existing staff, all of whom had been trained to help their clients overcome whatever had led them into crime in the first place so they could become useful and fulfilled members of society.

'I've not been in the job a year and I feel I'm outdated already,' grumbled Sue over lunch. 'If I wanted to punish people I'd have joined the bloody prison service. What's the point of taking social workers and training us as probation officers if we're not supposed to help people?'

Gordon sat down at the table with them and cast a jaundiced eye over the gathering. There was a distinct air of gloom about them all, not all of it due to the excesses of the previous evening in the bar.

'Well, I wouldn't take it too much to heart,' he said. 'Ideas and plans come and go. I've seen a lot of changes and a number of these new initiatives in my time and most of them get rubbed down a bit, smoothed off over time. As you say, Sue, the people doing the work are the same and we can't easily be changed, though I don't like this "top down" approach. We've always started with the client and worked with what we get from them not taken a policy and forced our clients to conform to it. This day centre, though, it could be really positive if we set it up to offer the right sort of thing. We might have the money for some education, a workshop, special groups for prisoners' families and alcohol abuse and all sorts of things. Don't go resigning in disgust quite yet.'

Alex nodded, somewhat cautiously. She trusted Gordon and if he thought they could still do a good job under the new system she was ready to give it a chance. Gordon moved on to motivate a few more glum colleagues and Alex realized she'd missed the chance to ask him why he was always cleaning his car. Sue shrugged, equally at a loss.

'Maybe he's a bit OCD,' she suggested. 'Tell you what, let's ask Lauren. She's bound to know.'

Lauren laughed aloud when they cornered her outside before the final session. 'Oh, now, he's just too nice,' she said. 'Last week was taking Mick's dog to the vet. Before that was a family off to see their Dad in prison. Three little ones, one without a proper nappy and two as got real car-sick. I hear he even gave "Cider" Rosie a lift once when she was legless and desperate.' She paused and added, 'Course, next week he had to get another car. Don't think even Gordon'll do that again in a hurry.'

The next morning was bright and sunny but Kevin struggled to stop himself from shivering as he sat in the little cell waiting to be called for his bail hearing. It was cool in the tiny, dim space but the constant sounds of footsteps, doors opening and clanging shut and voices from the corridor were making his head ache. He wriggled his shoulders and tugged at the tie his solicitor had supplied at their last meeting. The formal, unfamiliar clothing made him feel insecure, uncomfortable in himself, and Smythe had done little to give him confidence in the proceedings.

'I don't want you getting your hopes up,' he'd confided. 'We've got a decent enough young barrister and I'm sure he'll do his best, but we really don't have much to convince the court. I'm not even sure why we're here today . . . .' And he'd gone off, muttering and shaking his head.

Kevin had wanted to jump up and shout at him. 'We're here because I didn't do it! I was poaching, alright, I knows that, but I never killed no-one. And if I'm sent back to Bristol tonight I'm the one goin' to end up dead. So we is here to save my life 'cos I ain't gonna last much longer in that place.'

Of course he didn't jump up or shout. He just sat quietly with his head bowed, staring at his hands and hearing the whispers of his fellow remand prisoners: 'Better pray you'm not coming back boy 'cos we got plans for you t'night and 'tis a long weekend you've got coming.'

142

He'd marched to the prison van, their sniggering and hissing still ringing in his ears. Whatever the outcome today, he wasn't going back on to the remand wing. He pulled at his tie again and for the first time had an idea of what had made Biff do what he had.

Back in the office on Friday morning, Alex tried to concentrate, but she jumped every time the phone rang, grabbing at the receiver and even knocking it off the desk, so eager was she for news. As the day wore on she managed to bring the notes on several clients' files up to date, made a total pig's ear of a social enquiry report and stared in despair at the self-appraisal form she was supposed to complete for her next supervision meeting with Garry later on that month. Finally she shoved the whole thing into her desk drawer and went in search of Sue and some lunch. As she turned down the corridor into the other wing she heard Sue's voice coming from her office.

'Darren, get down.' There was a pause.

'I said get down!' Hovering outside the door Alex could barely make out a mumbling sound in response.

'If you don't get off that fucking window-sill now I'll push you out myself!'

There was a heavy thud and Alex flung the door open in time to see Darren, a most unprepossessing young man with greasy hair and spots on his spots, tumble to the floor, overturning a chair and knocking several books off the nearby shelf.

'That's not right,' he said rubbing his head. 'Girt assault, that.' He glared at Alex as if she were somehow responsible.

Alex nodded to Sue before saying, 'I know she's good but even she can't reach six feet over the desk and up to there.' She nodded to the window-sill set in the eaves. Sue smiled sweetly at them both.

'Well Darren, I expect you to be here next Friday to help with the workshop. Off you go now.'

'Fancy some lunch?' suggested Alex when Darren had left the room.

Sue sighed and nodded. 'Sounds good. I gather from your rather tense state there's no news yet?'

Alex groaned. 'Nothing. It all takes so long.'

Sue swept down the stairs ahead of her.   'Try not to fret so much. After all, there's nothing you can do.'

'That just makes it worse! Why does everyone keep saying that as if it's somehow comforting?'

Sue turned to her friend and shook her head. 'You have to admit you are a bit of a control-freak sometimes,' she said in tones of irritating sweet reason.

'I am not a *bit* of a control freak, I'm a *total* control freak. I always have been and it's the only way I manage to get this damn job done at all!'

At that moment Garry poked his head around the door and frowned at them.

'I can hear you right down the corridor,' he said. 'We aim to provide a calm and respectful atmosphere in which we can all work together. Please try to remember that. And Sue, perhaps you could moderate your language especially when talking to clients.'

He closed the door behind him and Sue and Alex looked at one another and began to giggle.

'God, what a tight-arsed dick he really is,' snorted Sue.

'Now then, please try to moderate your language,' said Alex.

'Ah, that's cheered me up no end,' said Sue filling the kettle. 'Go on, your turn to fish for mugs.'

Alex peered into the sink searching for some glimpse of what lurked beneath the scummy water. She picked up a brush and began to poke around hopefully but nothing recognizable surfaced. With a sigh she put the brush down, screwed her face up in disgust and plunged her arm into the cold, greasy water, rummaging for the plug. The water rushed away with a throaty gurgle and she stepped back, halfway up to her elbow in tea leaves and congealed fat.

'Oh yuck!' said Sue unsympathetically. 'Run it under the tap before you touch anything.'

144

Alex ran the tap until the water was as hot as possible, clearing the grease as it melted and floated away from the bottom of the sink. Leaning over the bowl she added a minimum of cooler water before scrubbing at her arm, her teeth gritted.

'Why don't people clean up after themselves,' mused Sue, as she absent-mindedly squeezed the teabags against the edge of the draining board and tossed them into the sink. Alex looked at her open mouthed as she drifted back towards the window humming softly to herself.

'Hang on – you just –' she was interrupted by Lauren flying through the door, gasping for breath as she stumbled into the room.

'Alex, quick, you're needed on the phone. It's the court in Bristol.'

Kevin knew it was hopeless the moment he stepped out into the box. No-one was paying much attention to him or what was going on, and the public gallery was emptying out after the last hearing, which had obviously been the main event of the day. The guard patted him on the shoulder and unlocked his cuffs before whispering, 'Steady lad. Won't be more'n a few minutes, right?' Kevin looked around, searching for a familiar face, only to find the two police officers from Highpoint who had arrested him all those weeks ago. Neither gave him more than a glance before resuming their whispered conversation, their pocket notebooks prominently on display in from of their seats. So they'd come to oppose his bail, he thought miserably. A lump rose in his throat and he felt like crying as he continued to look around, desperate for a friendly face. He knew she couldn't possibly get there but he really wanted to see his mother, proud and fierce in her shiny pink finery. She only owned one smart dress, he realized suddenly, and that was for court. For the first time he stopped thinking about his own horrible circumstances and considered someone else. He'd caused his mother nothing but grief, worry and expense from the moment he met up with the Johns boys and their hangers-on and he felt the rush of a strange and horribly uncomfortable emotion. For the first time Kevin was ashamed. He hung his head, overwhelmed by his helplessness, his inability to put any of it right. He might never even get the chance to tell her how sorry he was if he got sent back to Bristol.

He felt a brisk nudge in the ribs and scrambled to his feet as the judge entered, a stern-faced woman who reminded him of his English teacher back in school. They'd never got on, he recalled and he didn't expect this morning to be any different. It all went so fast, this one chance of his. Within minutes he was dizzy with the number of people standing, speaking, reading out charges and evidence and sitting down again after a flurry of questions. He tried to concentrate on the young barrister who nodded to him and kept putting arguments why Kevin was perfectly safe out in the community but he knew it was a lost cause. Suddenly the judge was speaking, saying how serious the charges were and what a heinous act the murder was. She threw in a few remarks about uncontrolled and shiftless lifestyles, pointed to the two coppers from Highpoint who had appeared to oppose bail and ruled there were no grounds to consider any change of custody arrangements. Kevin was struggling with the complex language but he knew it was all over when the judge rose and his guards stepped forward to put the cuffs on him again. He saw Smythe whispering something to an usher who relayed the message to the prison warders as they took him down the steps to the holding cell once more.

'Wait here then,' one said. 'Your solicitor wants a word before we go back.' Kevin sat in the cell as the key turned and wondered where the hell the guard expected him to be, seeing as he was locked in. The wait seemed endless, like the annual trips to the dentist or sitting outside the headmaster's office after school. Kevin fiddled with his tie and considered the bleak and terrifying prospect of returning to Bristol Jail.

Alex's hands were shaking as she took the phone from the desk, aware of the silence around her. The office abandoned all pretence at working and all gazes were fixed on her as she raised the receiver and said, 'Hello?' She listened in silence for a minute, nodded her head, listened again and then said, 'Of course, yes, I'll tell his mother. Thank you for letting me know.' She replaced the receiver carefully and seemed to sway as she reached behind her for a chair. Lauren was beside her in a second, Sue on the other side helping to steady her. The silence stretched on until Alison said, 'Well – was that about Kevin then?'

The sun rose hot and bright that Friday morning and Derek eased himself out of bed, leaving Iris still sleeping, the pills from the doctor rendering her deaf to the world. The kitchen was a mess again he noticed and the bin was still outside. He considered bringing it in but decided to leave it there. It wasn't his job, after all, and he was in a hurry to get back to the cottage. He'd taken to parking the car a bit up the road and cutting round by a patch of scrubby woodland behind his back fence. The car wasn't registered to him but even so, you never knew when some nosy copper might notice it outside his house and think to make some inquiries. Derek wanted to remain hidden for as long as possible, especially now with all the fuss over Big Bill. It would be nice to see Newt, he thought, as he bumped along the track to the cottage, but that was out of the question at the moment. If he'd thought about it properly he'd have realized his plans for the future were utterly unrealistic. His whole life was coming unravelled around him and the longer he stayed close to home the more likely he'd be caught. But Derek was no longer capable of looking further than a couple of days ahead. He was a man driven, obsessed by revenge and blinded by hatred.

The bridge by the sluice gate was warm in the morning sunshine as he leaned over and fed the fish. Below him the water roiled and churned as the pike fought over the meat, their numbers increasing every day. Quite a colony, he thought, tossing a morsel a little away from the reeds. It had scarcely touched the water when the open jaws and pointed head of a particularly large fish struck, tearing at the food and dragging it from sight in one movement. It was both a thrilling and chilling sight and he wondered what the collective term was for pike – perhaps a wolf-pack. Yes, that had a nice ring to it, a wolf-pack of pike – exactly what he had created in this still, calm-looking piece of the canal. He screwed up the empty papers and threw them into the water, watching as the hungry predators tore them to pieces before sinking back into the reeds to await his return. Picking up an old reed basket he's found floating by the bank he made his way back to the cottage wondering what his next move should be. There were still two names on his mental list but he was running out of time. Once more he cursed Alex Hastings and her interfering, busy-body visit. Everything had been going fine until she turned up. Well, she'd better just keep out of his way or she'd regret it, he thought, as he opened the door and stepped into the cool, dim and increasingly rancid kitchen.

'This is highly irregular,' said the judge, leaning over to consult with the court clerk.

'Yes indeed Ma'am, but I would request we reopen proceedings. It would be rather unfortunate were we to have the expense of another appearance not to mention the effect of the delay on my client.' The young barrister was at his most charming and persuasive, exuding concern for a young man he had barely spoken to and never seen before the day's proceedings. The judge stared at him, suspicious of the charm and the sudden concern, but as she looked around the courtroom her eyes met the frantic gaze of Smythe, so obviously concerned and equally obviously out of his depth.

'Would you approach please, Mr Smythe,' she said. Smythe jumped to his feet, scattering his notes in alarm. He hated appearing at the County Court, a world away from his familiar, comfortable place at the local Magistrates where everyone knew him and there were few surprises. He hurried over to the bench trying to conceal his anxiety.

'Were you aware of this information before requesting this hearing?' the judge asked.

'No, no, your Worship. This is the first I've heard of it, just now. I would certainly have asked my learned colleague here to raise it if I had.'

'I see. Thank you. You may be seated.'

Smythe stumbled back to his place wondering what the hell was going to happen now. He watched closely as the judge conferred with the two police officers from Highpoint, then a sergeant who had just appeared and requested leave to address her, then the clerk of the court again. After considering what she'd heard she beckoned the young barrister over and talked to him for a moment before nodding to the clerk. As the court was called to order once more, the barrister rose and said, 'In light of this new information and considering the probable formal withdrawal of the more serious charges against my client by the Somerset police force I would request he be released on bail, Ma'am.'

There was a murmur from the few people in the public gallery and the sound of frantic scribbling from the two sad members of the press, failed newspapermen suddenly confronted by some breaking news. This sort of thing didn't happen at bail hearings – that was the reason their papers sent them and not a real reporter. They leaned over the edge of the gallery, signalling to the police below. 'What's happened?' one of them asked, but his query was greeted by a determined shake of the head.

The judge frowned in their direction. 'We are still in session,' she snapped, and the reporter sank back into his seat.

'Please return Mr Mallory to the court,' she said.

Down in the cells the prison guards were fretting, waiting for Smythe to appear. Eager to get back to the prison in time to clock off, they were debating whether they should just collect Kevin and be off anyway when the call came to return him to the courtroom. They exchanged puzzled looks but hurried down the corridor to where Kevin was slumped on the bench in the corner of his cell.

'Now then, Mallory,' one of them said cheerfully, 'let's be having you.' Kevin was still, giving no sign he'd heard them.

'Come on, let's be on your feet,' the officer said. He peered into the cell and called for the holding officer, 'Can we have this door open please. Quickly!' The court officer ran down the narrow passageway, keys already in his hand. He turned the key and stepped back as the two wardens pushed past him. 'There's not a problem is there?' he asked peering round the door.

As the two officers tried to grab Kevin he exploded into frantic movement, kicking and lashing out with his arms as he struggled to free himself from their grasp.

'Hey, settle down – stop that you – OW!' The younger warden stepped back, bouncing off the wall in the confined space. His companion grabbed Kevin in a half nelson and held him, bent over, in the opposite corner.

'The bastard bit me!'

'Now just calm down Mallory. That's assault and you'll be in a lot more trouble if we report it, so I want you to sit down and we'll start again, understand?'

Kevin nodded, head down, his hair straggling over his face. All the fight had gone out of him and he almost fell onto the bench.

'What do you mean – *if* we report it?' demanded the younger warder. 'He bit me! I'll bloody have him for that . . .'

The older man stepped in front of Kevin and laid a restraining hand on his companion's shoulder. 'No, you won't. Let me see.' He examined the younger warden's hand. There were clear teeth marks on the back but the skin wasn't broken.

'You might have a bit of a bruise but that's all, so let's all get on with this in a professional manner. Come on, the court's waiting, and you . . .,' he glared at the court warder, 'you didn't see none of this, right?' The court officer nodded, stepping back down the corridor to clear the doorway.

'Your funeral if word gets out back to the jail,' he said.

Kevin lifted his head, his gaze sliding over the younger warder who was still nursing his wounded hand.

'What you mean, court's waiting?'

'They want to see you again. Don't know what for – we just do what we're told and if you know what's good for you so will you,' said the older man. 'Now, you coming nicely or do we need to cuff you?'

'Cuff him anyway,' muttered the young warder as he followed them back to the stairs leading to the courtroom.

As Kevin appeared, every head turned towards him and he hesitated, pierced by the stares of so many strangers. A none-too gentle nudge from behind delivered him to the box where he went to sit but was jerked upright again facing the bench.

'Kevin Arthur Mallory, I have been informed the police are now pursuing new lines of inquiry in the murder of Peter Smithson.'

Kevin frowned, wondering who the hell Peter Smithson was and what this had to do with him. For a second he wondered if they were going to try and pin a second murder on him but then the judge continued.

'In light of this the Crown Prosecution Service will be dismissing the charge of murder against you. You still stand accused of poaching but will be bailed to your home to await trial in the Magistrates' Court. Consequently you are released. Your solicitor, Mr Smythe, will explain the conditions of this arrangement to you and this court will expect you to adhere to them. Do you have any questions?'

Kevin stood with his mouth open, the words 'bailed to your home' echoing in his mind.

'I can go?' he stammered.

The judge smiled, 'Yes, Mr Mallory, you can go.'

Chapter Ten

There was silence in the office when Alex finished telling the story of Kevin's bail hearing, then Lauren piped up.

'So what is this new line of inquiry then? What's happened they is so sure suddenly?'

Alex shook her head, 'I don't know and they wouldn't say in open court. Obviously something's happened but they're not talking.'

'Don't want to foul up the investigation, probably,' said Eddie, who was leaning on the counter, soaking up every detail. 'Good job anyway Alex. If you'd not pushed so hard for him Kevin might have had to wait until they decided to volunteer the information.'

'Yeah,' said Lauren. 'Sometimes they don't bother letting one go until they's got the next one locked up, 'specially if there's another charge like with Kevin.'

Pauline stepped forward and waved her hand warningly at the room.

'Now then, let's not start speculating. And Lauren, we are

not here to take sides. We need to keep a neutral, professional stance with everyone involved.'

Lauren looked a little chastened but muttered, 'Was just stupid though, thinking Kevin Mallory killed anyone,' as she walked back to her office.

Eddie grinned and shook his head before turning to Alex. 'Can you spare a few minutes? I want to talk to you about the race, fill you in on what's going on, the training sessions and so on.'

Alex cleared her throat. 'Actually I wanted to have a word with you about that but I can't at the moment. I've got to let Ada Mallory know what's happened so she won't have a heart attack when he walks through the door. Only . . .' she stopped, remembering her shock that morning, 'some bastard slashed two of my tyres while we were away – I don't know how the hell I'm going to get out there.'

'Perfect!' said Eddie rubbing his hands. 'I've got a client I really should chase up. I'll take you out there and we can chat on the way.'

Alex sank back into the relative luxury of Eddie's new car, pondering how to broach the subject of the raft-race. As they bowled along the main road she was struck by the sudden and unexpected increase in traffic, most of it heading through town and going south.

'Oh yes,' Eddie sighed, 'the grockles are with us once more.'

Alex raised an eyebrow and he chuckled.

'Sorry. I've been here too long. A grockle's a tourist. They're a plague in the summer, droves of them just flooding down the roads on their way to Devon or Cornwall. Hardly any of them stop; they just jam up the roads and make life hideous.'

'Not a fan then?' asked Alex.

Eddie snorted. 'None of us are. It would be different if they visited places round here or stopped overnight or even shopped in the town but no, they just rush through chucking rubbish out of the windows and causing accidents because they don't know how to drive any road without a white line down the middle.'

Alex had never heard Eddie sound so vehement before. Generally he seemed determined to see the best in everyone, even the most hardened recidivist from his case-load. She was searching for a polite way to ask why he was so rabid when he changed the subject abruptly.

'So someone slashed your tyres?'

'Yeah. I came back from the stupid away-day and found there was a parking ticket on the windscreen and the two front tyres were flat. My fault about the ticket – the bloody council decided they'd help residents with their shortage of parking space by putting yellow lines down the road. Not quite sure how that's supposed to work but anyway, I meant to move it round the back for the day but I forgot. I'd love to know who did the tyres though. That jolly little jaunt of Garry's has cost me almost a hundred pounds,' she finished bitterly.

'Um, not a nice thing to come back to,' sympathised Eddie. 'Was there anything else – anything through the letterbox or signs anyone tried to break in?'

'I don't think so,' said Alex, alarmed at the thought. 'I didn't really check to be honest. Surely you don't think . . .?'

'No, no – if it's just the tyres it's probably a random thing. Someone rolling down the road late at night after losing at skittles or something.'

Somehow that didn't seem very reassuring but Alex had more important things on her mind. She was consumed with curiosity over Kevin's sudden release and although she was relieved to be able to give Ada such good news for a change she wondered how she was going to answer the flood of questions she knew she'd face.

'I don't suppose you know anything about these "new lines of inquiry" do you?' she asked. Eddie shook his head.

'No, not heard anything about that,' he said. 'Mind you, I wonder if it has anything to do with Big Bill. The timing is certainly suspicious.' He looked at her and continued, 'Big Bill – well William Boyd really – was found murdered out on the Levels the beginning of this week. His throat was cut apparently, a nasty way to go and not an easy way to kill someone especially a man as big and strong as Bill.'

Alex waited for more information but Eddie was focussing on the rough surface beneath his nice new suspension.

'And?' she prompted. 'What has that got to do with Kevin?'

'I'm not sure, but Bill's an important member of Derek Johns' gang – you know, Newt's dad? If someone is trying to make a reputation in the area they might be going after people they see as rivals. Now, the Elver Man was Peter Smithson, rumoured to be a didicoy from round Bath way and it's a very lucrative position. Maybe someone wanted him and Bill out of the way. Just a theory, mind. Whatever the police found at the scene, they're not saying anything to anyone just now.'

'So they might think the two murders are connected,' Alex mused. 'That would certainly let Kevin off the hook seeing as they had him locked up at the time.'

Eddie nodded. 'Pretty good alibi. Here we are.' He pulled up in front of the house and added, 'I'll pop back to get you in about an hour. I'll sound the horn if you don't mind. Ada and I don't quite see eye to eye on a few things.'

Alex climbed out of the car wondering what on earth Eddie had managed to do to alienate Ada. Eddie was the most easy-going person in the office, habitually cheerful and always willing to go the extra distance for his clients and their families, but the speed with which he took off down the track suggested it was more than a little tiff over Kevin's attendance. As she approached the front door she realized she'd not broached the issue of the raft-race and whatever that might entail. Cursing Eddie and his manipulations she sidled up to the house and knocked, calling out as she did so.

There was a clanking, a rattling of chains and Ada peered out as the door opened. Alex was hustled inside and Ada replaced the impressive collection of chains, turning the main lock – a deadbolt, Alex noted – before ushering her into the front room. Rather perversely, the back door was ajar and the back windows open to let the warm air flow in to the living room. Ada saw her puzzled look and said, 'I've the dogs out there, keeping eyes out. There's fence and hedges – come on, I'll show yer.'

The garden was bursting into life all around the house, a marked contrast to the shambles at the front. As she stepped out on to the cinder path the dogs rushed up to her, huge and menacing until Ada stopped them with a word. Mouse, the grey dog, took his place behind them and Alex had to stop herself glancing at him as they processed through Ada's little kingdom.

Rows of neat lettuces were interspersed with carrot tops, waving in the gentle breeze. She could identify potatoes and the tendrils of green and runner beans reaching greedily upwards towards the warmth of the sun, but many of the plants were unfamiliar to her.

'These here is radishes,' said Ada, picking her way along the path. 'In here,' she indicated towards the home-made cloches, 'there's marrow and a few cucumber. Got me some peppers this year, under that glass,' she waved towards a couple of old windows propped up against the greenhouse, 'and tomatoes inside of course.' The door opened reluctantly and the smell of earth and the tomato plants each neatly staked and beginning to put out the first bunches of fruit brought back a vivid memory of Alex's grandfather. Some of her happiest times as a child had come from long, warm afternoons spent pottering by his side, mixing compost and thinning seedlings as she helped the old man with his garden. She realized she was standing with her head around the door, a silly grin on her face and recalled with a shock the reason for her visit.

'Ada, I've some news about Kevin,' she said. Ada stepped back, closed the greenhouse door carefully and glanced around, wiping her hands nervously on her skirt.

'Come back inside then. Don't want to be blabbing on out here,' she said, shooting anxious looks over the surrounding fences.

'What are you scared about,' asked Alex once they were safe inside once more. Ada shook her head and scowled fiercely.

'Don't you be worrying about that now, What's you got to say about Kevin? He's alright ain' he?'

'He's more than all right; he's on his way back home. The court gave him bail today and Mr Smythe's driving him down right now. They're dropping the murder charge.'

There was a suspicion of tears in Ada's eyes as she stared fiercely at the front door, as if willing Kevin to walk through that instant. She turned her burning gaze towards Alex and said simply, 'Thank you,' and in that moment Alex remembered why she wanted to do this job, why it meant so much to her and how much she believed in it.

She was still on a high on the journey back to the office and nodded absently to Eddie's conversation until she realized he was talking about the raft-race.

'It's not all that far really,' he was saying. 'Maybe a touch under four miles . . .'

'Four miles?' said Alex, aghast at the thought. 'Four miles in the *sea*? Are you all crazy?'

'Now that's where you would be so valuable,' said Eddie. 'A qualified life-saver on board – and everyone has to wear life jackets so it's quite safe.'

Alex snorted in disgust. 'Eddie, you wear life jackets when there's some danger of actually drowning. Are we wearing life jackets at the moment? No. That is because we are quite safe, here in the car. Out on the open seas on a raft – oh no.'

'You're wearing a seat belt,' said Eddie calmly. 'Does that mean we are about to crash?'

'Of course not,' she snapped, all her good humour gone. 'It's just a precaution.'

'So is a life jacket,' said Eddie. 'The seatbelt of the waves. Anyway, there are life boats out and marshals around all the time. Come on Alex, you might enjoy it.'

'Eddie, the sea is freezing. I'm used to a pool – that's just water with no waves and preferably with heating. I learnt my life saving in a pool, not out on the sea. I don't even like those new wave machine things they're using in the big pools.'

Eddie sighed as he pulled in to the car park, turned off the engine and gave Alex the full force of his disappointed, teddy-bear look.

'We really need something like this to focus the lads,' he said. 'They've spent a good few weeks on the raft in the workshop and I don't know how I'm going to tell them it's all for nothing. You know what that sort of let-down can do to them. Please – I'll owe you.'

Alex tried to avoid those wide, brown eyes but she felt her resolve crumbling.

'Oh bloody hell – all right but – you never, *never* ask me to go yomping over the hills on walks. Ever. Deal?'

Eddie reached over and gave her a hug. 'Deal. And thank you so much.'

Alex climbed up the steps to the reception area and was confronted by Lauren, who was leaning on the counter, a sardonic grin on her face.

'Let me guess, you're doing the race,' she said.

Eddie hurried through the lobby behind her. 'I'll drop off the training schedule,' he called, as he disappeared up the stairs, taking them two at a time.

Lauren called over her shoulder, 'Told you all. Pay up now – 'tis a long while to pay-day!'

Alex scowled at her. 'Is there anything you lot won't bet on?' she growled.

'Likelihood of death,' said Lauren cheerily, 'but most other things is fair game.'

Iris woke as if from a long, nightmare-riddled sleep to find her world fractured and her home dirty, untidy and stinking. The morning was warm with a gentle breeze and she hurried around the house opening the windows, drawing the curtains back as far as she could to let in the light. She was hungry, desperately hungry, but could not bring herself to sit down at the kitchen table whilst it was covered in crumbs, splashes of tea and smears of old food. She wiped everything down with bleach and went to empty the bin only to find it was upside down, rinsed out as Bill had left it. She frowned at it for an instant, recalling his visit vaguely. It certainly wouldn't have been Derek, she thought, and there was no-one else around. Tears flooded her eyes and she felt her throat close up as grief threatened her tenuous hold on the present. She stood for a minute, eyes closed, with her face turned towards the sunlight. Then with a deep breath she righted the bin, took it inside and started on making breakfast. She knew Derek was not in the house by instinct. Some sense of calm told her he was not about to appear, scowling and wanting tea or toast or her complete attention for his stories. She had loved him once, been swept off her feet by his dark good looks and easy charm. Some part of her sensed the darkness he brought in his wake but at just eighteen that only made him seem more attractive. Her mother had disapproved, resisted the match as hard as she could.

'He's a wrong 'un that boy,' she'd said. 'He'll bring nothing but heartache and danger, you see.'

Iris had known in some tiny corner of her soul that her mother was right but it was too late by then. She was in too deep, already damaged goods and tainted by her association with the Johns clan. Even if she had found the courage to walk away, no-one else would have wanted her. No-one except dear, faithful Bill, that is. But Bill was a friend of Derek's, his best friend, and there was no way he could court her in safety. Even if they had run away Derek would have hunted them down. That was the sort of person he was. Iris sat at the table sipping her tea as she wondered what she was going to do with her life from now on.

The first thing Ada did when Kevin shambled through the door was to box his ears soundly. The second thing was to hug him, a fierce and protective bear hug that threatened to suffocate him.

'Mum,' he protested feebly, wriggling to get free.

'Don't you "mum" me, you stupid lad. Look at you!' She held him out at arm's length before giving him another hug. 'There's nothing on you. You'm skin and bone. Now sit down and I'll make tea for us all.' She turned to Smythe who was hovering in the doorway unsure of his welcome.

'You come in and sit and all. I don't know how to thank you, I really don't. You've saved my boy, I just know it.'

'Well, I don't know about that,' muttered Smythe, but his ears went pink as he blushed, pleased by the unaccustomed praise. It was not an easy life, being a defence solicitor in a small town like Highpoint and compliments were few and far between. Most days he figured himself lucky if they paid their bills. He sat on the sofa, glad to note the dogs were absent, and looked out over the garden with its vegetable plot and the occasional fruit tree. The row of books caught his eye and he was tempted to go over and have a look but wisely decided to stay where he was, for Ada swept back with tea, on a tray this time, and a fresh packet of biscuits.

'Now, tell me what happened,' she said, as she settled back in her armchair.

Smythe sampled his tea cautiously, placed the cup on the table and leaned forwards. 'Well, I'm not exactly sure of the details,' he said. 'The police say they are now "pursuing other lines of inquiry", which means they must have some evidence to suggest another culprit. They didn't say what it was in open court, so I'm afraid I don't know any more about it, but it does mean Kevin is now cleared of the murder charge. He will have to go to court for poaching, of course, but that will probably be a fine and maybe a probation order. There is a lot of concern over the dwindling number of elvers and the river wardens are pushing for the highest penalties at the moment, so the fine may be substantial.'

'They already got all my money,' said Kevin sullenly. 'They took it off I and never gave none back. 'Twas over two hundred fifty quid too, all my subs for the Watermen, so far as I'm concerned they can go whistle for they fine!'

Ada glared at him. 'You keep a civil tongue now. Is all this Carnival nonsense as got you in this mess in the first place. Well, 'tis going to stop now. You is staying round here where I can keep an eye on you and you is paying any fine and doing what that lovely probation officer says. Less you want to go back to jail?'

Kevin went white. 'They won't do that. I was in for nothing – wrongful imprisonment that was. Reckon they owes me a bit for that.'

Smythe cleared his throat. 'I agree it is very unlikely they will return you to jail, given the circumstances, but the option will be there if you fail to comply and I don't think you have any grounds for the return of the money. It is, after all, the proceeds from a criminal act and so will have been confiscated, I'm afraid.'

Kevin's response to that earned him another clout around the head from his mother.

'You go on upstairs and take them decent clothes off. I'll be making some tea and you can give me a hand. There's stuff needing doing, been waiting for you. Mind,' she said, looking at his lanky frame, 'don't know you'll have the strength. Goodness boy, didn't they feed you?'

Kevin stopped at the door and looked at her for a moment. 'Didn't like it. Don't fancy eating it when it's all full of spit.'

Sue waltzed into Alex's room that evening and said, 'Come on, we're going out to celebrate.'

Alex looked at her over a pile of half-completed Part B forms and asked, 'Celebrate what – me being suckered into this raft-race?'

Sue pulled a face at her. 'Now don't be like that. Anyway it's to celebrate your success with Kevin Mallory. You put so much work into that and you did it – he's out. That's amazing.'

'I don't know it's anything I did,' said Alex.

Lauren appeared around the door. 'You kept on, kept

believing in him. He was in court today because of you. Otherwise he'd still be in Bristol waiting for the coppers to notify the prosecution – could have been weeks before he finally got released. Come on Alex, don't you want to drink my winnings?'

'Winnings?' asked Sue as they headed for the door.

'Tell you later,' whispered Alex.

They headed for the Somerset Martyr, supposedly the hiding place for several rebels against the monarch in the aftermath of the Battle of Sedgemoor. Certainly it had the most gruesome pub sign Alex had ever encountered and she stared at it horrified until Lauren pulled her inside.

'Did they actually do that to people?' she asked.

Lauren shrugged. 'Them was traitors in the eyes of the King so that's the traitors' death,' she said. 'Was usually beheading for the important ones mind. Most of the little fry that survived was shipped off to the West Indies as slaves. Most of them was brought in front of Jeffries, though, so not that many didn't hang.'

'I remember reading about that at school – the Bloody Assizes, right?'

'Well, round here it's a bit more personal,' said Lauren. She spotted an empty table in the corner and hurried over, tossing her bag on to it before levering herself up into a chair. 'Go on, get some drinks in if you want all the details,' she added.

'I thought we were going to drink your winnings?' said Alex as she headed for the bar.

'Well now, I didn't know I was going to be giving a history lesson,' said Lauren.

They settled into the corner with drinks and several packets of pork scratchings and Lauren gave them a potted version of the history of the Monmouth Rebellion with a rather unnecessary emphasis on the gorier parts of the tale in Alex's opinion.

'But was not the battle but more the aftermath people

remember,' Lauren said, peering into her empty cider glass. Sue got another round and hurried back to the table.

'Was five hundred poor souls locked in the church up Westonzoyland overnight,' said Lauren. 'No food or water, not room to sit hardly. The next day they was taken out and some hauled off to prisons for trial but some was hanged round the village and across the Levels. They was chopped up and the bits put on spikes for a warning. Is said some nights you can hear them five hundred crying and screaming in the church,' she nodded thoughtfully. 'People round here remember that and never had no time for kings and such after. That's what Carnival's about. That first float is always Guy Fawkes, pulled by hand and lit by real flaming torches. That's how it all began.'

A shadow had fallen over the group and they drank in silence for a moment before Sue said, 'Come on, this is supposed to be a celebration. Kevin's out, justice triumphs and Alex gets to be a hero. Let's drink to that.'

They raised their glasses and smiled at one another.

'It's also the first time Alex has been out after work since I arrived,' added Sue.

'First time ever I reckon,' said Lauren, handing over the money for another round. 'Get some of them crisps too, will you? See if they's got any of them hedgehog ones left.'

Alex spun round from the bar, a look of horror on her face. 'You're joking right? Hedgehog crisps?'

The barman tapped her on the shoulder holding out a bag. 'Just the one then, my beauty?' he asked. 'Oh, don't be looking like that, there's not real hedgehogs in 'em. 'Tis just a flavour, see?'

Alex returned to the table considerably shaken and handed over the crisps between one finger and her thumb. Lauren tore them open and held out the packet. Sue took one, rather gingerly placing it in her mouth.

'Actually they're not bad,' she said, taking another. 'A bit salty and – not quite chicken more – a bit like thin pork scratchings. It's only the idea of it being hedgehog that makes

163

you think they taste odd. Go on – try one,' she said pushing the bag towards Alex, who leaned back and shook her head. Sue sighed and helped herself to another crisp.

'I was meaning to ask you,' said Alex to Lauren, 'you said the big boys at the pool called you "live bait". What was that about?'

Lauren pulled a face. 'You really does know how to have a good time don't you. Well, 'tis a fishing term. When they's out after some fish, big ones like pike, they need to get it to strike – come up fast and really grab at the hook. So they gets a little fish and fixes it by the tail and throws it in. The little fish, the live bait, it tries to get away and all that struggling brings the pike. So that's how they see me when I'm trying to swim – prey.'

Alex was aghast. 'God I'm so sorry. I didn't realize it was something as horrible as that. I didn't mean . . .'

'You know your problem,' said Lauren, waving her hand dismissively, 'You're too serious about everything. That's good for the job but you need to turn it off now and then. Like tonight, all that worry you've been doing for Kevin Mallory – it's all over.'

Alex felt a broad grin stretch across her face.

'You're right,' she said, 'it is. At last, it's all over.'

Chapter Eleven

To say Derek Johns was upset when he heard of Kevin Mallory's release would be a grave understatement. He was incandescent with rage, a red mist before his eyes and a ringing in his ears causing him to collapse into his chair in the front room of his house, the telephone clenched in his fist. Iris watched him from under her lowered eyelids, ready to react to whatever might come next. She tried not to flinch as he slammed the receiver down, tensing despite herself in anticipation of his fury.

'How's this then?' he shouted, struggling to rise from the chair. 'What's wrong with them? He was caught there, red-handed with a body in the back – what do they think happened then?' He began to pace the floor beating a path between the chair and the front window.

Iris waited until his back was turned for an instant and slipped out into the kitchen to put the kettle on. After a moment she reached into a cupboard and pulled out a glass and his bottle of whisky. Derek was hovering over the phone again and muttering to himself as she returned to the living room. Rounding on her, he swept the bottle and glass aside with a furious gesture. 'Bloody hell woman, I can't be drinking now. I've got work to do. Got to get the lads together and sort out what we going to do about this.' He turned back to the phone and began pulling out the drawers of the cabinet next to his chair.

'What you looking for now?' she asked, setting the whisky down a safe distance away.

'My book, the book with all my numbers in. Where's it gone to – can't find nothing in here any more.'

'I hope you're not thinking of bringing them all over here,' said Iris.

Derek stopped his searching and eyed her warily. 'What if I is then? What's it to you what a man does in his own house?'

Iris straightened up and stared right back at him.

'But this ain't your house, Derek Johns. This is my house. My name on the documents and my money paying the rent. You're not having your criminal friends round here trailing misery and the law behind 'em. I won't have it – no more now.'

Derek stared at her open-mouthed. He could not have been more surprised if the dog had started singing folk songs. It was inconceivable, this show of rebellion from his wife. After a long moment he turned away and went to pick up the phone.

'I mean it,' said Iris.

'You shut up if you know what's good for you,' he snarled.

Iris folded her arms and glared back.

'Or what? What do you think you can do to make things any worse, eh? One son dead and the other locked up and you back here about to lose me my home with the way you carrying on – what's left then?'

She was trembling and a voice in her head was telling – no demanding – she stop, shut up, sit down now but she couldn't stop. All the years of frustration and misery came boiling out in a great wave of fury.

'You sat here, all these years with those shiftless good-for-nothing cronies of your'n, talking about all the evil things you planning and doing and dripping poison into my boys' ears. You brought death to this door and you're never doing it again. I want you out, Derek. I want you out for good 'til you can show me you changed your ways and you can be a fit husband and a decent father.'

There – she'd finally said it. She realized she'd stopped trembling and a sense of calm filled her. For the first time in so many, many years she wasn't afraid. She watched her husband and felt nothing but a vague curiosity to see what he was going to do.

Derek opened his mouth and closed it again, stepped forward as if to strike her and, faced with those steady sea-green eyes, dropped his fist to his side. Without a word he pushed past her, grabbed his jacket and slammed out of the front door. Behind him Iris sank down onto the couch as her anger trickled away and the full enormity of her actions hit her. After a moment she reached for the phone and dialled a number, leaving precise instructions in a calm voice that disguised the shaking of her hands. Then she poured herself a stiff drink from the whisky bottle and waited for the locksmith to come and make her home secure.

Alex crossed the yard outside the offices and peered round the door to the refurbished workshop. The smell of sawdust and oil filled her nostrils and the radio blared in the background, assaulting her ears.

'Morning Alex,' came a cheery voice, booming over the music, and the general hubbub died down a little.

She stepped into the busy space and a couple of the young men turned towards her with wide grins.

'Tis you going to do the race with us, Miss?' someone shouted, and to her surprise there was a smattering of applause. Eddie hurried over wiping his hands on a piece of cloth.

'Come and look at her,' he said. 'She's not finished yet

but you can see her basic lines and the main framework is in place.'

Alex followed him into the body of the workshop where a large wooden structure was beginning to take shape. The raft was smaller than she had imagined and even taking into account its unfinished state it looked dangerously fragile.

'Rules say it must be at least four feet wide in the water,' said Eddie running his hands over the half-finished stern. 'We've gone for the minimum, so we'll sit in pairs here.' He indicated the centre of the structure. Skipping round to the front he pointed to an angled area. 'We've got a bow, to help with streamlining and our most experienced rower will be here, keeping stroke and helping to maintain the course.'

Despite her apprehension, Alex was impressed by the amount of planning and sheer hard work that had gone in to getting this far. She'd had a mental picture of a raft, something out of childhood stories of shipwrecks and Robinson Crusoe. Rafts in her mental universe were heavy, flat and square not hybrid rowing boats like this.

'How well does it move in the water?' she asked, and there was a hush around her.

'Well now,' said Eddie, 'we won't know that until we get her sealed and try her out on the river, but all the figures look good so she should float.' He caught sight of her expression and hurried on. 'Look over here, the model's been tested and it's stable and moves well.'

He indicated a plastic bowl on a bench where a tiny balsa wood raft bobbed and rocked in the centre. There were eight lumps of modelling clay spaced along the interior and she peered at them for a moment before asking, 'So which one is me?'

Eddie pointed to the back pair. 'You're left-handed so I've put you on the port side.'

All this nautical language was beginning to seem a bit over the top for such an eccentric enterprise, but the lads in the workshop seemed to be working and enjoying it too so she decided to let it go for now.

'We'll need to get some practice in paddling so we can put on a good show,' said Eddie. 'How are you fixed for tonight? We do half an hour or so a couple of times a week and the paddlers are using the gym equipment to raise their fitness level too.'

It was all too horrible, but Alex was stuck. She'd agreed to this and at least they were taking it seriously, which might mean she might not have to pull them out of the sea half-way to Minehead – providing the raft floated, of course, she added mentally.

Ada bustled around her kitchen, humming to herself and enjoying the warmth of the sunshine and the unaccustomed feeling of security from having Kevin back in the house. She was not an overly imaginative woman and she was certainly not easily scared, but as the weeks of Kevin's incarceration had dragged on she had felt more and more uneasy. The sense of being watched, followed by unknown eyes, had become stronger each day and she began to keep her doors locked and her windows closed despite the beautiful weather – and contrary to all the years of her life out on the Levels. With Kevin back she began to relax again, knowing help was close by should she need it, and now that she was no longer on her own she found the fear had lifted from her, drifting away into the sky to be replaced by a quiet contentment.

As she worked, she puzzled over what to do about Kevin. He was not a boy anymore, he was a young man and she couldn't keep him at home for ever. The thought of him leaving for good, setting out to make his own place in the world, nearly crippled her with anxiety, but she knew he would go sometime and better she helped find him somewhere with good people and an occupation than he just upped and went, heading who knows where. There was a sound behind her and she swung round to see the object of her musings standing in the doorway, clad in boxer shorts and a T-shirt, his hair sticking up every which way.

'What's for breakfast then Mum?' he said with a yawn.

169

'Breakfast? 'Tis almost lunch time you lazy great lump. Go back upstairs and put some clothes on. Is disrespectful, wandering around like that. Get off with you!'

She chased him upstairs and returned to the kitchen to set the little table by the window. Things were running low, she thought, as she rummaged through the larder. Time to head into town and restock. There was a travelling grocer who drove his van around the hamlets and outlying houses of the Levels bringing staples and occasional luxuries to busy smallholders and those without their own transport. When Frank Mallory had been around, Ada had patronized this mobile shop, but with him gone, money was very tight and she refused to pay the prices the van man charged.

'Daylight robbery,' she'd told him the last time he called. The argument was over a packet of shortbread biscuits, Kevin's favourite she recalled. The van man had protested; he needed to cover the costs of the van and petrol had shot up in price over the past year.

'You're getting a personal service,' he said, 'like your own delivery out here. I got to pay for the petrol and that's just going up and up. 'Twas £1.75 a gallon in that garage in Glastonbury. £1.75 – I asks you. Who can afford that then?'

Ada was brutally unsympathetic. 'That don't mean you can rob decent folk just 'cos you got to drive a little way. Them biscuits, they's ten pence cheaper in the supermarket. I ain't paying that for 'em.'

After suggesting Ada might like to walk to the supermarket to get her cheap biscuits, the man departed, never to return. Ada's pride had been saved by the introduction of a 'market bus' twice a week. Although it was supposed to be for customers of the main supermarket in Highpoint it was used by all the people on the Levels without their own transport. The first time that she used it, she'd been mortified when challenged by the driver over where she'd got her shopping, but the next time she slipped into the supermarket, helped herself to a couple of carrier bags and put her shopping in them, marching on to the bus with a flourish. They were good bags, lasting almost four months before Ada needed to replace them and the tattered remains still fluttered over her vegetable patch deterring the flocks of starlings that could descend and strip a garden in minutes. The bus driver had grown older and wiser and he and Ada had become quite friendly over the years. He often stopped the bus at the end of her small track, hooting the horn and ignoring his impatient passengers as he waited for her to appear. Bus was due tomorrow, Ada thought. She'd roust Kevin out of bed and they'd go into town. Was a market day too and she'd make sure Kevin got to see that young probation officer of his.

She glanced out of the window and spotted those cheeky grey ears, twitching at her from the field. Calling softly, so as not to disturb the grazing rabbits, she beckoned Kevin to look out of his bedroom window.

'I see him,' he said, and after a moment's rummaging above her head he appeared at the door holding the shotgun. Ada snatched it away from him, holding it pointed to the floor.

'What the hell do you think you doing boy?' she said, placing the gun behind her.

'Aw come on Mum, I'm old enough. 'Tis only a shotgun after all.' He tried to reach around her and she slapped his hand away.

'Yes, 'tis a shotgun that you got no licence for. I've got the licence and the last thing you needs now is to be caught poaching again – and with a gun. Will take more than Smythe to get you out of that. Here . . .' She reached into a drawer and pulled out a heavy catapult. 'Go on now – one for the pot and maybe a couple for the market if you can. Take Mickey with you an all so you don't get seen in the field.'

Kevin took the catapult with bad grace and slouched out of the door whilst Ada cracked the shotgun and removed the shells. She heard Kevin whistle softly to the dog and the creak of the back gate told her he was out of the way for a few minutes. She stood for a moment staring at the heavy red cartridges, rolling them back and forth in her hand before hurrying upstairs to her room. Separating the box of shells and the gun she hid them in different places, under the floorboards and behind a little panel in her bedroom wall. After a moment's thought she slipped the two cartridges she'd taken from the gun into her underwear drawer, just in case she needed them in a hurry. Then she went to the window and watched how Kevin was getting on.

Derek didn't stay away, of course. That would be too much to ask, Iris thought, as she heard the key scraping around the new lock in the front door. There was a pause, more scraping and then some muffled curses. She stood in the hallway, hesitating before she went to the door, then, checking the chain was fixed, she slid back the security bolts.

'What you want then?' she said, peering through the gap. He was drunk, by the look of him, drunk and not in the best of tempers. Hardly surprising under the circumstances, mind.

'What the bloody hell do you think I want, woman? Girt bloody key's not working – come on, hurry up and let us in!'

'I told you, you're not welcome here. Now be off or I'll call the police.'

Derek blinked at her, trying to read her expression, but she had her back to the light in the hall and her face was in deep shadow.

'You'd never – you'd not dare!'

Iris leaned forwards and lowered her voice. 'You listen to me Derek, I know you's up to something, out all hours and coming back with that funny smell on you. You is up to no good and the last thing you need is the police sniffing around you, asking awkward questions. I don't want to know nothin', for it's no business of mine. You leave me alone; you get out of my life and that's the end of it. Far as they's concerned I've not seen you nor heard of you since you was released and that's how I want it to stay. But if you come near me again I'll call it harassment and you'll be a marked man. And one thing more – you stay away from my son. I don't want you having nothing to do with Billy, you hear?'

172

'You can't do that! He's my son too and I got rights,' said Derek.

'Reckon you should keep your voice down unless you want to wake a few more decent folk, have them peering round they curtains and wondering what's going on,' she said calmly.

'You wouldn't dare try to keep me away from Newt!' Derek hissed.

'Oh, I would. You killed Biff and I'm not having you killing Billy too. What you going to do anyway – try an' visit him? Reckon they'd be right eager to let you in, 'specially as you got no visiting order nor nothing. You leave him be, Derek. He's no son of your'n now. I want my boy back and free of you and your kind.'

She went to close the door but Derek had his foot in the way.

'Where'm I supposed to go then?' he asked. 'Is the middle of the night.'

'You go where you been all those nights I needed some company,' said Iris. 'You go back there and stay away from me. Move your foot now, or I'll make you.'

She pulled the door back to the limit of the chain and Derek hastily jerked his foot clear, staring at his wife until she closed the door in his face. He listened as she double locked the latch and pushed the bolts into place. He was still staring as the hall light went off and the house descended into darkness. Derek Johns' life had turned to shit all around him and he couldn't understand why. He just knew someone was to blame and they were going to pay for all this.

There was great excitement in the workshop the evening Eddie turned up pulling a trailer behind his car. Alex watched from the rest-room window as the whole workshop contingent, paddlers, assemblers and instructors alike, heaved and wrestled the raft out of the doors and on to the flat bed, securing it with canvas straps. There was a moment's anxiety when it looked as if it were too large to get out of the door, but with some tilting and sliding and a great deal of swearing the raft emerged into the evening sunlight in all its patchwork and multi-colour glory. There was a scuffling at her elbow and Lauren nudged her, a wicked grin on her face.

'What was that poem we all used to learn at school,' she said. 'Something about going to sea in a sieve?'

'The Jumblies,' muttered Alex.

'Yep, that's it. Well, reckon you might be better off in a sieve. That thing looks a bit – well, amateurish.'

'Looks bloody dangerous to me,' said Alex. Eddie had spotted her at the window and was waving enthusiastically for her to go down and join them. As she walked across the room, trying not to appear too reluctant, she heard Lauren humming the 'Funeral March'.

In the yard the workshop gang were showing off their handiwork to a group of the other clients, who crowded around, touching and peering as the raft was prepared for the short journey to the river.

'Well,' said Eddie, rubbing his hands together, 'this is the acid test I suppose.'

Despite his smile she realized he was feeling nervous underneath, wondering what they could do if the raft didn't handle right or – worst of all – didn't float. She had a vision of the whole contraption tilting up and sliding gracefully into the muddy water, never to be seen again, and despite her reservations about the whole enterprise she found herself hoping it would be okay. Looking around her there was more energy and enthusiasm surrounding the raft than she'd seen since her arrival. This bunch really cared, they'd put in long hours and learnt new skills working as a group. She caught Eddie's eye and a flash of understanding passed between them. If it would just float then somehow they'd make it work.

'There you is,' said Kevin, as he walked through the kitchen door. He held three dead rabbits in his hand, clutching them by their back legs as he flipped them on to the table.

'Hang on now, let me get some paper down first,' said Ada

crossly, but inside she was proud of her son's ability to stalk and catch their dinner so well. Watching from the top window she'd marvelled at how silently he moved through the field, never losing sight of his target yet managing to remain hidden as he approached. His aim was something miraculous, she thought, as he seemed to fire the catapult without sighting, never needing a second shot. The rabbits fell one after another with no time to take fright and bolt, so fast could he fire, all in absolute silence.

'How'd you do it, so easy like?' she asked, as they sat at the table skinning one rabbit and cleaning the other two for the Saturday market.

Kevin shrugged, not really interested. 'Dunno. Just makes sense when I look – seems I just know the angle. Reckon I've always been able to do it. Remember when I was at school?' He glanced at his mother and back to his work. 'Some days I took on other boys, see how many cans we could knock off the fence. Always wondered why they was so slow, why they kept missing all the time. Got a girt bit of pocket money off the big lads in bets some days.' He grinned at her happily and she found herself smiling back at him. They bent to their task and soon there was a rich stew bubbling in a pot on the stove and the other rabbits were trussed and hung in the tiny back lobby ready for market.

'Tell you what,' said Ada. 'There's some sorrel out front, all fresh and ready for eating. You remember what that looks like?' When Kevin nodded she said, 'Go get me a bunch now and I'll make a bit of a salad.'

She wandered out to the garden and pulled a few chives, picked a small lettuce and lifted a few carrot thinnings before turning back to the house. As she walked through the door she gave a shriek and almost dropped the vegetables at the sight of Kevin staggering into the kitchen holding an enormous fish.

'What the hell is that you got, boy?' she asked.

'Found 'un on the doorstep,' said Kevin, dropping the monster on to the table with a thud. 'Girt heavy bugger an' all.'

175

They stared at the fish for a moment before Kevin stated the obvious. 'Got no head, mind.'

Ada placed her vegetables by the sink and stepped over to peer at the fish. 'Damn good job too,' she said. 'Is a pike, monster pike this 'un. They got real sharp teeth, vicious mouths all going different ways. Can cut off a finger even if they's dead.' She poked at the body tentatively and shook her head. 'Get him off my table now. I don't want that in my kitchen.'

Kevin pulled a face. 'Is lovely and fresh. Why not try a fillet eh Mum? I never seen one this big – reckon could be really tasty.'

Ada turned her back and lifted the lid from the pot on the stove.

'We'm not touching it, 'she said firmly. 'Firstly, 'tis a pike and they's not clean fish. They eat any old kind of rubbish, frogs and birds and filth from the drains. Don't know what's in there and I'm not fancying it.' Kevin opened his mouth to argue and she swung round, fixing him with a glare.

'Besides, we don't know where he's come from. Big ol' fish like that, worth something in the market I reckon. What's it doing on my doorstep? No, you take him out and find a ditch and you bury him. I don't want to be smelling him as he rots neither.' She stirred the pot and the rich aroma of rabbit stew wove around the kitchen.

Kevin sighed and began to haul the pike off the table, grazing his hand on the sharp scales as he lifted it. He dropped it again and rubbed at his palm. 'Maybe is a message,' he said.

Ada took a cloth and rubbed at his injured hand. 'What you talking about, message?' she said crossly.

'Like in that film, means something like "sleeps with the fish". Saying you drowned someone or something.'

'You don't half talk some nonsense sometimes. What film anyway – when did you ever see a film like that?'

Kevin was struggling with the pike again. 'In the picture house in town – me and Newt went one day. Was a good film but long and a bit nasty in places.'

Ada slammed the big spoon from the pot down on the table. 'You was too young to be seeing films like that! What was you – thirteen?'

Kevin looked stubborn. 'Fourteen,' he said. 'Was the second time round it was on and all the boys from the class went. Manager didn't say nothing, just let Newt buy tickets for us all.'

Ada snorted. 'Newt Johns! Well, he's safe away at the moment and *he's* not getting out in a hurry. Reckon there's no good coming from any of the Johns clan so you stay away from them all.'

'I like Newt,' said Kevin, as he disappeared out of the door, the pike draped over his shoulder. 'He was always good to I. Was Biff that was the bad'n.'

Ada watched as he made his way across the stream at the bottom of the garden and picked a path towards the main drain. Kevin was growing up and his experiences in Bristol had hardened him. She was afraid for him but she knew she couldn't protect him from the world much longer.

Waking that morning, the idea had appealed to Derek's sense of humour. He'd watched his pike colony grow from a few fish to a swarming, seething mass of hunger and there was something about their strength, their casual ferocity that he found fascinating. Often he would linger on the bridge and peer into the water to see his fish fight over their meal. They were not naturally shoal fish and as more arrived some of the originals, the smaller and weaker specimens, disappeared – probably down the throats of the larger arrivals. He developed favourites amongst them, identifying them by their scars or patches of colouring. There were two in particular, monsters both, that he watched for, two big, speckled boss pike that moved with the speed and grace but struck at the meat or any small fish foolish enough to get in their way with deadly force. He was driving down a back road late one evening when he spotted a jumble of fishing gear left on the porch of a rental cottage. Derek had no qualms about taking from the visitors, the grockles who swarmed over the area in the warmer months, pushing up the rents and paying the new, exorbitant fees for fishing licenses. He stopped the car a bit down the road, crept back and made off with the rod, a good size net and a box of assorted hooks and lures.

Back in the tumbledown cottage he now called home, Derek sorted through his haul the next morning. The rod looked strong enough and there was some decent line. He reckoned he'd need at least a 25 lb line to have a chance at one of the bigger fish, and some decent hooks too. At the bottom of the box he uncovered some trebles, barbed three-pronged beauties that he fixed to the wire rig. Reluctantly he went to the freezer and rummaged around inside until he found a joint with a decent chunk of meat on it, stripped the bone and slammed the lid down again. He opened the back door to clear the smell out, kicking the ancient freezer as he went past it.

'Girt useless bloody thing,' he muttered, breathing through his mouth as he assembled the dead bait that had once been Frank Mallory. One hook up at the top, one just slipped into the side of the bait, two bards protruding near the bottom and he was ready. It was a cool day with cloud cover and low mist over the water, which would make it easier for him to avoid the wardens. Not that they came out here often but it would be just his luck to run into one of them, him with no licence and his special bait. Best steer clear of them all, he thought, as he walked down the path and over the bridge.

There was a good thicket of scrubby hawthorn surrounded by willows a bit down the bank and he settled himself there, hidden from all but the most determined eyes. He cast his bait carefully and watched it drift towards the reeds where the pike waited. Nothing on the first cast nor the second so he set his rod on its stand and leaned over the bank, sprinkling a few scraps from a bag in his pocket. As they reached the edge of the reeds he saw the tell-tale ripple on the water and a moment later there was a flash of scales and the pieces were gone, snatched and consumed in one movement. He waited a minute and sprinkled a few more. This time they vanished closer to him, a few yards downstream from the bridge. Derek grinned to himself. He could afford to be patient – it was worth waiting for just the right fish, he reckoned. Gradually he teased the pike until it was within easy reach of him and he checked his dead bait before casting once more, a little upstream so the meat floated gently towards the waiting fish. The speed of the strike almost wrenched the rod from his hands and he wondered as he played the line out if it would hold. Then the thrill of the contest drove everything else from his mind as he and the pike fought to the death.

It was a close contest between two determined and predatory members of their species, but Derek was bigger and stronger and had the initiative. He waited half a minute after the bait had been taken before beginning to wind in the line, and the pike was hooked, the barbs pulling him slowly but inexorably towards the bank. First the fish thrashed, shaking his great head in an attempt to free it, then he dived, dragging the line against the rough bottom of the canal in an attempt to break it. Surfacing downstream from his tormentor, he rose up almost straight, tail walking on the surface, pulling and jerking with all his might as he set his 20 pounds against Derek's aching arms and burning hands. Again he dived, twisting and squirming as he tried to snap the line that held him. Derek hung on though his hands were scraped raw and blisters began to bloom on his palms and fingers. Sweat broke out on his face and trickled down into his eyes but he dare not let go of the rod to wipe it away. He let out a little more line, let the pike run and then slowly brought him back again. The third time the fish broke the surface and tried to tail-walk away Derek almost lost him. They had been fighting for almost twenty minutes and Derek was at his limit. He could not believe the pike's stamina, its burning determination to break free. Gritting his teeth he set his heels in the mud of the bank and began to pull once more, easing the fish closer and closer to the bank until suddenly it was within reach. Derek swung the net round and trapped it, lifting it clear of the water.

If he thought all the fight had been sucked out of the pike, he was mistaken for it began to thrash in the net, flinging itself around in an attempt to get back in the water. Derek leaned back trying to keep his hands away from the snapping jaws with their rows of wickedly sharp teeth. The long battle finally began to take its toll and the thrashing became squirming and then flopping as the pike struggled to survive out of the water. Derek experienced a sense of admiration, almost respect for such a fierce adversary. He felt suddenly that he didn't want to let it just suffocate, to die minute by slow minute in the air and he felt for his fishing knife. Taking a firm grip of the back of the pike's neck through the net he felt for the gills and cut. The pike gave a final heave and collapsed in a rush of blood from the sacs behind its head. Cautiously, Derek lifted it up from the bank, aware once more of time passing. He was exhausted, his body stiff and aching, and, despite all his care, one of his fingers was bleeding badly. But he had what he'd come for. The pike lay on the river bank, smooth and shining in the glittering sunlight, a fine and well-fed specimen. Serve the bitch right, Derek thought, as he carried it into the kitchen and removed the head – the bitch and her pathetic excuse for a son. Maybe he would drop them a note when he was on his way out of the Levels, let them in on the secret of the pike's diet. He packed the head carefully and put it in the boot of his car before setting off for Ada's cottage across the Levels.

Sue hummed softly to herself as she bumbled around the garden. On a tiny patch of cleared ground she had planted flowers, the brightest and boldest she could find, and they were bursting into a technicolour mat around the steps leading to the back gate. She was especially pleased with the sunflowers, carefully staked to support their weight as they stretched up towards the sky. The packet had contained a mix of types, she discovered, and the plants ranged from some only about three feet high to an extraordinary single bloom that towered over her. It was already nearly eight feet and still growing and she was giving serious consideration to entering it in the local 'tallest sunflower' competition. The garden was a sun-trap in the late afternoon and evening and she settled on the steps contentedly, blinking in the golden light and feeling utterly at peace.

Her good mood was shattered by Alex, who stormed through the house and into the garden snarling, 'What the bloody hell are you doing? Are you taking the piss or what?'

Sue peered at her, screwing her eyes up against the glare.

'What are you shouting about Alex? I've just got in myself and I've been sitting out here. What's the matter with you?'

'The curtains,' said Alex. 'I'm talking about the front curtains.' She pulled at Sue's arm but Sue stood up and shook her off.

'Oh for God's sake – I know you like the curtains pulled but it's still light. This is taking paranoia too far,' she said crossly. Reluctantly she followed Alex into the house and through to the front room.

'I didn't do that,' she said, looking at the bare window. The net curtain was pulled right back and the interior of the room was visible to all who passed by, just a few feet away on the main street. Alex was tugging at the curtain but it was stuck on the end of the bar.

'Well, I didn't do it,' she muttered, 'so how do you think it got back here then?'

Sue nudged her out of the way and with her extra height managed to free the tangled net.

'I don't know,' she said, 'but there, all fixed. I'm not a total idiot you know, I wouldn't do something like that. Who wants the neighbours peering in while we're at work anyway?'

Alex shook her head, still upset. 'Anyway, it's very odd. Was the door locked when you got home?'

Sue sighed. 'You know it was. You went out after me and I think your head would explode if you didn't double check everything. It was locked and so was the back door.' She held up her hand. 'And so were the windows.'

Alex stood for a moment, gazing at the window and then turned and headed upstairs. 'I'm going to get changed,' she called over her shoulder. 'Can you put the milk in the fridge? I'll be down and start on dinner in a minute.'

'Right – oh, what's on the menu for tonight?' Sue shouted as she carried the carton through to the kitchen.

'Surprise!' yelled Alex.

Sue opened the fridge and gave a shriek, dropping the milk all over the floor. Alex came running at the sound, 'What is it – what's the matter?'

Sue stood in the back room, her face screwed up in disgust.

'I don't know what you've got planned for tonight but you can count me out,' she said. 'I'm off to the chippy.'

'It's only a rabbit,' said Alex in disgust. 'Look at this mess – how did this happen!'

Sue went to the fridge and tugged at the door. 'Believe me,' she said, 'I know what a rabbit looks like.'

Inside, on the centre shelf, its jaws prised open to display the fearsome teeth, was the head of a pike.

Chapter Twelve

Alex was in court the day Kevin appeared before the magistrates for poaching, having fought hard to keep him as her client through several allocation meetings. She argued she had already built a rapport with the family, no easy task where Ada was concerned, and had managed to gain Kevin's trust. Garry had been grudging and suggested she needed a wider case-load if she intended to progress in her career. He seemed anxious to move Alex on to more difficult clients with more complex needs despite the fact she was still in her first year. After the meeting Gordon had taken her aside, looking at her anxiously.

'You are getting too involved,' he said. 'I know you feel a responsibility for this family but you can't do this for every client. It will wear you out, Alex. You need to step back and let others do their bit too.'

Alex knew he was right and she could feel the strain beginning to affect her work with other probationers, but she could not let Kevin down now, not after all he had gone through in the past months.

In the court she sat through the usual small-town litany of drunk and disorderly, driving whilst intoxicated, actual bodily harm (fighting whilst drunk on the pavement at closing time) and one case of attempted burglary where the perpetrator had made off with a record player and had to go back the next night because he couldn't carry the speakers in one trip. The court was half empty for most of the day, the public gallery hosting an ever-changing cast of family members and friends all watching helplessly as their loved ones were accused, chastised and sometimes taken away from them. Kevin's case was listed last on the day's order sheet and, as the hour approached, people began to drift into the courtroom. For the first time there was a crowd on the press bench instead of the lonely figure of the junior reporter who, sitting day after day, tried to make news from the procession of misguided misery that passed before her. Alex watched as she was boosted out of the front row by jovial men with spiral-topped notebooks and flashy ties – 'real' reporters who would write the only 'real' story of the week.

There was a ripple of expectation as Kevin was led into the court looking pale but surprisingly smart in his one decent suit. He'd put on a bit of weight, she noticed, and the suit no longer hung limply on him. His shoes were shined, his hair was lying fairly flat and generally he looked quite respectable. The only thing missing was a tie. She'd spoken to Ada about his clothes and Ada had shaken her head.

'He won't wear one,' she'd said. 'Don't know why but he's taken against 'um and there's no shifting him.'

Kevin sat next to Smythe who kept up a whispered commentary in his ear until the magistrates entered and silence fell over the room. It was over all very fast. The charges were read, Kevin's guilty plea was entered and suddenly every eye was on Alex as the magistrates turned to the social enquiry report. Alex had worked very hard on it and was quite pleased with her assessments, her brief but lucid analysis of Kevin's situation and her recommendations. After consulting with Ada and Kevin she had asked for a probation order with attendance at the fledgling day centre, one of the first compulsory orders in the county. She tried not to stare at the bench as the three figures flipped through the sheets in front of them, leaning over to check a point of law with the clerk before returning to the report.

Alex had made sure it was delivered a few days in advance, hoping they would have taken their copies home and read them, but at least one magistrate, a portly man in a suit that was slightly too tight, acted as if he'd never seen any social enquiry report before, let alone this one. After a few minutes the clerk called out to the room and they all sprang to their feet as the magistrates tripped off to discuss the report in private. The clerk returned after a minute or so and hurried over to her.

'Sorry about this,' he muttered, 'only two of them didn't make the last liaison meeting, so this day centre stuff is new to them. They want to know what it involves – classes or community work or whatever.'

'Yes,' said Alex. 'Yes, classes, a bit of community work sometimes, learning skills in the workshop, some specialist groups for driving offenders or alcohol issues – whatever seems the most appropriate for the client.'

'Do you have anything specific in mind here,' the clerk said. 'I know it's putting you on the spot but it would really make it easier to sell it to them . . .'

'I hope we can get some literacy classes for Mr Mallory,' said Alex. 'He's finding it very hard to get regular employment because he can't read or write. He would like to learn to drive and that would help him find employment, but he'll struggle to pass the test unless he can read. We're also offering metalwork and woodwork classes at present and vehicle maintenance comes on line soon.'

Alex hoped she'd sounded convincing because at the moment they were struggling to find instructors willing to work for the low wages and also had a chronic lack of space and funding. They'd been promised another building and several new staff posts but with the continuing squeeze on all government funded departments, giving a helping hand to young criminals came a very long way down the agenda. The clerk seemed convinced, however, nodding his head before hurrying off to share the information with the magistrates. Alex glanced over at Kevin, who looked terrified, and tried to catch his eye, smiling in what she hoped was a reassuring manner. Smythe saw her looking at them and hurried over, an anxious frown on his face.

'What do you think?' he asked, leaning a bit too close and putting his hands on the table in front of her. She knew it was just her imagination but she always thought he gave off a slight smell of mothballs and she had to resist an urge to shift away from him.

'The clerk seemed happy enough,' she said. 'I don't think there's much danger they'll send him back to prison is there? After all, he was there all that time and they had to drop the charges. Surely they'll take that into consideration.'

Smythe pulled at his earlobe and gazed over her head into the dim recesses of the courtroom ceiling.

'One would certainly hope so,' he mused, 'in the interests of justice. I'm not sure about this day centre idea though. If they decide it's a soft option they might decide to make an example of him, what with the concern about young men hanging around in gangs, not to mention the dramatic impact on elver stocks in the last few years.'

Alex felt her stomach clench at the thought of Kevin returning to jail. Smythe sounded more like a prosecutor than the voice for the defence and she wondered, not for the first time, if he really believed in his work.

'It's not a soft option,' she insisted, 'it's a higher tariff than an ordinary probation order. He'd have to attend every week or he'd be in breach and he'll hopefully learn some skills to make him able to earn a living some way other than poaching. Anyway, he doesn't belong to a 'gang'; he lives out on the Levels with his mother.'

'Ah yes, the redoubtable Ada,' Smythe murmured, but Alex

was saved his opinions on the Mallory family by the return of the clerk.

'All rise,' he called, as the magistrates trooped back and took their places on the bench. Kevin was white, visibly shaking as he remained standing to hear his fate with Smythe standing next to him. The press bench leaned forwards, their pens poised and their eyes darting from the bench to Kevin and back again, hoping for drama or despair. In the event, it was an anti-climax as the senior magistrate summed up his recent time on remand, set his guilty plea against his criminal activities and sentenced him to two years' probation with forty days attendance at the day centre. The only drama came as the clerk called the court to its feet. The magistrates stood up and headed for their room, the press turned to the door ready to head back to their respective desks and Kevin closed his eyes and collapsed in a dead faint.

Derek didn't feel safe in the cottage any more. Every time there was a car on the track he jumped, peering out of the window to see if it was Alex-bloody-probation or the police dropping by to check on Frank. He didn't worry about Iris. She wouldn't say anything about his return as long as he stayed away from the house. Well, that was fine by him, though he longed for the comforts of home some evenings as he sat in the almost empty front room reading the paper by the evening light. He used a couple of lanterns in the back room at night but the smell was pretty awful now and he was giving serious consideration to just dumping what was left in the freezer in a bog somewhere and taking off. There were a couple of bits of unfinished business he needed to take care of first however. It was all so much harder than he'd imagined as he lay on his bunk in prison, dreaming of his revenge. It had all seemed so easy when he planned it out, but now it was dirty and messy and nothing was going to plan. Derek was sick and tired of the whole business, but the anger at his son's death still burned in him, warping his outlook on life and disrupting his thinking. When he was done, he thought, when it was finished, he'd feel better. He'd be able to sleep properly, he'd go away for a while until all the fuss died down and he'd come back and patch things up with Iris and Newt. Just another few weeks and everything would be okay.

It was time for another little run out and he waited until it was dark before he slipped out to the car, now hidden past the sluice gate in an abandoned barn. He had dressed with care, all in black except for a navy balaclava stuffed in his trouser pocket. His trusty fishing knife was clipped to the back of his belt and he felt more confident this time. He'd planned it all out carefully and practised the moves in his front room over and over until he could do it with his eyes shut. The roads were empty until he hit the edge of town and he drove carefully, keeping an eye out for the police. But, as he rounded a corner on the approach to his turning, he suddenly came upon a figure, a young man, trotting down the middle of the road and had to swerve violently in order to miss him. His heart was pounding with the shock – if he'd hit him, well it didn't bear thinking about. He slammed his brakes on and flung himself out of the car, banging the door behind him.

Simon was still shuffling along, making engine noises and turning his imaginary steering-wheel, seemingly oblivious to his brush with death. Derek grabbed him by the throat as the lad made to pull out around him.

'You bloody little freak!' he snarled, shaking him like a terrier with a rat. 'You nearly got killed, do you know that? Can you even hear me?'

He dropped Simon on to the pavement where the boy rolled into a ball making little squeaking noises. Derek kicked at him before turning away in disgust.

'Stay off the road!' he called over his shoulder. 'Freak.' On an impulse he turned back and landed several more kicks before he got back into his car and drove off, his calm self-control shattered.

He took the back road again, slowing as he drove past Alex's house. The front curtains were drawn tight as usual, but there was a light on in an upstairs room. He must pay her another visit, he thought, and unconsciously licked his lips in anticipation. Not tonight though. He had other fish to fry tonight. He gave a tiny, high-pitched giggle as he accelerated down the street. Other fish to fry – that was funny. He giggled again as he drove over the bridge heading for the car park behind the Iron Beehive. It was almost deserted and he took up position in a dark corner where he could watch the car he was interested in. After a moment he slid out and wandered over to it, checked he was alone and swiftly punctured the two front tyres with his knife. Back in the shelter of his own vehicle he waited until the back doors opened and the few remaining drinkers were ejected into the night. Exchanging farewells and friendly insults they wandered off into the darkness, leaving one burly figure bringing up the rear. Derek hunched forwards over the steering wheel and grinned as the figure spotted the first flat tyre. Cursing and stumbling round the vehicle, the driver flung open the boot and leaned in searching for the tools to change the wheel. Derek pulled on the balaclava and checked his knife was loose in the sheath at his back before opening the door. Too late he realized his mistake as the interior light flashed on and the figure turned to face him. He closed the door and darkness fell once more as a voice called out to him.

'Hey, give us a hand mate. Some bastard's done one of me tyres.'

The man turned back to the boot, rummaging through boxes and the usual litter found in cars as he hunted for the jack. Derek moved up to stand behind him and pulled the knife from his belt, but at that moment the man straightened up and turned towards him, pulling a face.

'Phew, where you been then? Sorry mate but you smell . . .'

He saw the knife coming towards him and raised his hands instinctively. Derek lunged, but the knife hit an upraised arm. He pulled it back as the man shrieked in agony, then slashed at him once more as the man fell to his knees. The razor-sharp blade sliced through the hand and a spurt of blood hit

Derek in the chest, soaking his jumper and shirt. He stepped back in disgust.

'That's what you deserve,' he snarled. 'Maybe help you keep awake on duty!' He hurried back to his car, dropping the knife on the seat as he tried to wipe the sticky blood from his hands.

Behind him the man rolled on to his back clutching his ruined hand and moaning as he struggled to raise himself up off the ground. The sound of the car engine faded away in the distance and he fought for breath. However hard he tried he couldn't raise his voice above a squeak after that one great scream. It was so quiet he could hear the water lapping against the canal banks just on the other side of the pub. He was bleeding badly, he realized. He was going to die here, the victim of an unknown madman. His colleagues would be called and they'd all stand around staring down at his body. He didn't want to die here like this, alone and unnoticed in a pub car park. He gritted his teeth and struggled to his feet, the blood seeping through the fingers of his other hand as he tried to apply some pressure. There was a ringing in his ears and he thought he was going to pass out when suddenly the back door opened and a head poked out.

'You okay there?' said the barman's voice. There was the sound of approaching footsteps and the yard light came on again, harsh and white.

'Oh hell . . .' the barman stopped short as he got a good look at the gore-splashed figure leaning on the car.

'Call the police!' he yelled over his shoulder. 'Quick – police and ambulance. Sergeant Michaels has been attacked in the car park.'

The sirens and blue lights across the river woke Alex, and she stood at the back window watching the comings and goings with some concern. She'd thought about reporting the incidents of last week to the police but kept putting it off. As she'd said to Sue, when it came down to facts, her curtains were moved and there was a fish head in the fridge. Put like that it seemed more like a sick joke than a serious threat. Sue was not convinced and they had spent the evening arguing, parting on bad terms for the first time.

'It was a pike for heaven's sake!' said Sue, 'a big, mean ugly vicious bugger. And how did it get in there then? Maybe it swam in.'

Alex had been equally stubborn. She thought of all Garry's little digs at her competence, all the snide remarks about her ability to cope with the rural population and decided to deal with it herself. She wasn't going to run off scared to the police over a fish head. Hell, she'd once slipped a kipper down the back of her landlady's electric fire on leaving some particularly horrible digs. Bleating to the police was the probation equivalent of having the head teacher come in to quiet your class for you. Besides she was fairly sure she knew where it had come from.

'Suppose it was someone like Brian?' she said. 'What do you think would happen if I reported it then? I'd be a laughing stock amongst my clients but he'd never trust me again. Hell, none of them would. I'm going to ignore it and he'll realize he's wasting his time.'

Sue sighed heavily but could see her point. Running off to report to the police could mean the end of any authority an officer might have built up and some clients would see it as a breach of trust. In their eyes, 'them' meant the police and it was hard work getting accepted as part of 'us'. Finally, Sue had given up, but not before extracting a promise that, if anything else happened, Alex would report everything.

Nonetheless, since the incident Alex had become increasingly obsessive about locking up the house, closing the curtains at night and had changed the telephone number.

On the morning after they found Sergeant Michaels there was a knock on the front door and she opened it to find young Constable Brown outside.

'Oh, hello – I didn't know you lived here,' he said, blinking at her in surprise. 'You're from Probation aren't you.' Alex admitted she was and invited him inside.

191

'Would you like some tea?' she asked, but the policeman shook his head.

'No thanks. I've got the whole street to get through and a lot of people are off to work – or settling down after the night shift. I don't know which is worse. What do you think, making people late or waking them up?'

Alex smiled. 'And I thought I had a crap job,' she said. 'Is this about what happened last night?'

'Yes, did you see anything?' Constable Brown asked eagerly. Alex shook her head. 'Sorry, I just heard to sirens and then saw the lights. What happened anyway?' The Constable looked nervous, 'Well, I'm not supposed to say anything, but someone was attacked with a knife in the car park of the Iron Beehive, just after closing time.'

'Who was it?' asked Alex. 'Is he alright?'

'Do you know Sergeant Michaels – the custody sergeant at our station? It was him. How did you know it was a man?' he added suspiciously. Alex laughed. 'Only a man would drink at the Iron Beehive on his own,' she said. 'It's not terribly welcoming at the best of times and late at night it's a horrible, dark place. I know because I've had to drag a client out of there when he was drinking underage. Not my choice of venue for a quiet evening.' Constable Brown nodded and slipped his notebook back into his pocket.

'Well, yes it does have a bit of a reputation. It certainly lived up to it last night. Sergeant Michaels came out and found his front tyres had been slashed and as he was looking for his jack someone jumped him from behind and tried to cut his throat, they reckon. Was a terribly sharp knife anyway – almost cut clear through his fingers. If the barman hadn't come out he'd have bled to death. Are you okay?'

Alex sat very still, her mind racing over the words 'front tyres slashed'. 'It's probably a coincidence but someone slashed my front tyres too, about a month ago,' she said quietly.

Constable Brown had his notebook out again in a flash.

'Where were you parked?' he asked.

'Just outside the house. I was away and forgot to move the car. Came back to that and a parking ticket,' she added bitterly.

'I don't suppose you can remember what sort of damage it was? Were there a lot of cuts or just one, for example?'

Alex rose and went to the front door.

'I can show you if you like,' she said. 'I couldn't afford to get both fixed so I paid for one and I've been using the spare. The other tyre's still in the boot.'

The pathologist peered through his microscope at the photographs, made some tiny adjustments and looked again.

'Well,' he said after a moment, 'it is certainly the same type of knife. The wounds match, both were inflicted by a right-handed assailant; this blow was almost certainly aimed at the throat. Sergeant Michaels is a very lucky man,' he mused.

The Action Group Inspector cleared his throat. 'What about the tyres?' he asked. The pathologist picked up a sample slide and slid it into place.

'Ah, yes, the tyres . . . interesting. Single cut in each, more of a stab than a slash actually, and made with a single edged knife – either the same as the weapon used in the assault or one very similar.' There was a pause as he swapped samples. 'You say one of these comes from a second tyre incident?'

The Inspector nodded. 'Just over the river from the pub, but done a while ago – couple of weeks or so.'

'Well, the damage certainly seems to be remarkably similar. Was it both front tyres, do you know?'

The Inspector glanced questioningly at the corner where his sergeant stood consulting a notebook before nodding.

'Both front tyres,' he confirmed.

'So we do seem to have a pattern, albeit a rather unusual one,' said the pathologist, swivelling round to face the police. 'Three attacks with a fishing knife, a Normark if Constable Brown is correct, and I believe he is. Two of these were fatalities, both from slashed throats, both members of the criminal fraternity. The third, an attempted murder, is on a police

193

sergeant. In the same area as this attack we have two tyre slashings, one on the intended victim and one on a member of the public.'

'A probation officer,' the Sergeant interjected.

'I didn't know it was a probation officer,' said the Inspector. 'Is that relevant do you think?'

The pathologist smiled and shook his head. 'It's not my job to put it all together,' he said. 'I can tell you all these people almost certainly suffered at the hands of the same person and the tyres are very interesting. One stab to each tyre speaks of deliberation and control, not drunken vandalism. Whoever is doing this, they're following some plan. You might want to keep an eye on this probation officer or at least warn him.'

'Her,' said the Sergeant, 'warn her.'

'Ah,' said the pathologist. 'Now that *is* interesting.'

Alex was fretting, pacing her room and glancing out of the window every few minutes. She had very few clients who attended regularly without being constantly chivvied and reminded, and even fewer who attended regularly and on time, so the unexplained absence of Simon, the 'lorry boy' from Petherton, was a cause for some anxiety. After about fifteen minutes she gave in and rang down to Alison in the office.

'Oh, no, he's not down here,' said Alison brightly. 'Hang on though, I'll just check.'

There was a clunk as she dropped the phone on the counter and Alex waited, gritting her teeth in frustration. The waiting area was an open space, fully visible from the reception desk. There was nowhere for Simon to be unless he'd secreted himself under one of the chairs. She had a momentary vision of Alison lifting seat cushions and peering behind them and, despite herself, cracked a little smile. The phone was lifted again and she heard Alison's adenoidal tones.

'No, he's not here. There's a policeman to see you though.'

Slightly alarmed, Alex said, 'Did he say what he wants?'

The phone went down again, jarring through Alex's head, and after a brief pause she heard the faint tones of PC Brown. Maybe some news about the tyres, she thought.

'Send him up will you?' she said before Alison could convey her interpretation of events. 'And call me the moment you hear anything about Simon. It's not like him to be late.'

There was a knock on her office door and Constable Brown walked in looking unusually sombre. Alex waved him to a seat and offered him a cup of tea but he shook his head.

'No thanks. I'm just on my way out to Taunton, to the Saggers, but I wanted to have a word with you first.

'Saggers?' asked Alex frowning.

'Oh, sorry, Special Action Group HQ. I'd be in trouble if anyone heard me calling them 'Saggers', especially to a civilian, but to be honest they're so full of themselves and strut around – they've really pissed a lot of us off. You won't tell anyone will you?' he added.

Alex assured him his secret was safe with her.

'So, what brings you here?' she said. 'Is it to do with the tyres?'

The young PC nodded. 'Well, yes but it's a bit more than that.' He explained about the knife wounds and the match between the tyre damage and a blade used in two murders and one attempted killing of a police officer. Alex was horrified and intrigued in almost equal measure. 'So whoever cut my tyres killed William Boyd?'

'Yeah, Big Bill,' said PC Brown.

'And they also killed another man and attacked the custody sergeant at the pub.' Alex had a thought. 'The other man wouldn't happen to be this mysterious Elver Man, would he, the one Kevin Mallory was charged with?'

PC Brown looked uncomfortable. 'I can't confirm that,' he said. 'That's not supposed to be common knowledge – always saying it is the case, of course, which I'm not,' he added hastily.

Alex thought for a moment. 'Why would whoever killed the Elver Man mess about with my car?' she asked finally.

'We don't know yet,' said Constable Brown, 'but when we catch him I promise you we'll find out.'

Alex nodded, not much comforted by this. She opened her mouth to tell him about the curtains and the pike's head in the fridge but hesitated remembering her conversation with Sue. At that moment the phone rang. She snatched it up, expecting news of Simon, but instead it was Garry asking if she had a moment to spare some time that afternoon. Disappointed and a little apprehensive she replaced the receiver with a muttered apology.

'I'm waiting for a client,' she said. 'He's never late even though he walks all the way from Petherton. Well, runs really. He's amazingly fit – puts me to shame.'

'That wouldn't be Simon Adams, the lorry boy?' asked Constable Brown. Alex gave him a sharp look, 'Why?'

'Someone attacked him last night. Gave him a right good kicking by all accounts and left him on the pavement. He was lucky a passing motorist spotted him or he might have been out all night. I'm on my way over there later this afternoon to interview him.'

Kevin was looking out of the top window, wondering if he could get out of going with his mother to meet Alex at the day centre, when he saw a figure striding along the footpath, coming from the direction of Middlezoy. There was something familiar about him and Kevin leaned forward, pressing his nose to the glass to get a better look. The figure turned in to the front yard and Kevin jumped back out of sight as he recognized the florid features of Derek Johns. He slid across to the bedroom door and hurried down the stairs to warn his mother, but a hammering on the front door made him freeze like a trapped rabbit. He stood halfway down the staircase in his socks and boxers, afraid to move in either direction. There was silence for a moment and then the knocking began again, a steady pounding on the door which trembled in its reinforced frame but did not give way.

There was the sound of footsteps from the direction of the

kitchen and Ada appeared, hurrying over to the foot of the stairs, looking up at Kevin with disapproval.

''Tis Derek Johns,' he whispered, his voice coming out as a squeak. 'I seen him, coming down the path but you was out back.'

Ada flapped her hand at him, waving him up the stairs. 'What'd I tell you, parading around like that? You go put some clothes on now and leave this to me.' She turned her back on her son who retreated up the stairs to peer down at Derek Johns' head from the top window. Ada moved towards the door, running her eye over the bolts and locks as she did so. Everything was in place, just as she'd left it before going out into the garden. She stepped closer to the end of the hall and spoke calmly. 'You just leave us be now Derek. We is nothing to do with you so you go back home.'

There was a pause in the knocking. 'That you then Ada? You skulking and sneaking and hiding in there with that little runt of a son? Reckon you must be scared to show your face amongst decent folk.'

Ada stood very still, trying to make sense of all this. She had no idea what Derek Johns was talking about but she had worked out he was trying to rile her, to make her lose her temper and open the door. An angry, hostile man outside – that she could cope with. An angry, hostile man inside her house was another matter entirely and Ada wasn't about to let that happen. There was a scuffling from above and Kevin peered round the landing rails.

'What did he call me?' he asked.

'Don't you mind. You go back upstairs and leave this to me,' said Ada firmly, but Derek had heard their voices.

'Why don't you come out and face me, you little runt,' he called, 'or is you a coward like your Dad? Maybe you's a grass too an' that's why they let you out. Is that it – you a grass like your worthless Dad?'

Kevin flew down the stairs and lunged for the door but Ada planted herself in the way, fending him off with both hands.

'You stop and think now,' she hissed. 'He's just trying to get you mad so you'll open up and let him in. You want that snake in here with us?'

Kevin stopped pushing and stepped back shaking his head. 'No,' he said softly.

'Right now, you go into the kitchen and put the kettle on. Make some tea and don't you come back out 'til I say so.' She gave him a little shove. 'Go on now.'

She waited until Kevin was out of sight before reaching into the drawer of the hall stand and pulling out the carving knife. Derek was getting increasingly impatient and began to kick at the door, but Ada had taken the precaution of adding a metal thresh and extra bracings and it held firm. Derek landed a particularly hard kick and the force reverberated through the house.

'Shit! You bitch.' He staggered back, clutching at his toes. 'I almost broke my foot. You still there?'

Ada stood very still, waiting.

'Answer me you old cow,' yelled Derek, peering through the letterbox. He saw the knife at the last moment, as it snaked towards him, and jerked his head to one side. The movement saved his eyes and possibly his life as the blade sliced into the side of his cheek, emerging just below the bone to strike his right ear lobe. Derek leapt back with a shriek, slapping his hand to his damaged face as the knife vanished as quickly as it had appeared. He opened his mouth to shout but only blood came out. There was a rattling from the letterbox and the tip of the knife appeared, wriggled at him suggestively and disappeared inside once more. Derek staggered back, his head ringing from the force of the blow. The pain was unbelievable and as he shook his head to clear it blood sprayed through the wound in his cheek. Desperate to stop the bleeding he stumbled down the path and made off across the fields. His face was tearing and burning with every jolt and stumble but he did not dare be seen on the roads in this state.

Back in the cottage Ada heard the kitchen door open and a soft voice said, 'Mum?'

''Tis all done now Kevin,' she said, calmly wiping the knife blade on the inside of her apron before returning it to the drawer. 'No need to be telling anyone about this neither. 'Tis our business, not no-one else's. You get the tea ready – I'm gasping for a cup.'

'What did he mean, about Dad?' asked Kevin. Ada walked into the kitchen and ran her hands under the tap before sitting at the table and motioning him to pour the tea.

'Well now, I reckon you old enough to know about your father,' she said as she sipped the brew gratefully. 'He was never much good as a husband or much as a man, but he was trying to do something right at last, I reckon. Shame is he messed that up too and seems he's brought more trouble to this house. Still, he sent you a letter.' Kevin's head jerked up at this.

'Just shows how much he knows about you,' she added, 'sending a letter. I suppose you want me to read it then?'

Kevin nodded, his eyes staring and mouth open as he waited to hear what his father might have to say to him after almost fifteen years.

Later that evening Kevin and Ada sat in the front room and Ada took out her box of photographs and pictures, laying them out on the low table for Kevin to see.

'Let me see, this is your Grandma. Fierce woman she was, tried to do her best by us all but there was just too many of us – and my Dad, your Granddad, he was no help. Worse than useless he was. Here, that's him,' she said, poking a finger at a faded snapshot.

Kevin picked it up and stared at the figure lounging against a gate, an old crofter's cottage in the distance. 'Where's that to then?' he asked.

'That's where I was born and raised. 'Tis just down aways, across near them Roman works. Probably gone by now,' Ada mused. 'Dad never was one for keeping things in order and my Mum done her best, but was too much for her on her own.' She glanced out of the window. 'Is getting dark. Reckon you need to close up the greenhouse.'

Kevin rose to his feet obediently.

'Oh, while you out, check the front door. Make sure that great oaf ain't damaged nothing will yer?' She sat for a while, turning over photographs and reading old faded postcards, the tiny specks of a past life. She began to order the pictures, setting them out as best she could to show the family line, when Kevin came back in and stood in front of her, holding out his hand wordlessly. She looked up from her task and glanced at the outstretched palm. Nestling in his open hand was an ear-ring, a single gold hoop, still attached to the lobe.

Chapter Thirteen

It was hard to concentrate with the sense of impending doom hanging over you, Alex thought, as she sat in the office on a gloriously sunny Saturday, ploughing grimly through a pile of outstanding Part B forms. Record keeping had never been her strong point but in her first few months Lauren had kept her mostly up to date, chivvying at her heels like a fox terrier.

'You want to do them soon as you finish that bit of work,' she said. 'Don't do no good just letting it all mount up. You end up coming in of a weekend and trying to catch up with masses of notes and all them odd bits of scribble. Is no way to do things properly.'

As usual, Lauren was correct. Despite the open windows, Alex was sweating and the heat was beginning to give her a headache. On the desk in front of her were piles of paper, drifts of notes and memos all sorted rather haphazardly into cases and clients. She stared at the whole mess for a moment and rubbed her eyes, screwing them up to admire the galaxy of red and orange dots that danced in her vision. When she opened them again the jumble was still there and she sighed, reached out and picked up a handful at random, flicking through them with a sinking heart. Simon, the lorry boy, 'Cider' Rosie (she shuddered), a reminder to contact Andrew Hinton, dated several months ago – she was in real trouble here and it was all her own fault.

After PC Brown's visit she had made her way to Garry's room, her mind full of questions and her attention definitely elsewhere. It was always a mistake to underestimate your boss and on this occasion she ran straight into an ambush with no warning and no defences. There was a small pile of folders on his desk, a selection of her case files, and she had barely sat down before Garry was going through them one by one highlighting their inadequacies in a disturbing amount of detail. She wondered briefly how he had got hold of her files in the first place – they were kept in a locked cabinet and she was as careful about that as she was about her house. Then she realized, Alison had a key and could easily have handed them over. It seemed typical of the woman not to warn her and Alex was torn between fury at her assistant's betrayal and sick anger at the scathing appraisal to which she was being subjected. Somehow she managed to control herself, sitting in silence until Garry had run through her failings as a probation officer and the weaknesses in her working methods.

'I'm disappointed more than anything,' he said. 'You are a highly intelligent and well-trained officer with considerable potential, but you do not seem to be reaching it at this time.'

She was taken aback by this rather backhanded compliment, but before she could marshal a response he continued.

'There are some issues that must be addressed as a matter of urgency. Your records,' here he waved a hand airily over the folders, 'need to be brought up to date. I'm going to remove you from the court rota for a month to allow you some time for this. There are also some cases where, quite frankly, your response has been less than successful. Andrew Hinton, for example, seems to have simply disappeared. After your one visit, there is nothing.'

She leaned forwards to try and explain the difficulties but

he carried on. 'I know Paul can be rather over-protective of his charges, but after a promising start young Brian Morris has also rather slipped off the radar and that is a cause for concern. And there are some prisoners overdue a visit, Billy Johns for one.'

He had her there. She had neglected some of her more difficult cases as well as allowing those on hold – those in prison like Newt, for example, who certainly weren't going anywhere – to drift whilst she focussed on more immediate matters. He was right in most respects and she was not doing the best job she could, though she did feel he didn't seem to give her any credit for what she had done, what she was doing right.

'I wonder if this is the right environment for you,' Garry mused, staring over her head at the sparkling blue sky visible from his windows. 'Perhaps you would be more suited to a more, shall we say, *urban* environment.' He raised an eyebrow rather archly and glanced at her before resuming. 'I am aware your final appraisal is due at the end of this month.'

This was it, she thought, this was the end of all her hard work and years of struggling to quality. He was going to fail her and she'd never get another chance.

'I'm going to postpone the formal appraisal for three months,' he said. 'I feel I have been, perhaps, a little remiss in not ensuring you are more closely supervised. We will meet every week, check your records and see how you are progressing over that time. It is a two-way process of course.' Here he gave one of his slightly creepy smiles. 'I expect you will want to use my knowledge and experience to help you develop your practice.'

She suspected her smile was just as insincere as his as she agreed that would be most helpful. On the way back to her room she had to resist the urge to rush into the washroom and scrub every inch of visible flesh.

So here she was, on the third glorious Saturday afternoon since that horrible meeting, surrounded by the wreckage of her career and with no idea what to do. She was suddenly startled to hear her name being called from the yard below. Rising from her desk she peered down to see Eddie waving cheerfully up at her.

'Come on down,' he yelled. 'We're ready to give it a go!' Behind him half a dozen young men with their shirts off were wrestling the completed raft on to the trailer of Eddie's car. She hesitated, looked at her desk, and then guiltily slipped out of the office, locking the door behind her despite the fact the building was deserted. Life must be pretty tough, she thought, skipping down the stairs, if she would rather risk life and limb on a home-made raft in a mud-filled river than sit at her desk and work on her records. She emerged into the warm afternoon, blinking in the bright sunlight. The men had finished loading the raft and were milling around in a rising tide of excited chatter with a few playful scuffles on the outskirts. Eddie stood next to his creation, his square figure radiating pride and determination in equal measures as he checked the straps and made sure the paddles were secure inside.

'Right,' he said, 'off you go, you lot. I'll drive it to the landing stage. Coming with me Alex?'

She hesitated for an instant and then, feeling the eyes of the young men on her, said, 'No, I'll see you round there.' She walked over to the main group. There were a few nods and a mumbled greeting as they set off, and she felt at first as if she'd made a mistake, that she was in the way. Half way round a short man with powerful looking shoulders fell in beside her and said, 'Done much rowing then?'

'Some,' she said. 'At college. I was in the rowing club and we won a couple of cups and stuff. Don't expect it'll be much like that though.' She fell into the slightly stilted speech pattern of the group without thinking about it, and no-one seemed to notice. It felt more natural somehow, as if she had stepped into a different role. Another young man dropped back and joined them.

'I done it last year,' he said, 'and is terrible hard work. There's this current see, pulls as you turn towards Warren

Point. You is pretty well knackered by then so is a real battle. Lots of rafts, they try to get there early else you can get caught up in a bit of a crush 'less you goes round and out to sea a bit. I tells yer, I was girt glad to get back on dry land.'

Alex looked at him curiously. 'If it was so bad why the hell are you doing it again?'

The young man laughed. 'My brother, he's in another raft see. Reckons they's going to beat all comers. Well, he's younger than I, so I has to beat 'un.'

Alex had a number of brothers, older and younger, and to her this made perfect sense. They trotted on in companionable silence, hurrying over the bridge and down past the car park of the Iron Beehive before rounding a small shack to find Eddie with the trailer backed up on the river bank, ready to go.

There were several anxious moments as the group struggled with the finished raft, slipping on the muddy bank as they tried to lower it into the water. Finally, Alex looked at Eddie and said, 'How do we get it into the sea for the race?'

'We just sort of shove it,' he said, hanging on to one of the ropes that balanced the craft over the flat, silt-infested water of the Parrett.

'Maybe we should do that then,' said Alex. 'If it's going to make it in the sea it'll surely be all right here and if it's not, well at least there's only us around to see it.'

'And all them,' said the older brother, gesturing towards the far bank where a crowd of hecklers and supporters had gathered.

'You're right,' said Eddie. 'Okay, enough pussy-footing around. Let's get this raft in the water and see how it does. One – two – three!' And at the final shout the crew shoved together, propelling the raft down the ramp and into the water with a great splash. There was a cheer, mixed with a few jeers, from the other bank, and the audiences on both sides craned forwards to see what was going to happen. For a heart-stopping moment the raft rocked wildly, taking on water as it rolled and pitched, then it settled into a more measured rocking until at last it floated, a bit low in the water but not too far. Alex found herself grabbed and hugged by a jubilant lad who didn't look old enough to be on probation.

'Girt magic,' he chortled, showing a wide expanse of gum where his front teeth should be. Eddie intervened, gently prising Alex from his clutches.

'This is Jimmy,' he said, 'your rowing partner.'

Jimmy nodded enthusiastically. 'Right, right, you'm on the left, right?' Alex blinked at him uncertainly but was rescued once more by Eddie.

'As you say Jimmy, Alex is on the left. Now, let's try some real paddling shall we?'

Alex glanced down at her clothing ruefully. She wasn't wearing anything special but she was fond of these particular jeans and her tennis shoes were almost new. Eddie watched her expression.

'Sorry,' he said, 'I guess I should have warned you.'

'It still beats writing Part Bs all afternoon,' she said, and made her way to the bank where the crew were holding the raft steady.

'How come I'm first?' she asked, looking at them suspiciously.

'You'm lightest and got to get over there, see,' said Jimmy. 'I'll be right behind you – though actually I'll be next to you.'

Alex shook her head at him. 'I hope you're not the navigator,' she said. 'We'll end up in France.' She slid over the minimal sides and edged towards her place with the rest of the crew holding the raft steady. Someone passed her a single-bladed paddle and she sat for a moment trying to get a feel for the craft until it rocked alarmingly under Jimmy's weight. Resisting the temptation to fling the paddle away, jump into the water and swim for the far bank, Alex began to use the paddle to help keep the raft straight and close to the side as more of the crew took their places.

The raft dipped and swayed with every new body, but always righted itself, until they were almost all aboard. But just as the steersman was settling into the stern, Eddie suddenly called out, 'Wait, everyone sit still! Don't move.'

This did not have the desired effect, as everyone aboard jumped and swung round towards him, and the remaining rowers on the landing stage let go of the ropes. The raft drifted away from the bank, bow in the air with the weight still concentrated towards the back. Several people in the boat didn't have paddles and in the ensuing chaos the raft, with an almost natural grace turned 360 degrees in the current and slid over on to its side depositing the crew in the muddy waters of the river. Alex surfaced, keeping her mouth firmly closed and resolutely pushing any thoughts of what might lie in the murky depths from her mind. Several of the crew, those closest to the steps, were already scrambling ashore and the rest were swimming for the riverbank. She did a quick count of heads and realized they were one short – Jimmy was nowhere to be seen.

Risking a mouthful of river water, she took a gulp of air and dived past the raft, which was now bobbing merrily the right way up again. The silt was so thick she could barely see more than a few feet through the water, but she made a quick circuit round the raft before coming up for air again. Ignoring the calls and waving from both banks she breathed deeply once more and dived again, going under the raft this time. Her head bumped against something and she reached out and felt movement. A hand grabbed at her, seizing her shoulder and clinging on with the desperation of the drowning. Without thinking, her training took over and she reached over and bent the fingers back, pulling Jimmy by his arm as she prised him loose. She rolled him over on to her chest, holding him by the chin and pushed away from the raft and up to the surface. As they bobbed into view Eddie flung a lifebelt and the crew pulled them to the steps and hauled Jimmy, now coughing and retching, on to the bank.

Eddie held out his hand and helped Alex up the landing steps.

'Bloody good show,' he said. 'That was impressive.' Alex shook him off and hurried over to Jimmy to check he was breathing properly. He was blue with cold despite the sunshine and he was shaking and gasping. He cradled his hand against his chest and glared at her.

'You'm broken my fingers,' he said between coughs.

'I'm sorry but you were panicking,' she said. 'You could have drowned us both. I had to get free or we'd still be under there.'

Jimmy hunched his shoulders, nursing his injured hand like an abandoned kitten, and lapsed into sullen silence as Eddie rummaged through his car boot and came out with a rather tatty blanket.

'Sorry about this,' he said, as he tucked it round Jimmy's shoulders in an attempt to keep the shivering young man warm. 'It's the dog's.'

With commendable foresight one of the crew had run back to the Iron Beehive and called an ambulance and shortly Jimmy was being whisked away to Casualty.

'He'll be all right,' the driver had said cheerfully, 'less he swallowed too much water of course. 'Tis just shock and his hand is sprained I think.' He'd tried to persuade Alex to go too but she had shaken her head firmly.

'I'm fine,' she said. 'Just take care of Jimmy will you?'

The ambulance crew shook her hand and told her she deserved a medal. 'Girt brave I reckon,' said one. 'Wouldn't get me jumping into ol' Parratt. Not no way.'

Alex was glad when they finally drove off and she could sit in the sun and try to dry out a bit. She cast an envious eye over the other rowers, most of whom were stripped down to their undershorts, their wet clothes laid out on the hot concrete of the landing.

'What do we do now?' fussed Eddie. 'We've lost a rower and there's only a few weeks left.'

'You're not thinking of actually going ahead with this bloody thing are you?' she asked crossly. 'Anyway, what the hell were you playing at, yelling like that!'

Eddie looked sheepish. 'I remembered you're all supposed to be wearing life jackets,' he mumbled. 'In case you fell in.'

Derek had slept for a day and a night after getting back to the cottage, aided by most of a bottle of Scotch and numerous aspirin he'd found in the glove compartment of the car. When he finally woke he found the side of his face was stuck to the pillow by a mass of congealed blood. The pain was awful, a fierce throbbing made worse by the after-effects of the alcohol, and he lay for a moment wondering if he might actually be better off dead. As he tried to get up, the pillow ripped at his cheek opening the wound again and after several false starts he was forced to shamble into the kitchen with it clamped to his face. He cursed as he saw the pile of dirty dishes and hauled them out, pushing them along the wooden draining board with a fine disregard for those that fell off the end and smashed on the stone floor. Finally, the sink was clear and he filled it with water, dipping his hands in and trying to loosen the ticking. At last he was able to peel it off and he hurled the sopping, bloody mass of feathers across the room where it lay like a shot bird.

There was a small piece of a mirror wedged behind the water pipe on the wall and he peered at his reflection, turning his head from one side to another as he took in the full extent of his injuries. Whenever he moved his mouth the hole in his cheek threatened to open, an obscene second mouth with ragged, swollen lips. It even hurt when he blinked his eyes. He tilted his face away to the left and saw for the first time that he was missing his ear lobe. His fingers moved towards the mutilated ear but he jerked back before making contact. After staring at his ruined face for a long, long minute he emptied the water out of the sink, put the kettle on to boil and began to hunt through the kitchen drawers for something to cover the wounds. It took an agonising twenty minutes to wash his cheek and ear in water mixed with a little salt and a further ten to pull the torn edges into place and fix them with strips of old sticking plaster. He knew he should go to a hospital but that was out of the question. He'd just have to shift for himself and hope it healed, preferably without looking too bad. Not for the first time he wished he had Big Bill to call on, the ultimate loyal friend and support who would have seen he was fed, got him something a bit better than aspirin and been his eyes and ears out on the Levels. Without him, all Derek could do was stay out of sight and hope Ada hadn't set the police on him. If she had, it would be the last thing she ever did, he vowed. Her and that retard of a son too.

'You have got to be joking!' had been Alex's reaction to the news. Up early on Monday morning, and none the worse after her rather adventurous weekend, she had dropped in to the workshop to offer Eddie her commiserations on the end of the raft-race bid. Much to her surprise the place was humming with activity and there was an air of celebration about the gathering. She hesitated, standing in the door and watching before Eddie spotted her and beckoned her inside.

'What's going on?' she asked, looking around at the crowded workbenches. In the centre was the raft, cleaned of the mud and slime from the river and undergoing some modifications to the underside. The rudder was off and her colleagues from the aborted weekend test were sanding and planing the components before setting them aside to be varnished. They glanced up as she entered and both grinned broadly at her.

'Hey Miss!' one of them called.

'Oh for God's sake call me Alex,' she said. 'After all, we all nearly drowned together so this is no time for formalities.'

The pair laughed as if this was a wonderful joke.

'Right-oh,' said the short one of the pair. 'Well, I'm Chris . . .'

'And I'm Mick,' chimed in the other.

'So what's going on,' she said. 'I thought we'd lost Jimmy so we were still down a rower.'

Eddie beamed with all the confidence of a magician about to put a rabbit from a hat.

'We have another volunteer,' he said, waving towards the corner, where an all-too familiar figure lurked. Alex grabbed Eddie none too gently and hustled him out into the yard.

'If you think I'm getting into any type of craft with Brian, let alone a home-made bloody raft, then you are completely out of your mind,' she hissed. 'He's a drunk and a gluey! He's not safe on dry land let alone out at sea. I cannot allow you to do this – he'll put everyone at risk.'

'Come on Alex. He's willing to do all the training; he was in the Boys Brigade for years and he's cleaned up his act. This could be just what he needs to get him back on track.'

'Who told you he'd cleaned up? Him – or maybe Paul has put in a good word for his protégée. Well, you do this without me.' She turned on her heel and began to walk away.

'Pauline told me,' said Eddie. Alex stopped and swung round to face him. She had the greatest respect for Pauline and trusted her judgement almost as much as Lauren's.

'What does Pauline have to do with this?'

'She runs the Boys Brigade,' said Eddie. 'She's known him since he first joined as a Junior. He was a member up until early last year, all the way through the Company into the Seniors. Look, confidentially she's offered to put him up for a few weeks and keep an eye on him. I know it's frowned on but if anyone can get through to him it's Pauline.'

Alex stared at him very hard, using what several of her probationers called her 'death stare'. The silence stretched between them until Eddie blinked first.

'One drink, one sniff, one smart-arse remark and that's it,' she warned.

'Deal,' said Eddie smiling. 'Thank you – really, thank you. After Saturday I don't think I'd have the guts to send them out without a life-saver on board. We can't do it without you.'

Alex flapped her hand at him as she walked towards the front door. 'Flatterer'.

As the race day approached, the raft project became the focus of attention amongst staff and clients alike. Even Garry strolled over a couple of times to see how things were going, and as the crew got down to some serious training, a number of young women began to stray into the yard, standing in little groups as they nudged and giggled, casting appreciative eyes over the muscular torsos of the rowers.

Alex began to spend more time in the workshop too, a place of respite from the strain of her weekly meetings with Garry. Hidden in the depths of the workshop, and utterly focussed on what he was doing, Kevin had sketched out modified plans for the rudder and made a few doodles as he toyed with a smaller, lighter but more responsive frame to hold it. He didn't know exactly why he was changing some parts, but as he sketched, rubbed out and sketched again he knew it would work. He could almost feel how it would respond and he cast his eye around the workshop, identifying and mentally assembling the materials he needed. He hummed to himself, happily absorbed in this new task and entirely ignorant of the eyes staring hungrily at him from the shelter of the overhanging trees on the other side of the wall.

On the Friday before the race itself, Eddie was out in the yard, laying out the life jackets and checking each one carefully. He knew if anything went seriously wrong the lives of the crew could depend on these ungainly vests and he wasn't about to take any chances. Each rower in turn had their jacket fitted, adjusted and stencilled with their initials before they were packed away in a box. As he slammed the lid shut and locked it he had one last glance round the workshop where the raft, complete with Kevin's new rudder brackets, sat waiting on its trailer. They had trained on dry land, had several weekend sessions out on the river (considerably more successful than the first) and together had planned the strategy for the race itself. The only thing they'd not been able to do was try it out at sea. That was frowned on by the Lifeboat Service who had enough on their hands during race day proper without unsupervised launches going on all over the coast in the weeks before. Eddie ran his hand over the side of his creation and gave it a little pat before switching off the lights and heading for home. It was all up to the crew now. He'd done everything he possibly could.

As Eddie drove out of the gate a figure slipped over the wall and made for the workshop. There was one window at the back that didn't lock properly, he knew. He'd been watching on and off for weeks and it was the work of a second to lift the catch with the blade of his knife and slide it open. No alarm either of course. Really, they were just asking for trouble. Derek Johns had lost some weight since his encounter with Ada, mainly as it had been too painful to eat initially, and then he had had to live on what he could forage once his larder was empty. He had no problem slipping through the gap and lowering himself on to the workbench. There was a loud clatter as he knocked a tool off onto the floor and he froze, listening for any approaching footsteps. All was still and he breathed again as he stepped down and approached the raft in the middle of the space. He walked round it, casting his eye over the slightly ungainly looking craft. It was well made though, he thought, and a lot of care had gone into the construction. Not particularly beautiful, still it might actually make it if it didn't capsize half-way to Minehead.

He'd toyed with the idea of setting fire to the whole thing but that would attract a great deal of official attention. The coppers tended to get a bit riled up about arson and it carried a very heavy penalty if you got caught. Besides, he had nothing against most of the crew – apart from a general contempt for their brown-nosing and sucking up to the probation staff. No, he was after something a bit more personal. He examined the underside of the raft and chose several of the plastic tanks mounted on the left. These were empty to give a bit more buoyancy, the air acting to counter the weight of the crew. Choosing a place on the inside, near the top of each tank he made two deep cuts. Then he turned his attention to the lifejackets, picking the lock on the box in seconds. Rummaging through the contents he found what he was looking for, made a few adjustments of his own and put everything back neatly, closing the lock once more. He flipped the catch on the window behind him and set off through the park keeping in the shadows of the trees to avoid startling the natives. He'd done the best he could to repair his face but he knew he would never be considered handsome again.

Alex woke on the day of the race feeling sick. She'd resolutely avoided thinking about the actual day itself despite all the drills and practices, all the time spent with the small group who made up the crew and the larger supporting cast of builders, drivers, planners and general odd-bods who kept appearing to swell their numbers. Somehow she'd managed to keep the reality of this stupid adventure walled up in a tiny corner of her mind. Well, she thought, as she opened her eyes, the walls are down and this tiny voice is screaming. She sat up in bed and pulled an Edvard Munch 'face', mouth open, cheeks in and hands to the sides.

'You've not got toothache have you?' asked Sue, materializing at the door with a huge mug of coffee.

Alex dropped her hands hastily. 'No, sorry, just trying to calm my psyche,' she said taking the mug. 'Mmm, good. That's better.'

Sue eyed her suspiciously. 'Are you sure you're all right? You're never this calm and pleasant in the morning.'

Alex shook her head and took another sip. 'I think I'm going to throw up,' she said.

'Perfectly reasonable and sane reaction to this afternoon,' said Sue, with a distinct lack of sympathy. 'Hurry up and get ready. You need to eat something before we set off. We can't have the life-saver fainting and falling overboard now can we.'

Alex glared at her retreating back and wondered how the hell she'd got herself into this predicament.

On the beach at Watchet the crowds were already gathering and a holiday atmosphere reigned as families settled on the stony beach, unpacked picnics and settled in to enjoy the sun. Alex arrived just behind the minibus hired for the day to make sure the rowers and support crew all arrived safely and on time. It was driven by Paul Malcolm, who got out looking harassed.

'Hi Alex,' he said. 'Getting this lot out of bed was a joy I can tell you. Why did I agree to this? I'm dying for a pint but I daren't drink in front of the lads.'

The bus emptied out, a cheerful bunch, covering their nerves with jokes, insults and the occasional shove.

'Where's Brian?' she asked, looking over the group.

'It's okay, he's coming with Pauline,' said Paul. 'How's he done anyway?'

Alex had to admit she'd been pleasantly surprised by Brian over the last couple of weeks. He'd turned up, worked hard and fitted in with the rest of them with a minimum of fuss. Pauline assured her he'd not been drinking and the tell-tale spots around his mouth and nose had faded away. They were a little awkward with one another at first, seated crammed up against each other on the raft and having to work as a pair, but this faded as they developed a level of mutual respect. Brian had heard the story of the rescue and joked he was glad to be sitting next to her because she'd save him first. She watched how he picked up the unfamiliar art of rowing and was impressed by his stamina and his almost instinctive ability to adjust to the pitches of the raft. Above all he seemed to be enjoying himself despite the blisters, the aching muscles and the occasional ducking over the side. Perhaps he'd found what he was good at, she thought.

Paul distributed packed lunches to everyone and they sat down to eat whilst they waited for the raft. The sea was a bit rough, Alex thought, casting an anxious look over her shoulder as she munched on her sandwich. She was getting very nervous and the food tasted of nothing. She was just wrapping it up again when a familiar voice said, 'Are you wanting that?' and Lauren, their nominated first-aider, appeared, clambering determinedly over the piles of stones towards them, followed by Jonny who looked decidedly rakish in a pink vest and tiny cut-offs.

'Nice outfit,' she murmured, as he settled next to her, stretching out on the beach.

'Mmm . . . well, you've got to look your best. I often come down here. It's the perfect place to pick up things.'

Alex looked at him suspiciously and he gave a disarming smile. 'Fossils dear, the place is just lousy with fossils.'

Somehow she doubted Jonny spent his afternoons hunting for ammonites, but before she could think of a suitable retort a shout went up from the group and Eddie's car appeared down the road towing the raft. There was a scramble for the trailer as it slowly ground to a halt and in a few minutes the men had the craft unstrapped and were checking it over.

'Leave it on the trailer,' yelled Eddie, as he got out of the car. 'It can get damaged on the stones, so leave it there. We'll have to carry it down to the water after the inspection but it's safer up there until then.'

'What inspection?' asked Alex, who for one mad moment had hoped they would drop the raft on the rocks and scupper the whole thing.

'It's got to be measured and checked over to make sure it complies with the rules,' said Eddie.

'There are rules for this event?' Alex was incredulous.

'Of course there are,' said Eddie. 'You don't think you can just turn up with any old thing and paddle out to sea? There's rules about size, number of crew, type of paddles – everything really.' He handed her a piece of paper with a dozen bullet points printed in dark blue ink.

'At least four feet wide,' she read. 'At least two crew members. No oars or double-ended paddles and life jackets must be worn . . .' She turned the page over but it was blank. 'Nothing about it being seaworthy I notice.'

Eddie laughed and slapped her on the shoulder. 'I love your sense of humour,' he said. 'Oh, here they come. I'll get the life jackets out. Time to suit up.'

He almost skipped over to the car in his excitement, leaving Alex regretting even the minimal part of the sandwich she had just eaten.

About twenty groups were now gathered on the beach and rafts of every size, shape and colour dotted the pebbles. Some were strictly business-like with sleek lines and stern; several were almost playful with sea horses and mermaids fixed to the sides; at least one looked downright lethal, comprising several oil drums, some wood that appeared to have come from a broken fence and a pirate flag nailed to its stern. The harbour master stopped at this sorry craft and shook his head, consulting with the coastguard before, with a marked reluctance, handing the lads next to it an official number.

'Right,' said Eddie, giving a bright orange tabard with the number '7' printed on it to Pete their bow man, 'everyone ready? All checked your jackets? Now, remember, keep the raft up until you're a good way out. If a wave catches it and it hits the bottom that can damage the air tanks and we need those. You're allowed to go out above knee deep before you have to get in, so Alex and Brian – you hop in first and keep it steady for the rest. Tom,' he pointed to the steersman, a sleek, muscular man with long dark hair, 'you keep pushing as far as you can, but make sure you do get in. We'd be stuffed without you.' He grinned nervously and suddenly it was all very real and happening very fast.

Alex just had time to catch Lauren's eye and receive a quick thumbs-up from Jonny before a whistle blew and the beach was a mass of crews hauling their rafts towards the water. There was a lot of shoving as the teams jostled for position, the strongest and fittest standing ankle deep in the water whilst the less experienced took their places behind them. Alex gripped her paddle in both hands and took up position behind the rest, wondering how she could be so cold yet still sweat so much. The pause seemed to last for ever as the sun beat down and Alex's vision seemed to narrow to a tiny point focussed on the waves just beyond Mick's right shoulder. Then there was a second blast of the whistle and the teams lunged forwards into the surf.

The water was so cold it took Alex's breath away. In a few seconds she was up to her knees in it and soaked down one side from the splashing, as the crew plunged forwards into the waves. Disoriented from the shock of the sudden cold, the dazzling light reflecting off the water and the shouts and roaring from the sea around her, Alex stopped, stepped forwards again and almost slipped over on a small rock. A hand grabbed her elbow to steady her and then she was being dragged forwards, water up to her thighs and shoved unceremoniously into the fragile safety of the raft. Brian popped over the side next to her and slid into his place as the craft tilted alarmingly before righting itself.

'Come on,' he yelled, 'we got to keep it steady, else it's just us all the way to Minehead!' He dug his paddle into the water, pushing the raft around as Pete slithered in and set his weight to holding the raft against the waves that threatened to push it back on to the beach. Brian was grinning like a madman as he worked the oar and Alex took a firm grasp of her paddle and leaned over to help. The swirling water almost tore it from her grasp as she tried to find an angle that allowed her to make an impact on the raft's rocking. Suddenly the resistance was gone and she made a great swipe at nothing, almost overbalancing.

'Sorry,' chorused Mick and Chris, as they wriggled into position in front of her and Brian. 'Reckon we should have gone one at a time,' Mick gasped. There was now a fair amount of water slopping around in the bottom of the raft, but everyone except Tom was on board. With a final heave he tumbled over the stern and Pete began to set a beat for the rowers. After a few false starts they fell into the familiar rhythm, the hours of practice paying off as slowly and painfully they pulled clear of the surf at Watchet and began the long crawl round to Minehead.

It was nothing like their training runs on the river, Alex realized. The Parrett was relatively smooth and calm, and although it had a definite current it was at least consistent. The sea was rough, wild and tore at them every way it could, at least until they were clear of the beach. The raft, steered by the unflappable Tom, headed directly for the place where the waves formed into breakers and for a horrible moment they rose up and up, hovering on the peak before plunging into the calmer troughs behind. After three breakers Alex was feeling seasick, her head spinning with the noise and the constant motion, but she gritted her teeth and dug in with the paddle, determined not to disgrace herself. Then suddenly they were clear and the sea changed from frothing madness to hard, bright glass. The sunlight sparkled as it was refracted off the rippling surface and the roaring of the surf faded away behind them.

'All right!' shouted Pete. 'We is clear – off we go now,' and he began to chant a beat. Alex glanced around and saw relief on everyone's face and realized she was not the only one who'd wondered if they were actually going to make it out to sea. For the first time she felt a part of this motley crew and she bent to the paddling with a will. There was something almost therapeutic about subsuming your individuality, becoming part of something rather than being all of it, she thought. Despite her cold, wet feet, her terror and the lingering nausea she was actually rather enjoying herself. There were a number of other rafts around them and several lagging behind. A glance over her shoulder showed the first casualties, amongst them the pirate raft that broke apart, oil drums bobbing on the sea as the two young men tried to climb on to them to wait for the lifeboat. One of them waved the flag above his head, whooping and laughing.

''Tis our best race yet,' he called out, 'never made it off the beach before!' As the field began to open up, the crew bent to the serious task of propelling their frail craft all the way to the finish line.

In Minehead the crowds were gathering and a party atmosphere was developing as the pubs opened and friends and rivals massed to witness the finish of the race. There were occasional bulletins broadcast from the coastguard boat standing off from the race, and bets were laid under tables and in shady corners as the ever-changing odds attracted those wanting to chance a few quid on the outcome. Eddie parked the car and trailer in the nearest pub car park and made his way down to the quayside where he was joined by Lauren, Jonny and Paul Malcolm. They found a space on a low wall and settled down to wait, cool drinks and left-over sandwiches set out around them. Eddie squinted up at the sun, which was beating down fiercely and sending reflections off the water.

'Maybe they should have worn hats,' he said. 'I didn't think of hats. What do you reckon Paul?'

Paul stared out to sea and sipped his cola thoughtfully. 'I reckon it's a bit late to worry about that now,' he said. 'You did a cracking job Eddie, just getting them here. Let's just hope they make it eh?'

They sat in silence as the crowd swelled around them and a band began to play in anticipation of the triumphant arrival of the rafts.

For over a mile the Probation raft held its own against better trained and more experienced crews, and there was a quality of grim determination setting in by the time they approached Warren Point. Propelling a raft through the sea, even a relatively calm sea, is a very different prospect to paddling around on a river. The salt water splashed over them, leaving their hair and faces sticky with salt, and their wet clothes began to chafe in a number of unfortunate places. Their eyes stung from the spray, their hands were beginning to blister and they were all starting to burn from the fierce sun. Alex plunged on, although every muscle in her back and shoulders was starting to complain. A short while later Tom gave an anxious call.

'Pete? Pete, there's something not quite right about the steering.'

Everyone stopped paddling and looked round at him and the raft began to yaw to the left.

'Get on with it!' yelled Pete. 'You'm can't stop now – we is almost at Warren Point and there's a right strong current there. Reckon that's what you feeling, Tom.'

Tom shook his head but said no more as they inched their way across the unforgiving sea and out of the slight shelter offered by the Point. The smooth surface of the water began to ripple and then fracture as they turned towards the stiffening breeze and for the first time Alex felt the raft tilt a little to the left and recover just a bit too slowly. Although the sea was rougher, paddling seemed a bit easier and she dug in, still matching the men stroke for stroke until there was another dip and a splash of sea water rolled over her side and in to the raft. She instinctively stopped paddling and flung her weight towards Brian bouncing him off the pace.

'Heh, watch out now,' he protested, nudging her back and sticking out his elbow. Then he noticed the water spilling over the side again and he stopped paddling too. 'Oh bugger.'

Pete, still unaware of the problem, yelled at them to get working.

'Come on, 'tis the hardest part, but once we's round this 'tis easy into the harbour. Don't you bloody dare quit on us now.' He lifted the paddle and added his own weight to their forward motion, but the raft was listing more noticeably now and Tom joined Alex in leaning to the right in an attempt to lift the left side clear of the waves.

'We'm in trouble back here,' he yelled, but this had the effect of causing all the other rowers to swivel round towards him. Alex felt the raft dip as she overbalanced and tried to compensate by grabbing Brian as the first of the cross-currents hit the raft causing it to buck like an angry horse. The craft began to turn away from the current and she executed a neat back-flip into the sea.

Alex made a grab for the raft but it was already out of reach. Opening her mouth to yell she swallowed a great lungful of water and began to choke, thrashing wildly as she started to panic. A wave slapped her in the face and she went under for a second before her life jacket propelled her to the surface once more.

'Keep your mouth closed!' Alex thought, struggling for some self-control. The water was desperately cold but seemed to warm slightly as she ploughed through the waves towards the raft. The water dragged at her clothes threatening to pull her under again and she thanked Eddie for his insistence on decent life jackets. Suddenly she felt something give around her shoulders and to her horror the top strap of her life jacket pinged past her ear. Water snuck in between the smooth surface of the buoyancy floats and her body and she felt it begin to drag away leaving one side of her body supported and threatening to roll her over in the water. It was impossible to make any progress against the pull of the jacket and she stopped to tread water. Just as she gained some equilibrium the other strap went and the whole jacket began to uncoil around her. Her breath was coming in short gasps and her legs were getting heavy, exhausted from the effort involved in keeping afloat. Her head dipped under the water and she couldn't see when she surfaced, blinded by the salt and her own hair. The thought that she might actually drown out here flashed through her mind and then a familiar voice called, 'Got you now!' Eager hands grabbed for her and she was bundled unceremoniously into the raft as the lifeboat hove to, stopping a few yards away.

'Stand by to receive a tow,' boomed a voice, only to be greeted by jeers from the crew.

'Where was you a couple a minutes ago then?' yelled Brian. 'You wasn't that eager then. Well you bugger off now.'

'What are you doing?' gasped Alex. 'They've come to help us.'

'A big disgrace to need a tow. Don't count as a finish neither,' muttered Mick.

'Reckon we can make it,' said Chris, looking at Alex hopefully.

'We is past the Point,' said Pete. ''Tis a straight run in and we've got enough time.'

Alex sat up and looked round at the hopeful faces. She felt like total shit but she was damned if it was all to be for nothing.

'Oh sod it – let's give it a go. You're right, we can see the harbour from here.' She waved to the lifeboat. 'We want to row in if that's permitted. No-one's hurt and the raft's fine.' She tried to look confident, ignoring the water sloshing around her ankles.

'Right, Pete, get us moving again before they realize this side is probably sinking. And everyone, keep you life jackets done up properly. We may need them still.'

The lifeboat backed off a bit and followed them in as the little raft limped home to be greeted by cheers and wild applause from the crowd at the harbour who had had details of the drama relayed to them over the Tannoy.

As they arrived at the harbour wall Alex turned to Brian and held out her hand. 'Thanks,' she said. 'I can almost forgive you for the pike's head'. Brian shook her hand but screwed up his eyes and said, "Tis no worry. What pike though? I don't know nothing about no pike'. Before she could answer she was grabbed by Eddie who waded into the sea in his eagerness.

'Bloody hell, are you all safe? Everyone all right? Alex – what happened?'

Alex hauled herself off what remained of the raft and tramped wearily up the slipway, dragging the remains of her life jacket with her.

'You tell me Eddie. The whole of my side started to sink. And I thought you'd checked all of these.' She tossed the useless jacket at him as she headed for Lauren and Sue who were waving at her frantically.

'I did,' said Eddie. 'I checked them all.' He picked it up and stared at the straps, neatly severed apart from a small frayed strip in the centre and a frown settled on his face. He turned back to the raft and began to supervise the removal from the slipway, trying to keep his jubilant crew from disappearing into the crowds.

Alex made her excuses and got into the car with Sue to go home, trembling now with delayed shock and cold. The whole crew had crowded round the car to see her off, thumping her on the back and wringing her blistered and bruised hand in congratulation. She slumped into the seat and pulled the car rug around her.

'If I ever agree to anything like that again, do me a favour will you? Take me out and shoot me'.

Chapter Fourteen

Subtlety had not served Derek Johns well. It was all right at the beginning of his scheme to trap Kevin. It had been easy, scaring off all the other elver fishers by tramping like a plodding river warden along the bank in his heavy jacket, torch flashing at random into bushes and behind trees. He could almost hear them fleeing ahead of him, leaving one area unpatrolled and just one patsy to stumble on the body of the Elver Man. He had no qualms about doing away with Peter Smithson. Elver Man was a good little number and he'd had his eye on the business for a while. It was an affront, an outsider coming in and taking the big money away from local boys, but Smithson was strangely difficult to dislodge and most reluctant to disclose his contacts. No, Derek had no regrets about him.

He'd waited, hidden in the shadows until Kevin came shambling into view pushing his pram full of elvers. He knew the lad was a bit slow on the uptake but he couldn't believe his luck when he got into the front of the van and fell asleep. Derek had come prepared but he stuffed the chloroform-soaked cloth back into a plastic bag and lobbed it into the river where it sank out of sight as the police cars appeared, bumping their way along the unmade road in response to his anonymous tip-off from the village phone box. Derek had melted into the darkness as the police hauled the hapless young man out of the van and bundled him, none too gently, into the back of their vehicle. But how was he to know that dolt Brian Morris was fishing across the river? No-one bothered with that bend. Everyone knew it was a dead area but no – he had to be there and see Mallory on his way to the van.

Still, that had all worked perfectly until Alex-bloody-probation had started sniffing around looking for the corpse previously known as Frank Mallory. Once she'd seen him in the cottage he was stuck, unable to travel into town in daylight in case she saw him and his identity was revealed. He'd planned a much better place for Big Bill's demise but the snap choice of the bird hide had seemed safe enough until the 'twitchers' descended on him. It had all gone wrong since then and wherever he turned he seemed to see Alex. She'd helped to get Kevin Mallory out of prison, she'd been at Ada's and all that support had helped the old cow grow a backbone. Time was Ada would have run screaming at the sight of him, not nearly kill him on the doorstep. And despite all his efforts Alex Hastings refused to be frightened and didn't even have the decency to drown. Well, he was through with subtlety. He could feel the net closing around him as the police put the killings together and he wanted rid of the whole sorry mess. He was sick of living in the stink of Frank and he was sick of this poky ruin of a cottage. He couldn't get to Kevin any time soon and Ada had eluded him, but he had time for one more before he made his escape and this time he would be swift and merciless.

Alex sat with Eddie and PC Brown in her office listening to the preliminary findings of the Task Force.

'This is all confidential,' the young policeman said. 'We

hope to trap whoever is doing this but seeing as he seems a bit interested in you,' he nodded at Alex, 'we thought maybe you should know what to look out for.'

'What, so I don't miss some lunatic with a great curved fishing knife lurching towards me?' said Alex. 'Look, what the hell is this to do with me anyway? You say the first . . .' she hesitated, struggling with the word before taking a deep breath and continuing, '. . . the first murder was this Peter Smithson, the Elver Man as they all call him round here.'

Constable Brown nodded vigorously. 'Yes that's right. The pathologist is certain it is the same blade used to kill Big Bill Boyd and in the assault on Sergeant Michaels.'

'And now you're saying it not only matches my car tyres but also the damage to the raft? The same person cut my life jacket?'

There was another eager nod from the PC. He was like an overly keen dog, thought Alex rather uncharitably.

'The punctures in the air tanks on the left side match exactly,' he said.

'Sorry, but where do I come in. I know we can argue coincidence and stuff but, *shit*, in the last few months I've had my tyres slashed, someone's been breaking into my house and messing with things, I've almost drowned because my life jacket was sabotaged,' she swung round to glare at Eddie here, 'and it was my part of the boat where the air tanks were damaged. Not to mention that gruesome pike's head.'

Eddie and Constable Brown stared at her for a moment.

'What pike's head?' asked Eddie.

She told them, in terse, careful sentences while PC Brown took everything down in his shiny new notebook.

'Why didn't you say anything?' said Eddie, when she was finished. Alex snorted and pulled a face. 'I was going to when you called last time but I got distracted by a phone call. Then you were all busy with serious stuff and – well, I didn't want to seem like I was easily scared or something. Anyway, I thought it might have been a sick joke by a client but I don't think it was now. None of it seemed too bad on its own. It's just when you put it all together . . .' Her voice trailed off and she shook her head.

PC Brown closed his book with a sharp snap. 'I think you should be very careful for while,' he said, 'at least until we know who is doing this. There has to be some connection but we're not seeing it at the moment. At the meeting with the pathologist he said it was very interesting, you being a woman. As opposed to a man I mean.' He began to get flustered under Alex's hard stare. 'I mean, all the other victims are men and it's very unusual for someone like this to switch. So he thinks it may be something personal.'

Alex gave a sigh. 'So I've really hacked someone off, I don't know who, and the other people he's pissed off with have ended up dead or with body parts removed. Have I missed anything?'

Eddie leaned forwards and touched her shoulder. 'Alex, come on . . .' but she shook him off angrily.

'No, don't try to make it all fine Eddie. This is getting very weird and rather serious. I worked in London, in some of the toughest areas in Britain. I've visited a prisoner in *Broadmoor* and had less trouble. I just don't get this.' She stood up abruptly, pushing her chair over as she left the room. Eddie held out his hand to stop the Constable rising to follow.

'No, let her go,' he said. 'I'll talk to her later, see if she can make sense of it all when she's got over the shock. It's been a tough year for her without finding out some maniac is stalking her.'

'I wouldn't put it quite that strongly,' said PC Brown. 'If it is personal he's not been direct or confrontational, unlike the others. He's almost teasing her.'

Eddie stood up and glared down at the young policeman. 'Cutting someone's life jacket is not teasing,' he said. 'The raft was sabotaged and Alex could have drowned out there. I think stalking is just about right and I hope you will be able to impress on your seniors the seriousness of all this.'

PC Brown tried to maintain his dignity as he rose to his feet, but despite the fact he was a good six inches taller than

Eddie he looked like a truanting schoolboy standing in front of his form teacher.

'We certainly take it very seriously,' he said, struggling to get his notebook back in his pocket. 'I was going to suggest she might consider staying with friends for a few days whilst we resolve the situation. Perhaps you might pass that message on.' He walked to the door and pulled it open, his exit marred slightly by the fact the tips of his ears were glowing bright red. Eddie went to the window and looking down into the yard, just in time to see Alex slip into the workshop. He realized it might be someone in there, one of their higher-tariff clients, doing all this. Some of them certainly had the opportunity to sabotage the raft, though he couldn't believe any of the crew or builders would have done such a thing. Still, it was probably safer for Alex to stay away until all this was resolved, he thought, as he headed slowly for the stairs.

Kevin was desperate. It was Fair Week and he'd not been into town once. For the first time in his life he was going to miss the big opening of the festive season. From the arrival of the fair in September to the day of the town Carnival on November 5th everyone was in a festive mood. Pub hours became infinitely flexible as the Carnival gangs laboured in secret to create the huge floats that had so astonished Alex last year. Music seeped from upstairs windows as groups of performers developed and practised their routines for the Carnival concerts, the first indication most townsfolk had of the delights to come in the grand procession. The few remaining visitors were often startled by the appearance of a clown or several chaps dressed in shiny nylon with masks or a group lugging a giant model camel down the side roads of the town. Parts of Greek temples and diminutive pyramids sprang up in pub car parks, soon to be hidden behind tarpaulin tents and guarded jealously night and day by protective gang members.

Before all this however was the Fair. Not just any old fair though, no this was one of the largest in the country and attracted people from the whole community. All the little fairs that toured the country began to converge on the town in September until, like drops of mercury, they ran together to form the huge spectacle setting up on St Mark's Field.

'Please Mum,' he begged, 'I can't miss the Fair. ''Tis not like I'm banned nor nothin'. I've got a bit of money saved up. I just want to go and have a bit of a good time, maybe catch up with some mates.'

Ada looked at him suspiciously. 'And what mates would you have then, Kevin Mallory?' she demanded, standing in the doorway with her fists on her hips.

'They's from the workshop,' he said. 'All of us that made the raft and is working together. They's a good bunch, honest.' He watched her face hopefully and saw the first signs of her relenting.

'Well,' she grumbled, 'seems a strange thing when your most *honest* friends is a bunch on probation. Oh go on, but I'm coming too. Not to hang around with you lot,' she added hastily, seeing his stricken face. 'Think I want to be seen with a load of criminals? Still, I always enjoy the Fair and will be nice, getting out a bit more. We'll take the bus in tomorrow morning, make a day of it.'

'I don't want to miss the Fair again,' said Alex. 'I didn't know about it last time. I didn't really know about anything if I'm being truthful. Lauren's going with Jonny and we can all hang together in a bunch. There's absolutely no danger – it's all just nonsense.'

Sue watched her from beneath lowered lashes, trying to see just how serious her friend was and decided Alex meant what she said. She was stubborn enough to go to the Fair on her own if her friends wouldn't go with her, so she resigned herself to an evening of fried onions, vertiginous rides and crooked side stalls.

'But we let Eddie and Paul know,' she said. 'Let's face it, Jonny looks tough but in a scrap he'll squeal and run away if he breaks a fingernail.'

'Cruel,' said Alex, 'very cruel, but sadly accurate.'

The sheer scale of the Fair took Alex's breath away. It covered the vast open space of St Mark's Field and spilled down the side streets, tendrils reaching out almost to the market square. Although it was still early evening many of the rides had their lights on and music roared forth from dozens of huge speakers. The ground itself shook when the Ghost Train set off and all around there were smells of cooked food, oil, sawdust and hot metal to further confuse the senses. A long wooden wall painted in primary school colours had been erected along the side of the approach road and ambulances and the odd police car were parked on the dusty grass. Lauren was waiting impatiently near the main gate, Jonny lounging elegantly on the ticket booth as he chatted with the young man inside.

'Bout time too,' said Lauren crossly, as she scurried up to the entrance. Alex rummaged in her pocket for change, but the young man waved them through with a grin and a nod to Jonny.

'Friends in low places, dear,' he said as he sauntered towards the nearest hot-dog stand. 'Anyone hungry yet?'

Unusually for a family attraction the Fair had a beer tent and they fortified themselves before venturing out into the main area where the larger rides stood, a challenge to both nerves and common sense. Alex declined the beer and sipped on an orange juice as she watched the Big Dipper roar overhead, the cars turned almost horizontal for one terrifying second. Behind her came screams from punters in the huge swinging Pirate Ship and in the distance she heard the rattling of a chain as the Dive Bomber rose to the top of its arc and began the plunge to earth. She shivered and looked around for something less likely to make her lose her supper and spied her favourite, the Helter Skelter.

'Go on, that's just lame,' complained Lauren, who had returned from a fruitless but extremely vigorous argument with the owner of the Twister who refused her entry on the grounds she did not reach the minimum height.

'That's just prejudice,' she grumbled. 'Is intended to keep

kids off and nothing to do with real height. What am I supposed to do then – ride that stupid Carousel all night?'

'You didn't have to kick him,' Sue pointed out. They all looked over at the Twister where the owner was hopping around clutching his knee. Lauren shrugged, utterly unconcerned.

'Serve him right,' she said. 'Hey, look Alex, 'tis Kevin over there.' She pointed towards the rifle range where Kevin was attracting quite a crowd. Wandering over they watched as Kevin handed over his money and received a number of tiny pellets and an air rifle. He turned them round carefully, rejecting two and receiving a couple in exchange from the reluctant stall holder. Gesturing to the group around him to move back, he raised the rifle and squinted down the barrel, head on one side and the gun twisted over to the right.

'What the hell is he doing?' whispered Alex. 'He'll never hit anything like that.'

There was a sharp crack and one of the ever-moving duck targets flipped backwards to the applause of the spectators. Kevin loaded the gun again and repeated his feat.

'Two!' said a voice in the crowd. Alex watched, fascinated, as Kevin proceeded to score ten hits from ten pellets. He laid the gun down and turned to receive the congratulations of his friends and she noticed money changing hands as bets were settled. Kevin spotted her, gave a huge grin and turned back to the stall owner who was rather less enthused by his success.

'All right, that's enough,' he said. 'So you scored another ten – well that's sixty in all and worth ninety points.'

''Tis doubled for a full house with bulls-eyes,' said Kevin, 'so that's 180 points.'

There was a pause as the stall holder eyed him warily. 'Don't recall the bulls-eyes,' he said finally.

'First round, third and fifth shots, second time was second and ninth shots, third time was third, fourth and sixth shots, fourth round . . .'

'All right, all right – I can't remember all of that but just take your prize and get out of here. Go on, bugger off the lot of you.'

He handed Kevin the largest and ugliest stuffed animal Alex had ever seen and turned his back on the celebrating group as they moved on to the next booth.

'That's a bit of an eye-opener,' said Alex, impressed in spite of herself.

'Oh, that's nothing,' said Lauren. 'Hey, Kevin, KEV!' As he swung round towards them, she said, 'What's 97 times 13?'

Kevin blinked twice and said, 'One thousand two hundred and sixty one. Why?'

'No reason. Can you get me one of those coconuts?'

Kevin shook his head. 'They's glued on,' he said. 'I could maybe get you one of them boxes of sweets though.' He gestured to a stall with very sorry looking bows and arrows and tiny straw targets. Lauren twinkled at him and held out a pound note.

'You's a love,' she said.

Alex scrabbled in her bag for pencil and paper and hurriedly worked out the sum. 'He's right. Wow.' She looked at Kevin with new respect.

'Never wrong. Don't know how he does it but 'tis a good trick. Now, watch here.'

They sauntered over to the booth where Kevin was examining the bows and selecting half a dozen arrows from a bored-looking girl dressed in a vaguely medieval costume.

'Maid Marion,' Lauren whispered in response to Alex's unspoken question. Alex nodded and tried not to giggle. It was all rather ridiculous but despite that she was actually enjoying herself.

Derek pulled his cap down over his eyes and tucked a red and white scarf high around his neck to try and disguise the deep red scar on his face. He was a marked man in every sense of the word and his anger boiled and rolled inside him as he glared around at the crowds laughing and enjoying themselves. He didn't notice the slight but perceptible movement away from him as he pushed deeper into the Fair. He'd lived so long with the smell of Frank Mallory it had permeated his clothes and clung to his hair, and passers-by turned their heads away and stepped back when he came close, but Derek's attention was all focussed on one group. Ahead of him was Kevin, triumphant once more as he handed a huge box of chocolates to Lauren. The blonde, skinny probation officer was with them, but his eyes fixed on the figure behind her. Alex-bloody-probation, he mouthed silently. Got you.

After three goes Lauren refused to go on the Helter Skelter again.

'Not so much a ride, more like bloody physiotherapy,' she grumbled. 'Climbing all them stairs and it's just some big slide. Let's go find something a bit more exciting can't we?'

Sue agreed with her. 'Come on Alex, they've got a Centrifuge Cage. I've always wanted to go on one.'

The Cage was one of the scariest things Alex had ever seen. A huge drum spinning ever-faster on a single pole, it glued the riders to the walls as it whirled round until suddenly the floor fell away leaving them stuck like flies on a fly paper. Crowds gathered round to yell encouragement at the brave (or foolhardy) souls who dared to enter through the narrow doorway and stood up against the sides, placed at regular intervals by the serious young men in charge of the machine. Alex watched in horrified fascination as the door was locked and the whole contraption began to turn, slowly at first and then gathering speed until it was whipping around, the people inside a blur. Just as the floor fell away a hand grasped her elbow and her startled exclamation was covered by the much louder shriek from the Cage as the riders found themselves suspended in mid-air.

'I don't know anyone who's been brave enough to do that,' said Alison pushing in next to her. She sniffed loudly and treated Alex to a watery smile before staring down into the ride again. Alex hated crowds because she really didn't feel comfortable with close bodily contact, but even more she hated the feel of Alison, her bony elbows and damp skin wedged up against her.

'Oh, I don't know,' she said, 'it doesn't look too bad'.

Alison blinked at her. 'Go on then,' she said, 'why don't you try it.'

'All right – yes, I'll pay,' said Sue, and before Alex could protest she was hauled towards the ticket booth. Lauren trotted after them but more in hope than expectation. The man looked at her and shook his head.

'I'm sorry,' he said, 'I can't let you on. I know it don't seem fair but it's more than my licence is worth.' Lauren fixed him with a steely glare and then let out a huge sigh and turned away.

'I'll be watching,' she called over her shoulder. 'You tell me what it's like soon as you gets off.'

It was hot inside the Cage and the huge drum creaked as they walked across the tilted floor and took their places against the bleached wood walls. To her surprise she saw Jonny walk in after them and stand to the right.

'Always wanted to try it,' he murmured, 'and it will so impress my new friend.' He looked up at a strikingly handsome young man who was leaning over the railings and wriggling his fingers in their direction. Suddenly, Lauren's head popped up near him and Alex gave a feeble wave before the ride wranglers began to shift them all a few inches left or right to balance the cage. Her palms were sweating and she felt the blood singing in her ears as the door was closed and locked, leaving them waiting in anxious silence. As the drum began to turn she realized she was probably going to be sick and looked up at the faces turning before her eyes. A voice called out and she realized it was Kevin.

'Look at the pole,' he yelled. 'Don't look round, just at the pole.'

She fixed her eyes on the one still object in her now swirling universe and felt Jonny's hand grab her.

'I hear it's just like having a heart attack,' he said helpfully as a weight began to descend on her chest.

She risked one last glance at the crowd and her eyes met Lauren's just as another face, a familiar but changed face, appeared over her shoulder. The fury in the eyes of Andrew Hinton burned into her memory, a snap-shot of a moment she would never forget as Lauren vanished from sight, the machine shifted on its axis and the floor fell away beneath her feet.

The first thing Lauren knew was that there was a strange smell, when suddenly a hand clamped itself across her mouth and she was lifted off her feet.

'If you scream or try to struggle I'll break your back. Keep still and I'll not harm you. Understand?' said a voice in her ear, as the smell intensified. She had a momentary glimpse of Alex's face, white with shock and strain, before she was whisked round and hauled away through the crowds. She tried an experimental wriggle and the arm holding her round her waist tightened, squeezing the breath from her and threatening to crush her ribs.

'I warned you,' said the voice. 'Try that again and it'll be the last time you ever move your stubby little legs. You just as useful dead as alive so it don't matter to me.'

Lauren went limp and waited, eyes open, hoping someone would notice her plight, but fairgoers swirled around them oblivious, all bent on a final evening's pleasure. After a few minutes the crowd thinned out and they left the main field and entered the car park. She tensed, hoping to make a run for it when her abductor reached for his car keys, but he was ready for her. She was spun round and found herself dangling over his arm, her head bouncing up and down as he hurried to his vehicle. With one swift movement he opened the boot of a dark saloon car and pushed her inside, slamming the lid to leave her in darkness.

The smell was suddenly overpowering in the enclosed space and she gagged and felt around her hoping for something to hold on to or maybe wrap round her face to cut out the terrible odour. Her hands met metal warmed in the evening sun, the rubber of a spare tyre and then something sticky and wet. She jerked her hand back as the car engine fired and realized somehow the source of the smell was now on her. An abrupt turn flung her across the boot and she reached out again, desperate for something to cling to as she was bumped away to some unknown destination.

The moment the Cage stopped Alex lurched for the door, dragging Jonny with her.

'Oh come on,' he said, 'it wasn't that bad. You didn't even scream when the floor went.'

Staggering and trying to clear her head, she hauled him past the spectators and leaned on a clear section of the barrier.

'It's Lauren,' she gasped. 'I saw someone take her. Hinton – I saw Hinton take her just as the machine started.'

Jonny stared at her and shook his head. 'No, she's just over . . . over there . . .' He looked around to where his sister had been watching. There was a scattering of chocolates on the ground and the box lay on its side, trampled in the crowd. 'Who's Hinton? What did you see?'

'A probationer, released from somewhere – no-one seems to know anything about him and I've only seen him once but he gave me the creeps. He was just behind Lauren and I saw him grab her. Then she was gone. I couldn't see where with the damn machine spinning.'

Jonny grabbed her by the shoulders and shook her none too gently, 'Where did you meet him? Have you got an address? Think Alex!'

Alex pulled free and glared at him. 'The only place I met him was out on the Levels in some grotty tumbledown ruin. I can't believe he's still there though . . .' She paused. 'He looked different. It was definitely him, but he looked thinner and there was a horrible mark all down one side of his face.'

Jonny was off, hauling Alex after him. 'I don't care if he was wearing full make-up and a tutu, I want to find my sister!'

In her haste to keep up with him Alex tripped and stumbled over a figure on the floor.

237

'Hell, I'm sorry,' she said, wrenching her arm free of Jonny's grip. She bent over the hunched shape and recognized Simon Adams, the lorry boy. Simon lifted his head, his face contorted with fear.

'What is it?' asked Alex as gently as she could. 'What's the matter Simon.'

Simon shook his head and muttered something so softly she had to bend over to catch what he was saying.

'Was him again. I seen him, seen him take her, so I trying to hide so's he don't hurt me again.'

'Who was it?' asked Alex, 'You must tell me so I can rescue her. Who was it took Lauren?'

'She is always nice. Don't laugh like they others. He hurt us, that night. Crashed my lorry an' all.'

Jonny hovered over them in a fever of impatience.

'Bloody hell Alex, come on!' he yelled, and Simon promptly rolled up into a ball and covered his ears.

'Now look what you've done, you great oaf. He saw who took Lauren and if we asked him nicely he might have been able to tell us which direction they went.' She gestured round at the mass of people on all sides. 'Now we're on our own.'

Simon lifted his head, giving Jonny an anxious glance as said, 'Was Derek Johns. Big ol' nasty Mr Johns, it was. I seen him with Newt around afore so I knows him, but I never speak to'm. Not wise, asking questions 'bout they Johnses.'

'Oh shit,' said Jonny softly, then very gently asked, 'Did you see where they went?'

Simon looked at him suspiciously for a moment and then gestured to the rear car park. 'Was runnin' that way,' he murmured.

Alex looked around and saw Sue coming towards them looking worried.

'Look after him,' she said, pointing to Simon. 'We can't just leave him like this and I've got to go after Lauren. Jonny's in no state to drive and I think I know where he's taken her.'

She turned away and started pushing through the crowds

as Sue shouted, 'Who has taken someone? And who's been taken where? What's going on?' but Alex was gone.

The trip was mercifully short but brutally rough, and Lauren was half unconscious by the time the boot was opened and fresh, cool air rushed in.

'Right you,' said her abductor, and she was lifted out by her collar, hanging at the end of his arm like a rat. She opened her eyes as they entered the cottage where her sense of smell, briefly restored by the open air, registered that awful stink again. Before she could stop herself she looked at her captor's face and in that moment she knew he was going to kill her.

Derek Johns,' she said, pouring all the disgust she could into his name.

'What you doin' back here then?'

He shook her sharply but in an oddly impersonal way, as if his mind was on something else.

'Just you shut up so's I don't have to gag you,' he said. 'Reckon I'll tie you up though. Don't trust you not to do something stupid. I seen you with that gadjie at the Twister. Bold little thing aren't yer.'

'Why are you doing this?' she insisted, as he leaned over and grabbed a coil of old rope. He picked her up and carried her into the kitchen where the smell was strong enough to render her speechless for a moment. Derek grinned as he saw her face go white.

'You gets used to it,' he said, dropping her on to one of the kitchen chairs, 'and I've not had so many visitors to complain.'

He made a swift loop around her body and grabbed her hands, but her arms were too short to reach around the back of the chair.

'Dammit,' he muttered, and glared at her as if she were being deliberately uncooperative. He started to make smaller loops with the end of the rope, all the while glancing towards the door.

'Expecting visitors after all?' she asked.

Derek stopped fiddling with the rope and glared at her. 'I said you shut up,' he said. 'You's here to be all you is fit to be. Understand, little live-bait?'

Lauren went cold with fear, unable to offer any resistance as he pulled her hands into the loops in front of her body, but before he could tighten the slip knots there was the sound of a car in the distance, travelling at reckless speed down the track to the cottage. Derek spun round and stepped towards the window and Lauren seized her chance, flexing her arms and sliding out from under the rope binding her to the chair. In a second she reached the back door and grabbed at the handle. As he turned and saw her, she flung it open, slammed it shut behind her and grabbed a rusty hammer off the workbench in the porch. Lauren was small but she was deceptively strong, especially across her arms and shoulders, and with two blows the door handle and latch were in pieces. Derek tried to turn it from the inside but the spindle spun uselessly in the broken door and he kicked out in frustration.

'Big mistake you little rat,' he roared through the door. 'You'll ask me to kill you after I've caught up with yer.'

Lauren didn't wait. She turned and fled as fast as she could, her feet pounding on the path leading to the canal, but she wasn't built for running and she knew he'd catch her in seconds if she remained in sight. She stopped at the end of the garden and looked around, desperate for cover or some kind of hiding place. The old towpath ran off into the distance in both directions and between her and the long, safe grass of the deserted water meadows lay the ominous width of Kings Sedgemoor Drain. Her lungs already burning with the unaccustomed exercise, she set off, grimly forcing herself towards the footbridge and some chance of escape, but a shout behind her told her it was already too late. As her feet pounded away on the path she looked around frantically and spotted the reed basket Derek had been using to transport the meat for the pike lying in the mud on the bank. Gritting her teeth she swerved towards it and after a brief struggle pulled it free. There was no time to hesitate, as Derek Johns thundered down on her and gritting her teeth she dropped it into the canal, slid in after it and pushed off. The basket lurched, span round and almost delivered her back into his grasp as he flung himself flat on the bank and clawed at her, but then the current caught her and she began to slide away towards the middle of the water.

Derek plunged into the canal in pursuit. An indifferent swimmer, he was driven by adrenaline and blinded by hatred and it was only when he felt his feet sink with the weight of his boots he paused to reconsider. Swearing and spluttering he hauled himself back on to the canal side and unlaced his footwear, discarding his jacket and the concealing scarf in a heap on the tow path. It had only taken a few seconds but Lauren was already half way to the bridge, the basket twirling merrily in the current as it bobbed along. At the last moment Derek unclipped his precious knife and laid it on his clothes before plunging into the thick, grey water. No point in ruining a good blade, he thought, and he was going to need it again soon. Then he struck out after her as fast as he could.

Lauren's car with its specially adapted hand controls and high seat had been the nearest vehicle when they got to the car park. Alex's was back in town and Jonny had cadged a lift with his sister in anticipation of a pleasant evening in the beer tent. Sue was still back in the main field, and as Jonny gave a potted biography of the man who had kidnapped his sister they both realized they had no time to mess about looking for something better.

'Guardian of the spare key,' he said, fishing in his pocket. 'You drive. I've had a beer or three and Lauren'll kill me if anything happens to her car.'

Alex took control of the car as best she could and sped off in the direction of the cottage where she had met the man she knew as 'Andrew Hinton'.

As they lurched across the Levels towards the cottage, she struggled to keep the car between the ruts in the track.

Woah! Watch where you're going,' shouted Jonny.'

'I challenge you to drive this bloody thing any better,' she said through gritted teeth.

Finally, they skidded to a halt and, as the dust settled, she grabbed Jonny's arm. 'Be careful,' she said. 'If it is him and he is here, then he's very dangerous and I don't think he'll hesitate to kill us – or Lauren. Let's go round the back and see if we can spot him.'

On reflection it was a bit late to try the stealthy approach, but anything was better than charging through the door into an ambush. They stepped out into the fading evening light and walked warily through the remains of the garden gate. It creaked loudly as they shoved their way through, and they froze, looking at one another, before the sound of splashing drew them to the canal behind the house.

'Oh, no, no. Lauren's terrified of water,' said Jonny. He began to run in the direction of the splashing, and attempted to gallop across the overgrown bank to the towpath beyond. Alex followed, looking around in a desperate effort to spot her friend.

Lauren clung to the rim of the basket as it made its dash down the canal. She was sick with fear, dizzy from the constant spinning and she could hear Derek Johns gaining on her as he ploughed through the water behind her. The basket began to slow as it came to the footbridge and she realized it was letting in water, tilting over towards the far bank as it began to wallow. She was reaching out to try and grab one of the bridge footings when the basket gave a lurch and the shadowy outline of a fish passed by under her outstretched arm. Lauren froze in terror as a second pike crested the water, bumping at the basket before sinking into the reeds again. She shoved as hard as she could as her tiny, fragile craft lodged against the piers of the bridge and it spun away from the nightmare of the pike and off towards the sluice gate waiting just ahead.

The pike were hungry. They had been gathering in greater numbers, but their food supply had almost dried up and so, in keeping with the laws of survival, they preyed on one another, the younger and smaller feeding the smarter, meaner and tougher fish. Now there were about a dozen left, monsters all of them, and they had scented the lingering odour of Derek's special bait from the basket. First one and then another, they glided downstream after Lauren.

The basket hit the metal gate with a resounding bang and promptly fell apart. As her feet slid into the water Lauren felt the cold nudge of a fish and glanced down. The pike swirled around her, mouths opening as they seized the remains of the basket. She shrieked and clawed at the gate, hauling herself up by the bolts and clinging on to the lintel above the main sluice. There was the sound of ragged breathing behind her and she knew Derek was almost on her. She struggled upright, searching for a handhold on the hot metal surface and felt, almost out of reach, the big circular wheel that opened the gate. She jumped, grabbed at it and felt it stir an inch or so. Derek gave a growl of triumph and anticipation as he swam doggedly towards her, ignoring the pike that nudged him from all sides.

'Got you now, you ugly little runt,' he called as Lauren, with the last of her strength, flung her whole weight on to the wheel.

There was a screeching as the metal barrier lifted and a rush of water as the canal flooded out into the Huntspill River. Derek was sucked through, unable to save himself as his head hit the gate and he went under. Lauren clung on, her feet slipping off the narrow ledge so she swung over the foaming water. Her whole weight was now on the wheel and her hands began to cramp as she gripped the damp metal. Glancing down between her feet she saw the last of the pike roll helplessly into the main stream and a part of her felt relief that at least she'd drown and not be torn apart by merciless teeth. She felt her grip beginning to loosen and her hands were slick with sweat. She closed her eyes, took a deep breath and prepared herself for the end. Just as Lauren's strength finally failed, Alex grabbed her wrist from above, hanging on grimly over the top of the sluice until Jonny could shimmy up and lift them both off to safety.

Chapter Fifteen

'I really don't think you should be here,' said Alex, eyeing Lauren who was seated in the most comfortable chair in her office. Lauren shrugged.

'I'm fine,' she said. 'Just a few bumps and stuff. Anyway, 'tis a big day for you today and I reckon you need a bit of support.'

Alex grunted, unconvinced, but secretly grateful for her friend's loyalty.

'Tell me,' she said after a few minutes of futile rummaging through her desk, 'did Hinton – sorry, Derek Johns – ever tell you why he took you?'

Lauren grinned. 'Well now, he never did, but Dave – he explained it all whilst I was in the hospital.'

'Dave? Who the hell is Dave?' demanded Alex.

'Oh you know, Constable Brown. He said to call 'um Dave. Nice bloke he is. Anyway, you was the only person as saw Derek Johns when he was in the cottage so he had to pretend to be this Andrew Hinton person. You was the only one as could identify him, link him to all the stuff there. So you had to go and he was using me, figuring you'd come after.' Her face went still for a moment as she remembered his mocking words. 'I was the bait,' she finished.

Alex considered this for a minute. 'Does anyone know who Andrew Hinton really was?' she asked.

'Was Frank Mallory,' said Lauren cheerfully. 'Poor old bugger, right dumb too. He was dying and wanted to see Kevin, so he bubbled, but he chose the wrong people to bubble on.'

'*Bubbled?*'

'Grassed up Biff and Newt Johns. Then Biff went an' killed hisself and Derek went on the rampage. They was all right sick when they opened that ol' freezer in the kitchen. Dave says 'twas probably Frank in there but most is gone or just rotted away. He was dead proud when they got Derek Johns' knife though. Was a Normark, just like he said, with that little fish tail bit missing. If he could a' got rid of you I reckon maybe ol' Derek might have just gone away for a bit and slipped back quietly – 'cept for his face of course. Someone done a right number on that. He was right girt ugly, I'll tell you.'

Alex was having trouble following a lot of this and it was with a sense of relief she answered the phone as it rang up from reception. She'd not had time to replace the receiver when the door opened to reveal Ada bearing down on her, Kevin trailing in her wake.

'We need to talk,' said Ada, plonking herself down in the nearest chair and folding her arms.

'Well, I've got an important meeting to prepare for,' Alex began. 'Couldn't it wait until . . .'

'No it can't,' said Ada firmly. ''Tis urgent and needs your say-so.' She nodded her head and caught sight of Lauren in the corner.

'Nicely done girl,' she said. 'Good job too. 'Tis the only way with some of 'em – real crazies – you got to just do away with 'um.'

Lauren managed a tentative smile and slid further back in her chair.

'Now, about Kevin and this probation thing,' she continued, fixing Alex with her fiercest stare. 'He's got to leave.'

'But Kevin's done really well at the day centre,' protested
Alex. 'He's made friends, he's got some real skills and we are
confident we can help him into employment eventually.'

'No need,' said Ada. 'He's got a job. Got offered it last
week, but is not here so he'm not able to come any more.'

Alex looked at Kevin, who raised his eyes and for the first
time gave a real smile, a smile full of confidence and a little
pride.

'Tell me Kevin,' she said, ignoring Ada and focussing on
the young man, 'what's this job and where is it? Maybe we
can transfer your order if you're moving away.'

''Tis with the Fair,' he said. 'They wants I to be on the rifles
'cos I don't never miss. To encourage 'um see. And they was
girt impressed with my numbers. Called me a "human calculator", they did. Said maybe I can do a stint in one of them
show tents when I'm settled.'

Alex looked at Ada. 'What about your Mum?' she asked,
but it was Ada answered, her jaw set.

'Reckon most of what's gone wrong is about round here,
what with them Carnival gangs and all that silliness every
year. Kevin's grown now and he can't be staying at home
with his mother all his life. Them fair people, they's like a
big family and they'll keep an eye on him, teach him stuff.
Is a chance to see places I only had pictures of and I'll not
stand in his way.' There was a tiny wobble in her voice but
she held Alex's eyes, pleading for the chance she believed her
son needed.

It was against all the rules and would be devilishly difficult
to organize, but suddenly Alex didn't care. She'd get the route
from the fair owners and set up meetings with other offices,
she decided. He'd finished his day centre order and if he had a
chance to go abroad she'd get his probation discharged early.
It was too good a chance for a lad from the Levels to miss.

'Give me a day to sort it out,' she said, ushering the pair
out.

She glanced at her watch and realized it was time. There was a knock and Sue stuck her head around the door.

'Just wishing you luck,' she said. 'He'd be nuts to fail you after all this. You're too good at the job. Honestly, it'll be fine.'

Alex looked at her friends and picked up her final self-evaluation, her diary and all the notes from the weekly 'support and supervision meetings'.

'Right,' she said, 'well, whatever happens, I'm ready.'